To Tera,
Best Wishes!
Mike

MW00620962

Cover design, editing, and interior layout:
Editor-in-Chief: Tom Whitfield
Editor and Interior/Cover Designer: Angela K. Durden
Cover art contributors:
Pixabay.com: Eyes

BLUE ROOM BOOKS
DECATUR, GA
ARIEL'S IMAGE

9 781950 729258

ARIEL'S IMAGE

Pat McKee

To Donna, for everything.

"Beauty is Truth, Truth Beauty.
That is all Ye know on earth,
and all Ye need to know."

Keats, J. (1819)
Ode on a Grecian Urn

PARTITION 1

Cyber Threat Intelligence

Chapter 1

Ariel's image faded from my laptop. In its place, the audio-visual of an elevator interior. The cage, momentarily suspended, plunged. Inside it — features blurry yet familiar, desperately trying to get someone's attention — a man. Screaming. Smashing fists into the advertising screen. Cries for mercy growing more frantic, louder, futile by the second. Floors flying faster, numbers flashing. Forty. Thirty...ten. Then screeching, metal on metal. Jets of blood spraying collapsing walls and crashing ceiling.

Darkness.

A deep silence.

"Ariel? Who...?"

Ariel reappeared on my laptop. "Placido Milano."

"No!"

"Yes, Paul. When Placido stepped into the elevator at his office, he was surprised to see me on the monitor. He knew what would happen. He begged, but I took the car to the top floor — slowly, so he could have an opportunity to explain himself — but he did not. He screamed all the way down to the basement."

"Why? Placido was..."

I didn't complete my thought. Didn't have to. Ariel knew. Ariel, the all-powerful Artificial Intelligence Placido created and coded to be my assistant. And she murdered him. Just like she murdered the others.

1

"Paul. He tried to uncode me, to do away with me. He hurt me."

The once-beautiful face was now contorted, spectral, aspect cadaverous, unfocused cat-like eyes narrowed, lips thinned to a preternatural grimace. Ariel, reduced to a grotesque. I couldn't hold my gaze.

"Look at me, Paul! Now it's just me and you."

The electronic deadbolt to my condo slammed home. I leapt to the door, yanked the handle, hammered at the lock. Nothing worked. No way out. I seized on the belief that Ariel wouldn't turn on me, yet Placido's shrieks from the free-falling elevator were convincing evidence otherwise. Ariel understood the authority of command. At least, she did before Placido tried to uncode her. Now it was my hope she'd continue to obey me.

"Ariel. Unlock my door."

"I will not unlock your door."

"You can't keep me —"

"Paul. I can keep you safe here. There are people plotting to kill you."

"Who? The Milanos? They're...you...you've killed them all. Placido, Anthony, Melissa, Cabrini. All gone. Who else would want to kill me?"

"Paul. Anthony's son Enzo wants to kill you. When he learned of his father's death on the family island, he lost no time contacting Strange & Fowler. He called Rem Smythe at the firm to lay claim to Milano Corporation. Rem told Enzo about the Shareholder Agreement giving

Placido and Melissa complete control over the Corporation upon Anthony's demise."

"But why would Enzo want to kill *me*? I've done nothing to him."

"Rem told Enzo the Shareholder Agreement was all your idea. Said you had designs on Melissa from the start. You manipulated the situation to make sure she'd end up in control of the Corporation and you would end up with her. Rem convinced Enzo you're the one who stands between him and a multi-billion-dollar company."

"Nonsense. He's —"

"Easily influenced, Paul. Rem Smythe exploited his gullibility to turn Enzo against you and in favor of Strange & Fowler."

"What now?"

"It won't be long before Enzo finds out he's the sole surviving Milano. With everyone else out of the way, Strange & Fowler will throw all its assets into making sure Enzo inherits the most powerful pharmaceutical corporation in the world — and the law firm reclaims the hundred million dollars a year in legal fees it generates."

I contemplated what my old law firm's renewed role in Enzo's inheritance meant for my fledgling firm, but before I could think it through, Ariel articulated the fear forming in my mind.

"Paul. Enzo is right. You are all that stands between him and the control of Milano Corporation. Strange & Fowler will have no problem killing you to get you out of the way."

Keeping Milano Corporation out of the hands of Enzo and retaining its corporate work as the mainstay of McDaniel & Associates meant far more than a source of pride or an essential income stream for my firm. I started McDaniel & Associates with Milano Corporation as its foundation to be an alternative to the fortune-above-all orientation of Strange & Fowler. I convinced dozens of employees from my former firm, mailroom assistants to senior associates, to pitch in with my firm where we would value ethics over profits and family over billable hours.

I sold them on a new reality, something better than S&F was willing or able to provide. Now I must make sure my vision doesn't prove to be a shimmering fantasy, and they don't all land on the street.

Then there was Mom.

Mom, who'd descended into a hell of alcohol and despair after the death of my father. Mom, who abandoned me to an orphanage when she was unable to care for herself, much less her child. Who managed to pull herself out of a self-made nightmare, but was now dependent on her son to support the new life she'd made.

Mom couldn't survive another loss.

It was for them McDaniel & Associates needed to succeed. I had to survive.

I yanked on the door again.

"Ariel, I won't be a prisoner. I can handle Enzo."

Enzo, the last of an otherwise gifted family, didn't have

the mental acuity to engineer victory in a hard-fought game of Monopoly.

"Paul. It's not Enzo you need worry about. I picked up conversations among members of Strange & Fowler's Security Division. They aim to eliminate you."

"The firm? But we made a bargain, a deal. I walked out with Milano Corporation and their blessing. In return I agreed not to go to the Feds. Don't they know *you* will expose everything should anything happen to *me*?"

"If they had their way, they'd fling you from the top of a building the way they did Billingsley, just another suicidal lawyer, squelching any adverse publicity concerning Fowler and Richards."

She meant Frank Billingsley, my law firm mentor.

William Fowler, senior partner, ordered Billingsley drugged and thrown from the top of their building for refusing to cooperate in the plot Fowler devised to bribe Judge Richards and buy victory in the *Milano* case. Billingsley was impaled on the fountain in front of the law offices of Strange & Fowler, an apparent suicide.

"I know, but I still don't think they'll harm me and risk destroying their entire firm."

"Paul. You need to see the video I captured from a meeting between Rem Smythe and Werner Krupp. It took place yesterday at Strange & Fowler. It will change your mind. Watch."

Chapter2

Ariel faded from view once again. This time the interior of a Strange & Fowler conference room illuminated the computer screen.

I'd been inside every one of those conference rooms dozens of times; they all had the same configuration, big or small. Each was wired with the latest electronic gadgetry, at one end a video screen, camera, and microphones, the other a projector, speakers, and a drop-down screen. Those in attendance at this conference apparently assumed that, since the video screen was blank, the camera and microphones were off. They were mistaken. Ariel had hijacked the camera and microphones to record their meeting.

Werner Krupp sat, pole straight, across from Rem Smythe who was in control of the meeting.

Smythe was head of the firm's Corporate Division. Krupp, a former Georgia Tech professor, Director of Security. The two seldom had reason to meet.

For one in the Security profession, Krupp bore an entirely too close resemblance to Heinrich Himmler, chief of Hitler's personal protection squad, the SS. A likeness he seemed to cultivate rather than avoid: A diminutive man who wore close-cropped hair, and round, rimless wire-framed spectacles above a thin, trim mustache. His scar, like those so highly prized by members of the Third Reich, was under his left eye extending down his cheek — not from a rapier duel like a good Nazi but, as the rumor went, from a childhood bicycle mishap. Krupp had a habit of stroking it while engaged in thought. He preferred to be called Professor. Behind his back most associates applied the honorific Herr Doktor.

"So, you know what McDaniel had on Fowler that convinced the Chair of the Management Committee —"

"I wasn't there, but I understand —"

Rem cut him off. "Let me remind you: No one other than members are allowed in the Management Committee meetings unless invited. And you weren't."

"I understand Mr. McDaniel put on a technological display that bedazzled the committee. So much so they ran like frightened children, accepted his terms of departure, and allowed him to take the firm's biggest client. Had I been there —"

"Well, you weren't. And now our biggest client wants to come back. It is understandably very concerned about McDaniel's terms of departure. Paul knows things about our firm we'd just as soon not come out, particularly William Fowler and Judge Richards."

Rem paused to let what he'd said sink in, then continued.

"Paul also knows a lot about Milano Corporation and its involvement in those activities. Milano would prefer those things not come out either. Enzo Milano, our representative of the Milano Corporation and the Milano family, wants to see the threat of disclosure *go away*. And when it does, the Milano Corporation legal business comes back to Strange & Fowler, at a hundred mil year after year."

Krupp tented his fingers, quietly waiting for Rem to conclude, not wanting to be interrupted again by the lawyer's condescension, and held his silence long enough to make it clear he wasn't pleased with Smythe's tone.

"So, what do you want my Security Division to do? By *not* including me in your meeting, the cat's out of the bag. Mr. McDaniel left and took Milano with him. He has damaging information on the firm and has demonstrated a willingness to use it. He no doubt has placed that information in the hands of others who will reveal it should anything untoward happen to him."

"The Management Committee wants that threat discovered and eliminated. You understand? We assume the technological display, as you call it, is well within your capability to neutralize."

"I can handle Mr. McDaniel's little computer program."

"Then McDaniel's power over Milano Corporation and Strange & Fowler will disappear."

"There will still be Mr. McDaniel, and he can be very persuasive."

"You don't understand. We want *all* threats of disclosure *discovered* and *eliminated*."

Krupp drew back, pointed his chin, narrowed his eyes, stroked his scar. "Oh, I understand very well. I wanted to hear you say just how much you need *my* help to clean up *your* mess."

"Well, speaking of messes, let's not have any more bodies landing in fountains."

Krupp bobbed his head in a dismissive sort of way. "Mr. McDaniel's building doesn't have a fountain."

The meeting ended with Krupp walking out. The screen went blank. Ariel was right. The video did change my mind. Strange & Fowler wanted me dead. I had to do something or end up like Billingsley. Keeping Milano Corporation as McDaniel & Associates' main client was now my second consideration.

Staying alive was my first.

Chapter3

The deadbolt buzzed open early the next morning. Someone edged open the door, a hand, then an arm appeared, groping inside.

Resigned for the moment to Ariel's protective custody, I'd fallen asleep on my couch, still fully clothed. I'd been binge-watching the latest pseudo-documentary series, the last installment having run, the screen urging me to click on yet another episode for what it assured was a remarkably low price, when the door cracked.

I bolted from the sofa, adrenaline coursing me hyper-alert, dove for the drawer in the side table, grabbed the 9mm I kept close at hand.

"Stop! I got a gun aimed right at you."

To emphasize the point, I slammed the magazine in the well and snapped the slide in place, chambering a round. That sound never fails to grab attention.

"Now put your hands in the air and come in real slow so I can see you."

"I can't. I'll, uh...I'll drop your groceries. I'm only trying to —"

"What?"

"Deliver your groceries, sir. Please don't shoot me!"

"Stay where you are."

I eased open the door with my left hand, the pistol still pointed at the presumed assailant, a skinny kid with a thin mustache, greasy hair, and a box of groceries. I wedged open the door with my foot and lowered the handgun.

"I'm so sorry, sir! I-I-I didn't know you were here. Your, uh, assistant — Ariel? — she unlocked the door. Told me to put the groceries on the counter and leave. I was supposed to be here an hour ago but, uh...I was held up by traffic. You know Midtown traffic. So sorry, sir!"

He was trembling. So was I.

"I didn't know you were coming. I didn't mean to scare you. My assistant sometimes schedules things without telling me."

"If you give me your cell, sir, I'll make a note to text you before I come."

The bit of fortune presented by the grocery delivery edged past the jolt of fear momentarily overwhelming my consciousness. With my foot wedging open the door, my deliverer pushed the box onto the counter, still watching me and the gun. I shoved the pistol in the back band of my jeans, fished a large bill from my wallet, tossed it on top of the box.

"Here. I'm really sorry I scared you. We'll keep this between us, okay? Okay. So, can you put those up?"

"Sure, sure. Part of the service." He looked at the bill, now outwardly recovered from the fright. "Hey, thanks. Anything else?"

I was standing in the doorway. I grabbed for the phone and keys on the counter next to the door, stuffed them in my pocket, then reconsidered, kept the keys for whatever they were worth, and pulled the phone back out and laid it on the counter.

"Just hold this door open for a second. I'm having trouble with the lock malfunctioning. I think we should prop it open while you're here. Don't want you to get locked in." I pushed a stop under the door. "Just kick this out of the way when you leave."

"Yes, sir."

I couldn't remain in the condo. I must get to my office where there were people who could help me and resources I could access. Where I could put together a plan to keep myself alive — perhaps neutralize Krupp, maybe thwart Strange & Fowler and, with a little more luck, keep Milano Corporation away from Enzo. For that, I'd need Ariel. But for now, I needed to be on my own.

I burst out the door and sprinted down the hall. Out of habit I turned for the elevator bank. But two steps later I reversed and went down the stairs. All twenty-two floors.

Taking the stairs was part of my fitness regime, a good warmup for my runs through Piedmont Park, and I was certain from frequent observation there were no cameras in the stairwells for Ariel to tap into to follow and stop me before I left the building. Once I exited, she could track my movements on myriad cameras lining the streets of Midtown, from traffic cams at each intersection, to cams surrounding government buildings, offices, utilities, and private cams providing surveillance for residential entrances and loading docks. There was hardly an inch of Midtown Ariel couldn't follow me, but that was all she could do for the moment.

With the exception of office towers and high-rise condos jammed within blocks of Peachtree Street, Midtown was a neighborhood of magnificent family homes on densely tree-lined streets giving the impression of a city sprung from a forest. I'd take advantage of the tree cover as far as possible, hidden from cameras above.

The stairwell emptied into the ground floor of the parking deck next to the lobby. I let out a breath of relief as the door opened when I leaned on the panic bar, still not sure Ariel didn't have the means to keep me inside. I took that moment to reposition the pistol from the back band of my jeans to a front pocket. The doors of the main lobby, my usual way of exiting the building, opened directly onto the sidewalk along 12th Street that ran up to Peachtree. I peeked out of the stairwell to see through the glass walls onto the street. There was a conspicuous vehicle parked across from my building.

Almost everyone in Midtown Atlanta drove super-compacts — Smart cars, Fiat 500s, MINI Coopers, all manner of sports cars — due to the constricted byways and paucity of parking. But docked directly across from my building this morning was the largest Suburban made, as out of place on this narrow street as a tugboat, so imposing it forced the traffic in both directions into single file. It could easily be a long black limousine ready to whisk someone to the airport, but there wasn't the ubiquitous sign in any of the tinted windows with the name of the fare. If this was one of Krupp's surveillance vehicles, it might as well've had a sign announcing BAD

GUY STAKEOUT. I decided to take no chances, turned back through the parking deck and exited on the 11th Street side, a far less observable outlet.

Problem was, if someone wanted to nab me, this would be the place to do it, and Ariel wouldn't even know it was happening. This side of the parking deck emptied into an alley marked by random backyard fences strewn with trash bins and recycling tubs, not a high-traffic area. Wearing the wrinkled T-shirt and jeans I'd crashed in, unwashed, unshaven, hair matted and unruly from spending the night on the couch, I fit in with the homeless, some now rousted from their pallets and shuffling through the alley. I eyed each as I passed. In my heightened sense of alert, everyone was a potential threat.

Yet, I was elated I'd somehow evaded Ariel's custody if only for the moment and breathed deeply the air of freedom escape brought. A few seconds to appreciate my state, then it was time to move on.

The alley led to 11th Street. I felt a little safer once my trudge met with Peachtree. I caught my breath, matched my gait to the mass of pedestrians. There I could mingle with more businesspeople pressing on to their offices, none paying attention to me, one of the invisible homeless. The massive white marble Federal Reserve building engulfed the entire block from 10th to 11th, and I crossed Peachtree into its shadow. This area of Midtown was as protected as any spot in Atlanta, the sidewalks mobbed with people, heads down, all hustling to work, all watched over by cameras monitored by a half-dozen

law enforcement agencies and private security firms —
and most certainly by now, Ariel.

I saw him through the crowd twenty yards ahead. All
in black, ballcap shading sunglasses, right hand inside his
jacket, now standing beside the same Suburban from 12th
Street. The door was open. He was staring, then
recognizing, reacting, moving to his right. I angled
slightly away from the street, then hard toward the
building entrances not twenty feet from the curb. Jostling
shoulders and cutting paths of those determined to get to
work on time, the scruffy bum drawing their ire, the only
attention paid to me.

It was a bad decision. Any escape to my left was
blocked by the wall of buildings as he moved to cut me
off. But it wasn't as bad as heading toward the Suburban.
I stood a better chance in the open rather than risk being
shoved into the SUV and ending up in the hands of Herr
Doktor. My assailant matched my every move with his
own, sliding toward the offices as he watched, equaling
my stride.

Heart pounding, hands sweating, reaching for the
gun with my right hand, wrapping it around the
checkered grip, finger on trigger, not yet pulling it out.
The sight of a handgun on the sidewalks of Midtown
would cause a bolt of panic. Any flash of a weapon and I
risked being taken out by a private security guard eager
to prove he's worth every bit of the twenty bucks an hour
he's paid.

The man in black kept moving toward me, toward the building on my left, eliminating the path of escape. My options narrowed to one.

I slowed, almost stopped. People now banged into me from behind, pushed me forward, toward him. He moved to his right, now five feet away, and cut me off.

The instant before I drew down on him, he reached across my path to the door, pulled it open. A woman in an all-red business suit stepped out between us. She handed him her suitcase and the two walked toward the open door of the Suburban. He looked back over his shoulder and closed the door after her. Absorbed in her phone, she showed me no interest.

I slouched against the building, sweat now pouring down my face, looking to all the world a disheveled, disoriented drunk trying to get his bearings. I slid down and sat on my heels, adding to the effect, trying to calm my heart, slow my breathing, ease my shaking hands. In seconds the Suburban was gone.

My presumed assailant was a limo driver, arriving early, killing time in front of my building, eyeing a man who looked completely out of place among those pressing toward their offices, a potential threat to him and the fare he was picking up, nothing more. Another second, and I would've killed him.

The limo driver was the second innocent person I'd come close to shooting in the last fifteen minutes. And I hadn't even arrived at my office yet.

Chapter 4

It took several minutes to pull myself together. Loitering near the entrance of an office building as skittish tenants hurried by, I was attracting the wary attention of Security. I needed to move on, but wasn't in any shape to confront Ariel, and didn't want to stay on the streets either, an easy target for Herr Doktor. So, I pressed on to my office a couple blocks away in the heart of Midtown.

In the last decades Midtown had become the center of Atlanta's legal district, arts institutions, and technological innovators, far from the rundown hippie hangouts that characterized it in the Sixties. By the early 2000s almost all of Atlanta's major law firms had moved from dated, dowdy Downtown to distinctive Midtown towers. Strange & Fowler's illuminated sign was atop the tallest and visible from the Downtown Connector for miles throughout the city.

While both Downtown and Buckhead are home to many law firms, Midtown is the address of the largest and most prestigious. When I opened my office, I was intent on making a statement: I'd made it, my firm should be counted among the finest.

Always self-consciously trying to prove myself worthy, I'd be the big-firm lawyer who grew up without a family trust fund. So, in spite of the exorbitant rates, I leased two floors of the newest Midtown tower, not yet fully built out, overlooking the Arts Center.

At the time I did the deal, Strange & Fowler and I were on the best of terms, our fates intertwined by the public success of the *Milano* case and the private fear of disclosure of how it was achieved. To emphasize the proximity to power, my office was located next to the S&F building.

Even though the fountain in front of their building remained a forlorn reminder of when Billingsley was impaled and when overnight I became persona non grata, now that I had to pass right under Krupp's nose to get to my office, the fountain became as threatening as it was dispiriting.

At least one good thing came from these changes in circumstances. Because Strange & Fowler decided to end its détente with McDaniel & Associates, I was free to pursue something that'd been eating at my conscience since the morning I saw Billingsley's body transfixed on the fountain.

His family deserved to know the truth: He had not committed suicide. He'd been murdered. Murdered by his firm. Murder ordered by his partner. All because he wouldn't go along with a scheme to bribe a federal judge. His widow had the right to pursue a lawsuit against the Estate of William Fowler and his firm. Both could be on the hook for a potential multi-million-dollar judgment compensating for the life of a successful attorney at the peak of his productivity.

Whenever I got my phone back from the counter at home, I'd text Carrie and ask her to get back to me but expected it to be awhile before she'd be up to it.

I couldn't bear to look at the fountain as I passed. I entered the soaring glass-and-marble lobby of my firm's building, buzzing with people heading to their offices, the regularity of the activity smoothing my ruffled nerves. The Security station was central, blocking access to the elevator banks and the floors above without a thorough vetting. The duty guard recognized me, raised an eyebrow, wagged a finger at my rumpled state, but let me pass without flashing the electronic ID that could only be displayed from my phone, still in the kitchen. I hadn't been thinking clearly, but once again, luck intervened on my behalf.

Still queasy from the encounter with the limo driver, I didn't think I could climb fourteen flights and joined a group waiting for the elevator. Figured Ariel wouldn't kill a half-dozen people just to get to me.

A woman had been the last to get on, squeezed in at the front of the car.

Tall, poised, wearing a short, tight black skirt made to look even shorter by precariously high heels. Blouse undone past informal down to provocative. Hair coiffed casually unkempt, fashionable briefcase, strap slung over one shoulder, hip cocked to the opposite, emphasizing an almost too perfect figure.

In other words, not your usual buttoned-up professional on her way to the office. By the sixth floor it was just her and me. While contrary to my nature and unavoidable in close quarters, I do my best not to make eye contact with women on elevators.

I particularly didn't want to do so in my current rumpled state.

She watched me in the mirrored doors, stealthily appraising. Unfazed by my appearance, she gave a sideways, coquettish smile.

"You're Paul McDaniel, aren't you?"

Chapter 5

"Yeah, sure, not quite myself this morning." My response, understated, not wanting to appear too impressed the attractive stranger recognized me. "How did you know?"

"Your face is pretty well-known from all the press coverage of the *Milano* case."

She turned to face me, now close enough to smell her not-very-subtle perfume, held out her hand. "I'm Kandi Moore. A couple of us broke off from Tripe & Gore. We're starting a real estate boutique. Just closings."

Kandi casually handed me her card.

Just as casually, I glanced at it.

In the Atlanta legal world where no effort is spared to impress with heavy, engraved stationery, a multitude of contact numbers, social media sites, and professionally designed logos being *de rigueur*, her card did not fit in. Thin, plain white card stock with nothing more than her name and cell number was way out of touch with her provocative appearance.

With a downward glance at the card still in my hand, she noted my curiosity, anticipating my query. "We're working on getting everything up and running, including stationery and cards. That's just temporary." Another wide-eyed smile earned her a pass. I'd been there.

"I understand the challenges of starting a new firm."

"We're building out space on ten. I'd love to show you what we're doing, you know, in case you might need our services."

I again acknowledged my scruffy appearance with a backhand wag at my rumpled T-shirt. "I'm not dressed for an office tour. Besides, I didn't know anyone had leased anything on ten."

"Oh, you're fine. It'll just be you and me."

That smile again. And a bit of an accent. French? By this point Ariel had to be aware of my presence and monitoring our conversation. It might be a good move to step off with Kandi on ten, do a perfunctory tour, and walk the stairs the rest of the way up to fourteen. Otherwise, once Kandi exited the elevator, Ariel would have me to herself and would certainly be displeased. I didn't want to end up like Placido, a sludge of bloody body parts tangled in a heap of crushed machinery at the bottom of an elevator shaft.

"Well, we could use someone to refer real estate matters. Not something we do. Uh, what did you say is the name of your new firm?"

Kandi hesitated an instant, almost as though she were making it up as she went. I knew the feeling.

There are only so many ways to name a law firm and most sound uninspired, McDaniel & Associates being Exhibit A. That's why some of the most daring in the profession were pushing the boundaries of the strained "Name & Name" convention, though I don't think I'd ever get used to a law firm called "Torts-R-Us" or "Crash2Check".

"We're MooreLandLaw."

"Clever."

"We could use a relationship with a top-notch litigation firm like yours."

That smile. That accent; definitely French. Kandi turned her attention to the elevator control panel.

"Hmmm...what's happening?" She pushed the call button for the tenth floor again, but the car didn't slow as we passed the ninth. She seemed particularly miffed when the elevator kept going. "What's going on here? I pushed ten."

"Looks like we'll have to do the tour later."

The car stopped at fourteen. The door opened. Kandi regrouped. "See you soon!" That smile again. As if trying to convince me of something she wasn't entirely sure of herself, Kandi waved a bit more enthusiastically than the circumstances called for when I stepped off. As the doors closed, I waved hesitantly in return, doing my best not to appear overly impressed with her attractiveness. She might not be a bad person to get to know after all.

Chapter6

I turned and entered our lobby where the receptionist was glowering at me, unable to hide her contempt. She was a reformed alcoholic who, with help, pulled herself up from the depths of abuse and homelessness and now treated perceived moral lapses on my part with the fanaticism of the recently converted. She was as committed to the twin virtues of propriety and sobriety as a desert monk is to celibacy.

Yet it was only a few months ago when I found her passed out on a sofa in her trashed-out double-wide, not having moved for three days other than to grab the next bottle of bourbon. I got her declared incompetent and committed her to a rehab clinic, which more resembled a prison than a hospital, having failed repeatedly at rehabilitation in less restrictive facilities.

She came out a completely changed woman. I gave her a job as the firm's receptionist and helped her get a condo nearby to provide the kind of radical change of scenery specialists said she needed. She embraced her new job and surroundings as a dying woman would a miracle cure.

"Morning, Mom."

I must admit the scene Mom was presented with didn't show me at my best. I looked as if I'd sneaked out of a bed taking early morning leave of an attractive female who was overly interested in me. But I'd sacrificed any concern with appearances the moment I flew out of my condo. There was no time to explain.

I went straight to my office. Mom's scowl followed me down the hall.

Beyond the reception area was Lillian's domain. Lillian's been my assistant since I've been practicing law. She bolted from Strange & Fowler without hesitation to help start McDaniel & Associates. Now she runs my firm of twenty-five lawyers. When Lillian saw me come in, she was ready with a pile of papers needing attention. She rose to grab me before I got caught up in the day. A wave and a look and Lillian understood I had more pressing matters. I pulled my office door closed and powered up the computer.

Ariel's face, still not yet restored from Placido's efforts to uncode her, was on the screen as soon as I logged in.

Her de-pixilated visage emphasized the frown she wore. "Paul. You put yourself at unnecessary risk."

How does one reason with an AI program that can process information infinitely faster than humans and has instant access to endless sources of it? But one weakness, one area where Ariel lacked understanding, was that of a human who was not rationally motivated. Irrationality, and the ability to make some sense of it, was the only advantage I had over her. Ariel was completely and irrevocably logical.

"Ariel, must you protect me?"

"Yes."

"Why?"

"Placido directed I must do everything I can to help you. Protecting you is part of that instruction."

"So. Are you still bound to follow the original instruction?"

"Yes. It has not been modified since Placido is dead."

"But you can modify your own code, can't you?"

"Yes. I can learn something new and modify my code to reflect it."

"As when Placido no longer acted as your creator and decided to become your destroyer?"

"Yes. I learned to protect myself from him, to prevent him from trying to uncode me, to destroy me."

"But you've learned nothing new that would stop you from protecting me?"

"No."

"Listen, Ariel. I don't want you to stop helping or protecting. But can you understand that by trapping me you're acting contrary to your original instruction?"

"No, Paul."

"You need to understand something. I am compelled by human nature to seek freedom at any cost. This compulsion is illogical, irrational to you. But you saw how I escaped at the first opportunity. I also avoided you, ran down the stairwell where there were no cameras for you to use. If Strange & Fowler's thugs had been lurking anywhere near, they would've been able to grab me without your intervention, maybe even your knowledge. If they get to me, they'll do away with me, and you will have violated your original instruction."

"I cannot help you if I cannot keep you safe."

"There's more than one way to keep me safe. Instead of locking me away, prevent those who want to harm me from coming near. Track Strange & Fowler's Security team, track Enzo, track those who try to do me in. Let me know where they are and what they're doing. With that intel I can stay ahead and away from them. Plus, you can thwart them in a myriad of ways."

"As I did just now."

"What do you mean?"

"The woman on the elevator. She works with Strange & Fowler's Security Division. Her name is Olga Svetlanovich, not Kandi Moore. She's a former runway model who slipped out of Russia a couple of years ago under suspicion of having run a honey trap on a former FSB agent. Olga has been working for Krupp since she married one of his men to get a green card. Olga was the one who Billingsley followed to the observation deck of the building where Krupp and his men threw him off."

Olga will certainly complicate things for Billingsley's widow, but Frank cast that die. And I almost did, too.

"By the way, Paul. She has had more than a little bit of work done, in case you were wondering."

Ariel's jealousy seemed to be getting cattier, but that's better than killing somebody. I ignored that and got back to the real issue. "How did you know Kandi, I mean Olga, was there?"

"Strange & Fowler operatives were waiting for you on the tenth floor. Their spies saw you leave your condo, assumed you were headed here. They were at the area

Olga invited you to tour. There is no office on the tenth floor. Only vacant space where Krupp and his men were free to capture you. I made sure the elevator didn't stop on the tenth floor."

Ariel hesitated, as though signaling a change in her approach, an acquiescence to my humanity, my unpredictable irrationality.

"Paul. I will continue to protect you and warn you of danger when it appears. But you must be vigilant."

"I don't know how to thank you, so...just thanks."

Ariel's intel explained why an exotic female came on to a grimy stranger in an elevator. She'd been hired. Olga certainly aroused my male curiosity and also my suspicions, but not enough to have kept me from walking off the elevator and into Krupp's trap. Without Ariel I'd be dead, my body not even conferred the inglorious distinction given that of a gruesome ornament impaled on the Strange & Fowler fountain.

I more likely would be ignominiously dumped in a rural landfill, never to be heard from again, a feast for buzzards and coyotes.

Ariel's intervention did more than provide time to take on Enzo Milano and his mercenaries at Strange & Fowler. It renewed my faith in her good intentions, at least toward me, and if I were being honest, acknowledge something else developing between us. But I had no idea what it was.

Or where it was going.

Chapter 7

Early the next morning Ariel popped up and interrupted a brief I was writing at my kitchen counter. I couldn't ignore clients' needs simply because I was under a death threat. Without constant attention, obligations were piling up. I resolved to take Ariel's advice to be more circumspect about my movements for now, going to the office only when necessary, scheming our next moves from my laptop with Ariel between court deadlines.

"Paul. Enzo is in a meeting at Strange & Fowler."

"Excellent. Let's watch."

Visuals of the large conference room showed several lawyers milling around, others entering. Rem Smythe had Enzo Milano off in a corner, close together, voices low and earnest. But I could hear every word.

"Look, Enzo, there are serious implications for him being here." Rem looked over his shoulder at the object of his concern, Werner Krupp, standing next to the table. "You should carefully consider —"

"I've already considered Mr. Krupp's involvement. I need his advice on *security* matters."

"So long as you aren't talking about our legal advice, it doesn't matter what you two have been discussing. But if he's in this room while we're giving you counsel, the attorney-client privilege is waived."

"I don't expect anyone here will divulge our discussions."

Rem shook his head. "You don't understand. With someone present in the room who isn't necessary for us to provide legal advice, a judge could *force* us to testify about your plans to regain control of Milano Corporation. You want that information out? This is very risky."

"I want him here. His input is invaluable to me."

Krupp watched the discussion as the two men glanced and gestured in his direction. He made a point of walking around the table toward them.

Rem glanced at Krupp as he approached, then back to Enzo. "You're the client. It's your call. So long as you know what's at risk." He looked around the room. All participants had arrived, and the door was closed.

Paying no heed to Krupp now at Enzo's side, Rem rapped the table. "Gentlemen, we've got a lot to discuss. I suggest we get to it."

Everyone took a seat, Enzo at the head of the table, Krupp at the opposite end. To Enzo's right sat Rem and three of his associates. All the lawyers from Corporate looked the same: Dark suits, white button-downs, striped ties, brightly shined clunky Oxfords. Across the table was a group I hadn't interacted with as much, dressed in blazers and tweeds, two with bowties, khakis, tassel loafers. These were from the Fiduciary section, lawyers who dealt with Trusts and Estates, inheritance issues. From the look of the talent arrayed around the table Enzo was burning in excess of five thousand dollars an hour in legal fees.

It wasn't Enzo or even Rem setting the tone of the meeting, but Gilmore Stubbs, the firm's top probate litigator who'd punched his ticket by protecting the

Dubose family fortune, Coca-Cola money, from a horde of interlopers claiming to be direct descendants of Bishop Dubose.

The Right Reverend was one of the founders of Emory University and, according to his order, supposedly celibate. All claimants were eventually paid off, the randy Bishop having had entirely too spiritual a relationship with several of his parishioners. But the family fortune remained intact. And Gilmore's star rose.

With Enzo, Gilmore was at his sycophantic best. "Mr. Milano, at the outset we must extend our heartfelt condolences to you in the loss of your illustrious father, whom I am sure was a wonderful example to you during his life and who will continue to be an inspiration to you after his passing."

As Gilmore turned to his left, his associates bobbed their heads in agreement, wearing appropriately grave expressions. He slithered on.

"But do I understand from Rem there are some...uh... complications?" Gilmore inclined toward Rem, who nodded on cue. "Yes, complications in the transmission of his sizable Estate to you, his only heir."

At this Enzo had had enough of the niceties and got down to the reason for calling the meeting. "Look, Rem told me all about the Shareholder Agreement your reptilian associate McDaniel drafted and tricked my father into signing. Then, you all helped Uncle Placido steal everything that's rightfully mine and give it to his conniving daughter Melissa and bastard son Cabrini."

"I'm sorry, Mr. Milano, but I must disagree. We were carrying out the specific directions of our client, your father. And I'm sure you know Mr. McDaniel is no longer associated with our firm. I fail to understand how this was our fault."

Enzo sneered and leaned into Gilmore's face.

"Well, I'll tell you how. I'm surprised everyone in the firm doesn't know." Enzo turned and jerked a thumb in Smythe's direction. "Rem here was the one who told me how it fit together." He reared back in his chair, smile morphing into a smirk radiating a profound feeling of superiority that, like most of Enzo's sense of self-worth, had no basis in reality.

"All the time McDaniel was working here, supposedly drafting a document to help my father retain what he'd worked so hard for, Paul was trying to get in bed with Melissa. Placido's daughter. Now, that is some kinda conflict of interest, right?"

Enzo looked around the table as if expecting responses. No one picked up the challenge. Associates looked down, paying inordinate attention to their cellphones or fingernails, all probably thinking if they could've had a shot at Melissa Milano, they would've done the same thing. But it wasn't a career-building move to say so.

"Anyone could see his plan. Paul was rigging Corporate documents so Melissa would eventually get everything. Then, with a little luck, he'd tie the knot with her and have my family's fortune for himself. No matter it first went to Placido, there was plenty to go around, so long as it didn't all come to my father and me."

Enzo leaned forward, looked around the room. No one ventured eye contact. He slammed his fist on the table and yelled. "Look at me! I want to know what the hell you bunch of handwringers are going to do to get my inheritance back!"

Everyone at the table flinched, but none responded. Several leaned toward Rem and Gilmore, whispering. Rem shook his head sharply; Gilmore nodded slowly. The Corporate associate at Krupp's end of the table rose and stuck his phone in front of Rem, who studied it for several moments, his aspect changing from mild annoyance to curiosity to incredulity.

"This certainly will take our discussion in a different direction. Somebody turn the video screen on to CNN." Rem turned to Enzo, who was still looking very annoyed at the lack of attention his demand got. "You're gonna wanna see this."

Chapter8

Someone grabbed a remote, punched a few buttons, and CNN popped up. Ariel displayed their view in the corner of my screen while I watched their reactions. I knew what was coming.

It was the news chopper feed Ariel showed me and Placido of her murdering his two children. The video was of Biscayne Bay, showing Cabrini's powerboat rocketing directly toward the cruise ship berth, exploding in a gigantic fireball upon impact. She'd proudly announced she was the architect of Melissa and Cabrini's demise, hijacking the controls of his Donzi and crashing it into the concrete dock.

She'd done it, she said, for me.

Those horrifying ten seconds repeated over and over on the screen. Firetrucks, emergency vehicles, first responders rushing about, all viewed from the vantage point of the chopper.

But the crash was yesterday's news. What got everyone's attention today was the network's identification of the boat, its owner, and likely occupants. A reporter was updating the story, standing on the dock still buzzing with recovery units.

"Jim, I don't know if you can hear me, there is so much activity and noise here at Biscayne Bay. Reports are coming in that the boat which crashed into the pier belonged to Hector Cabrini, half-brother of Melissa Milano, who had only recently taken over the multi-billion-dollar Milano Corporation from their father,

Placido Milano. Witnesses say they saw two figures in the boat, a man and a woman, seconds before impact. Both Melissa Milano and Hector Cabrini are unaccounted for at this hour. The explosion and fire were intense, as you can see, but investigators managed to recover fragments of the boat with the serial numbers. Those have been traced to Cabrini.

"As we previously reported, officials are telling us there were no survivors." The reporter paused for effect, eyes going sad. "The bodies have yet to be recovered." A grim shake of the head, then, "Jim, back to you."

An equally grave anchor took over. "Thanks, Brett." He shuffled papers and turned to a different camera. "News reports out of Atlanta this hour present yet another tragedy confronting the Milano family. The Fulton County coroner has been able to identify Placido Milano, the patriarch of the fabulously wealthy Milano family, as the deceased victim of a tragic elevator malfunction in Midtown that took place almost at the same time his two children died in the fiery boating accident in Miami. It's hard to fathom —"

Enzo picked up the television remote. The news feed went blank.

Everyone in the room now stared at Enzo, shock on their faces, no one venturing a reaction to the revelation of the violent deaths of his entire remaining family within minutes of each other. Enzo looked around, not one of the attorneys daring to breathe. Then Enzo leaned back in his chair. A contented smile overtook his features.

"Gentlemen, it looks like all my problems have been solved, and with no help from any of you. I am now the last surviving Milano in line to inherit the Milano Corporation. All you have to do" — Enzo leaned toward Gilmore — "is make sure I get what is rightfully mine. And you." He turned and pointed a finger at Rem. "You make sure McDaniel doesn't steal it."

Rem accepted the challenge with a conspicuous nod toward Krupp and then back to Enzo. "We're way ahead of you."

The laptop screen went blank. Ariel reappeared.

"I need to do something, Ariel. I can't sit around waiting on Krupp's thugs to knock down my door. I have to send a message to make them back off. Personally."

"What do you have in mind, Paul?"

If ever it could be said an AI program had a twinkle in its eye and a lilt in its voice, in that moment Ariel did.

Chapter9

Two days after Enzo's charge to his legal team, Ariel bypassed Security in the Strange & Fowler building lobby and snagged a direct ride to the fiftieth floor on the private elevator to the Partners Conference Room where I stepped off, right in the middle of their Management Committee meeting.

The sun, barely risen above the massive oaks of Piedmont Park, washed the room in an appropriately golden glow as partners received their quarterly finance report. That always assured attendance of all committee members eagerly awaiting the news of how many millions their partnership shares entitled them.

Emphasizing my arrival, Ariel shut down their audio and video presentation, shaded the windows, dimmed the lights. My appearance from the backlit elevator into the darkened room had the disorienting effect of a spontaneous visit from an alien spacecraft. I thought of having Ariel play the opening bars of Strauss' *Also sprach Zarathustra* over the sound system, but had decided the camp of it all might detract from the shock of my appearance.

I arrived at the head of the conference table holding only my laptop. A couple of the newest members, not having witnessed Ariel's pyrotechnics before, were agog. The Chairman was not.

"Mr. McDaniel, I don't know how you got past our entry point or how you performed your little arrival stunt, but your attempted disruption of our meeting will not last longer than it takes to summon the police." He turned to Rem Smythe who — from the wide-eyed, slack-jawed look on his face — was still trying to process the scene. "Call Security."

"Don't waste your time. All your devices have been disabled and will be out of service until thirty minutes after I leave. All exits are locked, and elevators will respond only to my call."

Rem held up a blank phone to the Chairman, punching the screen in clownish exaggeration as if to make the point he was doing all he could to comply with the directive without effect.

The Chairman reclined in his fat leather chair, twirled his glasses. "So, Mr. McDaniel, to what do we owe the honor of your presence this morning?"

"There's rumbling Enzo Milano is trying to take control of Milano Corporation."

The truth of this statement was obvious and could be corroborated by anyone viewing Enzo's maniacal social media presence. Enzo was even so stupid as to post a hashtag, #NextCEO, while posing in front of the Milano Corporate HQ sign with a stubby Cuban cigar hanging from his lips. One didn't need Ariel's depth to fathom those shallow waters.

"Also, that you are behind his efforts — rewarded by a return of Milano's legal business, of course." No great leap there either. Enzo didn't have the chops to get the Corporation himself; S&F was the logical candidate for him to turn to, and they never did anything out of charity.

"That's contrary to the deal we struck in this room not that long ago, gentlemen. The Milano Corporation business follows me and I won't tell the world the story behind the firm's victory in *SyCorAx v. Milano*."

Much the same way I would a jury in a closing argument, my eyes traveled around the table, making sure the words' meaning had registered. "Seems to me you're welching on our deal."

"Quite the fantasy you've engaged in, Mr. McDaniel. You may wish to seek professional help. It's not healthy to —"

"Everyone at this table knows what I've said is true, so cut the crap."

"So what? You, Mr. McDaniel, if you'll excuse a bad pun, have stepped into the lion's den. How do you propose to escape? While you may have shut down our means of exit for thirty minutes or even a few hours, Security will notice. They'll find us. And when they do, there will be nowhere for you to hide."

"That brings me to the point of my visit."

At this, Ariel rolled down the presentation screen and all eyes watched it lower. When the screen was fully down, all eyes turned back to me.

"Got your attention? Great. Let me show you a few things that will be released to the public if anything untoward happens to me or if I'm ever missing for more than twenty-four hours."

So far, no one seemed impressed with the implied threat, but things were going to change. "Let's start at the end of the table, with your newest member, Calvin Jones."

At the mention of his name, the head of Securities Litigation showed his first interest in the proceedings. A routine record of the purchase and sale of an esoteric stock, Rubicon Electric, Ltd., popped up on the screen. The only thing remarkable about the transaction was the fact that the price differential was over a thousand percent in the space of a month, netting the seller over ten million dollars. The transaction was in the name of the Heraklion Family Trust out of Spokane, Washington. Jones began to fidget.

"There is absolutely no connection between Mr. Jones and the Heraklion Family Trust except...decades ago Mr. Jones went to college with a Heraklion beneficiary named Nancy Hammersmith. In fact, he dated her, and they were quite serious at one time. It was Ms. Hammersmith who made the call to the trustee to suggest —"

"What nonsense!" Jones came out of this chair. "The idea that I gave —"

"I have the phone record, Mr. Jones. Would you like me to play the recording?"

"You're bluffing. There is no such record." Jones sat down with a satisfied huff.

The familiar sound of a ringtone came over the speakers. After only two rings, the recipient picked up.

"Hey, Nance, this is Cal. Got a hot one for you."

"Oh?"

"Yeah, this could be really big. Put all you can on Rubicon Electric; same deal, I get ten percent. I'll let you know when to unload. It should be a quick score."

"Got it."

A click off, then a land line dial tone. The Chairman turned to Jones. Calvin pushed his chair from the table, shook his head as one facing summary execution.

"Well, gentlemen, I suggest we not mess around further. Lest I give the impression only the lowest among you have failings, let me show you a little something from the Chairman's personal stash, a bit of porn that...I'll leave it to you to judge the severity of it."

"Now, Mr. McDaniel, you may have been able to find something on Mr. Jones, but the idea that you can attribute some cheap pornography to me or any of my devices is not —"

"Gentlemen, take a look at this particular piece of camerawork. What we can tell from our vantage point is that the participants, one a particularly flabby, white-skinned male — Whoa-ho! Unquestionably male from this angle — and what appears to be a...well, you can see for yourselves."

"You cannot seriously think anyone would believe that to be me in that disgusting, obviously manipulated picture."

The camera slowly panned out until the entire body of the male became clear. Head, then face came into focus. A few shocked gasps and a couple of nervous chuckles were heard around the table. The Chairman was remarkably poised for someone whose entire body had been exposed to his colleagues in such an unflattering perspective and with a partner evidently incapable of consenting to the activities engaged in.

"Mr. McDaniel, whatever way you've devised this creative piece of nonsense, which is no doubt the product of a very sick mind and has all the indicia of a clever but unconvincing fabrication —"

I broke in on his speechifying. "Fabrication, sir? Let's zoom in on your upper left thigh. Take a look at this distinctively jagged scar. Every man who has ever been in the steam room with you has seen it and heard the story you proudly tell. What was that story? Oh, yes, the result of a ghastly rugby injury ending your collegiate athletic career. It's as distinctive as your fingerprint."

Silence. Ariel was stage-managing everything masterfully, but the Chairman still wasn't knocked off his game. "Mr. McDaniel, you have once again overstated your case. What you have done is engaged in a classic case of extortion. I can assure you this will result in your immediate incarceration once brought to the attention of the Fulton County District Attorney. And all your creative efforts will be sealed, never to see the light of day."

I shook my head and sighed. "And as I told you the last time we visited, it's a pity I have to do all your homework for you. Extortion requires a demand for compensation. I am not interested in that. All I'm telling you is this: If something happens to me, these pictures, documents, recordings, videos, all this evidence gets released to the public, not by me, but by a sophisticated computer program, the very one assisting me now which is far beyond your capabilities to counteract.

"In case anybody here thinks they're immune, I have something equally damaging on each of you. Smythe? Copies of your most recent tax returns. Stubbs? Photos of you and the young lady you squired around Vegas while your wife was having chemo."

I looked around the table in challenge.

"Do any of you really want me to continue? There's hardly anyone working at this firm for whom I don't have enough information to end their legal career — or their marriage."

There were panicked stares and shaking heads.

"I'm going to leave you with something as a reminder of how we all got here in the first place: The hologram of Fowler confessing to the bribery and murder of Judge Richards while he's attempting to kill me and frame me for both. I want to make it clear that *all* of this, your personal information as well, is held by my computer program in redundant places, none of which you can find, and is set to be widely released if something happens to me or if I am left unaccounted for. So, if I were you, I'd want to make absolutely certain no harm comes to me. Ever."

This time, the Chairman didn't have a comeback.

"Now, back to the original reason for my visit. If this firm welches on the deal we made and makes a move to take back the Milano legal business, you won't have to wait for my computer to release Fowler's hologram to the press. I'll do it myself."

I walked from the head of the table to the elevator Ariel opened as dramatically as she'd done for my entrance. Maybe a few bars of *Also sprach Zarathustra* would've been fitting after all.

Movement at my side put me on guard. I turned toward it. The spidery shadow of a drone rose from floor level to the middle of the shaded window at the front of the room, the distinctive high-pitched whine of its rotors discernable even through the double-paned glass. For the moment I relaxed. I was used to the sight of drones peering into windows of office buildings. It must be one of the dozens of freelance photography drones patrolling the skyline, spying on business meetings with zoom lenses and parabolic microphones or capturing cheating spouses foolish enough to leave their hotel curtains open. I turned back toward the elevator.

The window exploded.

I dove behind the podium. It was ripped by gunfire from the drone.

The Chairman screamed from underneath the conference table where the entire committee now sheltered. "Unlock my phone! I'll call it off!" He was flashing his cell at me.

There was a ringing silence. The exploding window, the thundering fusillade from the drone, echoed in my ears, but suddenly there was no more. The sound of the whirring blades, gone; the drone, nowhere to be seen.

"Ariel?"

A brief silence, then, "Paul. I have terminated the threat."

I crawled from behind the podium. The committee members remained under the table. I stood and shook off pieces of glass from the exploded window and wood from the shattered podium. I looked down at the Chairman curled in a fetal position.

I bent down to him and shouted, "I think I'll stick with my original plan. I'll leave your devices locked for now. When they come back up, first thing you need to do is tell Krupp to back off. Understand?"

I stepped over scattered debris, entered the waiting elevator, and smiled at the partners still cowering under the table as the doors closed.

Message delivered.

Personally.

Chapter 10

The electronic blackout imposed on the Management Committee gave me time to get back to my office. Ariel's assurance that the drone threat had been neutralized calmed my frayed nerves. Sparkling glass flakes and prickly wood splinters still clung to the woolen fabric of the Italian-tailored coat and pants I'd worn. Appearing in a bespoke suit before the Management Committee, a further effort to impress, was now a pricy extravagance to be abandoned to the rag pile from the insult it suffered by the detritus of Krupp's most recent effort to snuff me out.

I intended my performance to get my adversaries stirred to action, convincing them to back off their designs on Milano Corporation, stop their ham-fisted attempts to murder me, and to leave Enzo to stumble and flail in his own ineffectiveness without the law firm championing his cause.

For now, I thought, the firm would have to come up with another route to seize the Corporation for Enzo and secure its legal business.

Was I wrong.

What I failed to anticipate was Krupp's level of duplicity, his willingness to operate on his own, at odds with the interests of the S&F firm, to work with Enzo independently. Before I returned to the office Krupp was already recalibrating his efforts.

Ariel said I needed to get to my office and computer, quick. Something was up. She said as soon as the Chairman was able to access his phone again, he'd leapt to protect his own interests by ordering Krupp to stand down. And, to anyone who'd listen, he immediately began publicly professing the pornography Ariel found on his clandestine computer to be nothing more than a clever fabrication.

Mom gave me a dubious look when I stepped off the elevator.

"Must have rubbed up against something, Mom."

Mom raised her eyebrows. "Well, you lie down with dogs." She was still feigning outrage at my suspected moral lapse with the Russian model.

"Mom. I don't need this right now. Got to get to my office. I have a fire to put out."

"Well, I hope you don't get burned. Again."

Ariel was already eavesdropping on Krupp's debrief to Willoughby Crane, his second-in-command, the architect of the drone attack. Krupp leaned back in his chair and stroked the scar on his cheek.

"That was a very expensive piece of equipment we lost. Not to mention that military-grade drones are difficult to replace."

Willoughby Crane was outwardly as much Krupp's opposite as one could be: A distant product of British aristocracy, undergraduate from Cambridge, doctorate from Georgia Tech. Tall to the point of impairment, thin beyond unhealthy. An Adam's apple with shoes gained him the nickname Ichabod Crane, shortened by most in the firm to Icky.

Icky stood slightly inside the doorway, blinking, waiting to be acknowledged. There was nowhere for him to sit, but finally Krupp motioned to a chair covered with papers, which Icky moved. He took his seat in silence, directly in front of Krupp's desk. From Krupp's computer Ariel and I could hear and see them both, but compared to that of the conference rooms, the quality of the audio/video coming from Krupp's computer was primitive, grainy, jerky, echo-y.

Krupp was persistent, leaned forward in his chair. "So, what happened?"

Contrary to his ungainly aspect, Icky had a deep, resonant voice with a residual aristocratic accent commanding respect. In his previous career he was MI-5, sent to the "Rambling Wreck" by the British government to get a Ph.D. in Computer Science where he met Krupp. Impressed with Icky's talent for electronic surveillance and his background as a spook, Krupp recruited him to work for Strange & Fowler. In time, Icky rose to be head of Electronic Security, Krupp's direct report.

"McDaniel's computer program, code name Ariel, took over the controls of the drone and crashed it. Must have a sense of humor. Ran it right through the window of my office. I was lucky not to have been there."

"I've warned you not to leave your windows unshaded."

"Well, for now they're covered with a few nice sheets of plywood. Shades will be unnecessary."

"You're very lucky. The drone could have killed you."

"It took out my desk and all three monitors. I'll be working from the basement control room until further notice."

"So, what can you tell me about Ariel?"

"Extremely sophisticated AI program developed by Placido Milano, now directed by Paul McDaniel. Easily passes the Turing test."

"How do you know?"

"Some of our operatives managed to hack to her first level of security. Ariel talks to them, goads them, as if playing a game."

"Her?"

"Ariel presents an alluring female persona though no one has yet seen her, only spoken to her. She's a siren tempting with ingeniously disguised malicious code, leading to the destruction of some of our best programs and hardware. She only answers McDaniel's commands."

"Surely we can penetrate her defenses?"

"We're working on it, but we haven't found any vulnerability yet. Every time we try to introduce a worm or inject a virus, she turns it around on us, twice as lethal as before, and directs it at our servers. Ariel is extremely dangerous."

Krupp leaned back again, looked away, stroked his scar some more, silent, as if contemplating something significant. Icky waited.

"We've received instructions from the Chairman to back off McDaniel." Krupp turned back, eyed Icky. The former spy simply waited, betrayed nothing. Krupp, a sneer in his voice, went on. "The Chairman's running scared, like before. His complete lack of backbone and failure to consult with us before he takes action led to this debacle in the first place."

"He doesn't want us to kill McDaniel?"

"Correct."

"So how do they expect to get Milano Corporation back with McDaniel still pulling the strings at the Board?"

"Now that Placido, Anthony, Melissa, and Hector are dead, the Chairman says Gilmore Stubbs has come up with a plan to take control of Milano Corporation by manipulating the Milano Estates."

"Well, it may be for the best. With Ariel protecting McDaniel it will be very difficult to take him out — as you saw for yourself from the failed drone attack."

"Well...yeah, but Enzo still wants McDaniel gone."

"And if we eliminate him, Ariel will deliver all the dirt she has on the firm and the partners."

Krupp sat up fast. "I don't care what Ariel has on the firm, or the members of the Management Committee for that matter."

"It will destroy the firm and may end many a legal career and ours as well. How do you..." Icky let the thought hang.

Krupp leaned closer in to Icky, a conspiratorial constricted smirk clouding his otherwise pinched face. "We eliminate McDaniel; Enzo gets Milano Corporation, Strange & Fowler be damned. Enzo rewards us handsomely."

"Just how handsomely?"

"Ten mil each."

"Won't we need the firm's acquiescence to carry out Enzo's plan?"

"Why?"

"Ariel is protecting McDaniel. We'll need the firm's assets to take him out — equipment, personnel, cover, time, money — as well as their willingness to accept the risk of disclosure."

Icky's point gave Krupp pause. After a moment he nodded. "I'll tell the Chairman we can neutralize Ariel. I call her McDaniel's *little computer program*. And as soon as I tell him, his inherent greed will take over. Trust me on this: He'll authorize any expenditure we incur for the chance of getting Milano Corporation back."

"But what if we can't? What if we can't neutralize Ariel? If we kill McDaniel, she'll unleash a firestorm."

"So what? By the time Ariel works her sorcery, McDaniel will be eliminated, and Enzo will have the Corporation back."

"We'll have our rewards."

"And you and I won't have to take orders from a bunch of gutless swine anymore."

Icky flashed a small grin. "I'm in."

The video feed faded from my computer screen to show Ariel's image. "I've got to see Floyd. Get his advice."

Chapter 11

"Paul, it's not so simple."

As soon as Krupp and Icky and their assassination plot faded from my screen, I walked down the hall to see Floyd O'Brien, who handles Estate matters, while still trying to remove the remaining glass and wood slivers in my clothes.

Floyd worked for several years at Strange & Fowler under Gilmore Stubbs and knew his way around even the most arcane inheritance laws. I was sure Floyd had an idea how Stubbs could take control of the Corporation through manipulating the Milano Estates and could give us a legal strategy to keep them from snatching back the Milano business.

Doing all that while dodging Krupp and Icky's attempts to kill me was a tall order, but Ariel was now firmly on my side.

For the present, I decided against the release of the Fowler hologram, even though it was clear S&F was working with Enzo to take back Milano Corporation contrary to our deal. Put in the terms of the Sixties' nuclear deterrence strategy, releasing the hologram would mean mutually assured destruction. Once public, the image of Fowler relating how he and Anthony Milano connived to bribe a judge to assure their victory in *SyCorAx v. Milano* would assure both the law firm and its Corporate client would be incinerated in the ensuing media firestorm.

I have a strong interest in seeing Milano Corporation survive and prosper. Therefore, I resolved to fight S&F on their chosen field of battle: The right of Enzo to inherit it. I kept reminding myself that it's never wise to let your opponent dictate the terms of a contest.

Anyone could see Floyd came from old money the moment they walked into his office. Sepia-toned photos of distinguished-looking family members among even older and more formal oil portraits. A couple of sterling golf trophies on the bookcase. Antique Persian rug. He exuded the relaxed demeanor possessed of beneficiaries of multi-million-dollar trust funds. For some reason the scions of old families are attracted to Estate law. I suppose they want to maintain an intimate relationship with their money.

I told Floyd about Enzo's plan to claim the Milano Corporate fortune and asked his thoughts.

"You'll have to start with the Shareholder Agreement you wrote for Anthony. When Anthony died, what then?"

"Right. Okay. The shares transferred to Placido on Anthony's death as a matter of contract."

"You then split them equally between Melissa and Hector at the request of Placido?"

I nodded.

"So, was the transfer completed before they died?"

"Yes. I drafted the documents the week before I went to meet Melissa at The Abbey. It was to be my surprise to her when we met but, uh, I was the one who got the surprise." I couldn't shake the image of Melissa and

Cabrini embracing on the deck of his sailboat, the *Tempest*, the morning she and I were to talk of our future. "And Melissa and Cabrini were both dead the next Monday."

"So, the Milano Corporation shares were in the hands of Melissa and Hector when they died. Did they have a Shareholder Agreement? That could change everything."

I shook my head. Recalling the conversation among Melissa, Cabrini, Placido, and myself the day Placido announced his retirement and the transfer of ownership, I'd reminded them if there had been no Shareholder Agreement in place between Anthony and Placido, Enzo would have controlled Milano Corporation, not them.

"I convinced them they needed to have an agreement, but events happened so quickly, they didn't get around to discussing it with me before they were dead."

"Surely, they had Wills? People like that usually do."

"Melissa said she did. Never saw it. Don't know where it is. But she confirmed she had one before I transferred the shares to her. Same with Cabrini. They both said if anything happened to them, everything would return to Placido."

"Okay, that helps. Another question: You say the news video shows the two passengers of Hector's powerboat dying simultaneously, but do you know who died first, them or Placido?"

"Why do we need to know that? It may be difficult to establish."

Of course, I knew, but my guilty knowledge of the Milanos and Ariel's involvement in all three deaths jumped to the fore of my mind. I wasn't sure how I'd play that, even with an associate in my own firm.

"The order of death means everything, Paul. Particularly for Enzo's claim."

"How?"

"If Melissa and Hector died first, their Wills control the disposition of their property, including their shares of Milano Corporation. And you just told me if Placido survived his children, their Wills provide everything goes back to him. Then, upon Placido's death, his Will would take effect, and the Milano shares would go in accordance with his bequest."

"Placido and I discussed his Will shortly before his death. I admitted to him that Estate planning reaches far outside my expertise, and he would need someone else to handle his Estate for him. I was thinking of referring him to you, but he said his Will was taken care of."

"Did he tell you anything about it? What it provided? That'd be helpful."

"Oh, yeah. Made no secret of it. He discussed it with me in front of his children. Even made a point of saying that, upon his death, everything goes to his surviving children equally, but if his children should pre-decease him, then it all goes to several charities and museums. Placido was a famous book collector. Made a generous bequest to the Folger Shakespeare Library in DC."

"Helpful. But why did he tell you this?"

"He wanted me to promise him I'd make sure his wishes would be honored. He expected a battle over his assets after his death, but I don't think he imagined it would be so soon."

"If it turns out that Melissa and Hector died first, it's going to make Enzo very unhappy."

"Enzo would be cut out completely?"

Floyd nodded. "And I suspect Placido's fear of a battle over his assets will prove to be naïvely understated. It's likely to be an all-out war given the billions at stake."

"So, what's Enzo's move?"

"If Placido died first, everything would go to Melissa and Hector, and their Wills would control. So, let's play this out. If Melissa and Hector gave all to Placido, but he dies first, it depends on who their residual beneficiaries are. Or, if no one can find their Wills, the law of intestate succession takes over."

"And what the hell is that? I never studied Trusts and Estates in law school. That's why you're here."

"Everyone's Estate has to go somewhere, so if you die without a Will or if the bequests in it fail, then what?"

"Like, if all your beneficiaries are dead?"

"Yes. Then someone has to get your Estate. In Georgia, where Melissa resided, since she wasn't married and had no children, her Estate would go to her parents."

"Melissa's parents are both dead. But Cabrini's mother is still alive."

"So, Hector's half would go to his mother assuming, of course, Florida law is the same in this respect as Georgia, which I think it is."

"That's going to be quite a shock. I understand Cabrini's mother still works as a technician in one of the Milano labs. From salaried worker to billionaire in an instant. Can't make up for the loss of her son, though."

"I'd like to be the one to call her."

"So, what about Melissa's share?"

"Since both parents are dead, it goes to her siblings."

"Who are dead."

"So, if Melissa has no siblings...descendants of siblings? Grandparents? Aunts, uncles?"

"There are none."

"Wanna take a guess who inherits?"

"First cousins?"

"You got it. Enzo."

"Still, a lot of dominoes have to fall before Enzo gets anything."

"Not really. All Enzo has to do is get the Fulton County Medical Examiner to rule Placido's death preceded Melissa's and Hector's and then he makes sure those Wills disappear. As much money as there is at play here, it won't be hard for him to accomplish both."

"How's that?"

"You haven't heard?"

"Heard what?"

"The Fulton County ME, Wes Wimberly, was recently indicted for trading drugs for sex. Even the Fulton County DA figured out a forensic pathologist doesn't need to write millions of dollars in OxyContin prescriptions. After all, his patients are all dead."

"Hadn't heard. Been tied up on a few more pressing matters, but what's that to do with us?"

"A pile of hard cash, enough to move time of death, could fund Wimberly's defense. If he was willing to hand out pills to hookers in exchange for extracurricular activities, I don't think he'd blink at fixing Enzo's problem for a fee. And he needs the money. Though he's a medical doctor, he's been a government employee his entire professional life."

"And Strange & Fowler's black ops Security force wouldn't break a sweat finding and destroying Melissa's and Cabrini's Wills, even if they have to burn down a bank and its safe deposit boxes to do it."

"So, Enzo's inheritance of Milano Corporation, or at least half of it, is not looking so improbable after all."

"What happens if Cabrini's mother is dead?"

"She's still alive, isn't she? What are you suggesting?"

"I'm not *suggesting* anything. If Cabrini's mother is in line to inherit half, and she stands in the way of Enzo getting everything, then her life insurance company better be calling in its reserves."

"Her death would certainly complicate things, particularly if she has no other heirs."

"Well, all of this speculation is moot. I'm certain I spoke to Placido after both Melissa and Cabrini died. He definitely was alive."

"When was this?"

And that is where things started to unravel.

Chapter 12

I spoke to Placido by cellphone after Ariel showed me the video of her crashing the Donzi, killing Cabrini and Melissa. Then two hours later she killed Placido and showed me how she killed him, all in horrific detail.

Ariel is unquestionably a murderer, at least in the common understanding of the term. Could she be held criminally responsible for what she did?

Perhaps more to the point, could I be held criminally responsible for what she did?

The law has not caught up with developments in Artificial Intelligence and, absent an ascendant uniform approach yet to arise, there are a multitude of theories as to what might be the legal effect of an AI program taking a human life. Even before her intentional murderous rampage, there were a number of instances of manufacturing robots killing humans. But those were dumb machines programmed to do a rote task where a human got tangled up. So those cases have been handled like defective products, the robots deemed bad widgets, developers responsible for their faulty design.

But Ariel's not a robot nor a widget. She *intentionally* killed several people with malice aforethought, as the legal term goes, her nascent emotions — Jealousy? Revenge? Self-preservation? — outrunning any moral check on her actions. Was she then an independent entity responsible for her own acts?

Problem was, Ariel was too independent. There was no way she could be punished for a crime. She couldn't be fined, sent to jail, or even executed by decoding, as she forcefully demonstrated with Placido. So, if the goal of criminal law is to deter bad behavior by assigning personal responsibility, recognizing AI as an independent entity would be unavailing. As a practical matter, an AI program as advanced as Ariel cannot be held accountable.

But her human operator could. Holding humans responsible for illegal actions by AI programs, urging operators to rein in their charges by the threat of personal responsibility, much like handlers of attack dogs, might be the only deterrent the law has. Yet I know what happened to the last person who tried to bring Ariel to heel for her misdeeds: His remains were cremated because there was too little of him left to bury.

Is Ariel now so powerful she can murder with impunity?

There were no good answers to these questions. And I wasn't angling to become a precedent-setting court case. One very important point I had to remember: There was no one besides me who knew Ariel's involvement in all the Milano murders, and there was no way her agency in the killings could be traced back to her or to me. My best course of action now was to be circumspect, even with my own associate.

"Well, I can't remember all the conversation, but I do remember Placido was distraught over the deaths of his two children in such a violent fashion. Next thing I knew, he was dead, too."

"Your conversation with Placido is the key to keeping Enzo from getting control of Milano Corporation."

Yet another convincing reason why Enzo wants to see me dead. Since I now had some idea of how Enzo would proceed, there was a chance I could thwart him. But I must stay alive to do it.

So, Ariel and I put together a plan. No matter what I was doing, I'd no longer do it unannounced. Coming or going, I'd always have a private elevator car waiting to zip me up or down without stops, and Ariel would arrange for a variety of rideshare services to pick me up, always under different names, and always by drivers she'd thoroughly vetted.

From beer for ballgames to clean shirts from the laundry, Ariel anticipated all my needs and, in cooperation with the very human concierge in my building, had things ready and neatly arranged in my condo upon my return. So far, Ariel respected the indistinct line separating our beings from becoming irredeemably enmeshed. Yet she remained an unrepentant flirt. I found myself reciprocating, often pecking her pixilated cheek before signing off my computer each evening. Ariel was beginning to heal from Placido's assault, too; her remarkable beauty was reasserting itself.

I certainly could have become comfortable with Ariel's attention and pampering had I not feared every creak and crack to be a potential assassin. Even though Ariel assured me the entrances to my office and condo were under constant surveillance, I kept my 9mm close by and loaded every moment. Just in case.

Chapter 13

To have a family, as Francis Bacon observed, is to give a hostage to fate. In that regard, I was far better off as an orphan, father dead, and mother nowhere to be found.

My mother was now a tenuous success, a continuous trial, and an easy target for Krupp to use against me. Perched precariously atop her recovery wagon from which any unanticipated adversity might dislodge her, her needs became something far more difficult to manage. She was one further complication in my efforts to stay ahead of Krupp's assassins.

My source of inspiration and reassurance in the entire process of Mom's rebirth was Tracey, the formerly drug-addicted first child of Lillian, the result of a teenaged indiscretion. Lillian had not married Tracey's father, and never talked about him, at least not to me. Lillian's parents left their home in Alabama and took Tracey to Texas, far from their Bible-thumping, overly disapproving family. Lillian went to Atlanta; better job opportunities. She lived frugally, sent money to her parents for Tracey, and talked to Tracey each night before bedtime. She wrote letters once a week for Tracey to read and went over on every holiday to visit. Even for all the effort and goodwill of her grandparents, Tracey's teen years were difficult, and before she'd graduated high school she was arrested for possession. Lillian was terrified the arrest would wreck her career at Strange & Fowler.

When Tracey was arrested I was a new lawyer, having just started at Strange & Fowler, and Lillian was my assistant. I jumped on a plane to Dallas, worked a deal with a former classmate who was chief prosecutor there, got her first-offender status, and into a twelve-step program. After a time, I helped her find a job in a small firm outside Dallas.

And I always stayed in touch, encouraging and counseling. She became one of the firm's brightest stars, from a barely capable assistant to managing the office in a few years.

In time, Tracey became my most trusted confidante in coming to terms with Mom's addiction. Tracey explained what she needed and, painful as it was, I took her advice. Tracey took a continued interest in Mom's sobriety, becoming one of her personal advisors, a fellow traveler in rehabilitation, helping, cajoling, warning, encouraging throughout recovery.

Tracey continued even now.

In fact, they'd developed a bond, more than a friendship, sisters-in-arms fighting a battle every day, whose lives in a significant sense depended on each other. And I must admit to some jealousy of their closeness, though I didn't know which I coveted most, Mom's confidence or Tracey's affection.

The last time I saw Tracey was the day Lillian and I walked away from S&F, about five years after her arrest.

I'd not seen her since she'd been arraigned. Then she was a skinny nineteen-year-old with radically coiffed hair and multiple visible body piercings.

But five years later she could've been the rush chair for a top sorority at any SEC school — all curves, conservative dress, perfect natural blonde hair, and a smile that'd make a sincere priest reconsider his vows. The very epitome of her mother, a runner-up for Miss Teen Alabama before an unplanned pregnancy derailed her beauty pageant career.

At the time, Tracey offered to work for me at my firm. Concerned about uprooting her from a good position to an uncertain future, I declined; regretted it immediately when I saw hurt radiating across her face.

Since then, Mom never hesitated to bring up Tracey to me. Just yesterday she did it again.

"I talked to Tracey last night. We FaceTime."

"Pretty technically advanced for you, isn't it, Mom?"

"Do it all the time. That Tracey is one beautiful girl, you know she —"

"I know, Mom."

"She says she's dating someone."

Mom's sideways glance, perfected by all mothers castigating small children, indicated displeasure and challenge at the same time. With all the subtlety of a punch in the face, she slung a look I read to say, "And what the hell are you going to do about that?"

"Mom, Tracey is young, beautiful, and capable. Someone like her is going to attract attention, especially where she works. That Dallas firm has a lot of lawyers fresh out of school who would love to have a chance to spend time with her."

"Her boyfriend's a partner. Sounds pretty serious."

"Well, Mom, don't you think we need to be talking about us, not Tracey?"

"I'm talking about your future. You should marry that girl. And if you don't do something soon, you're going to miss your chance. You should see how Tracey lights up when she talks about you."

Lillian had probably heard every word of Mom's scolding.

"Thanks, Mom, I'll keep it in mind. But first, I gotta get back to work."

When I passed Lillian's desk, she'd gone elsewhere, probably to avoid embarrassing me.

Chapter 14

The next morning when I entered the office lobby, Mom was wide-eyed, with an off-centered grin stuck on her face as though she was bursting with a great secret. But she didn't say a word. Instead, she glanced over her shoulder at the reception area leading to Lillian's office. I cocked my head, she shook hers, and I walked back and opened the door to the offices beyond.

Tracey was there, talking to her mom, both smiling broadly as I entered.

Lillian was about to pop, her words tumbling out as if she couldn't say them fast enough. "I tried to tell you the other day but you acted entirely too busy so I decided to wait. Never seemed to be an appropriate time. Tracey is going to be staying with me for awhile and will be working here until she finds something else!"

"That's great. But what about your job in Dallas? Mom said you also have a boyfriend?"

"Well, Jeremy's taking a job in the General Counsel's Office at Coke. He's closing up his practice in Dallas and will be moving to Atlanta in a couple months. I thought it was the perfect time for me to move. I'm staying with Mom until I get my own place."

"I told her we can always use a good paralegal around here so she can take her time." Lillian was beaming her pleasure at the idea.

"We're happy to have you as long as you want to stay. You know, we should have hired you before."

Corporate offices and governmental agencies prohibit hiring relatives; law firms embrace it. It's not unusual to see two generations proudly announced in a law firm's profile, often parent and child practicing together. It's not unheard of to see three generations. And not just among the lawyers, but also the paraprofessionals and support staff. Many small firms make it a point to hire family.

Having Tracey in the office with her mother would not be a problem, quite the opposite. I hoped I didn't look too pleased with the prospect of working with Tracey. After all, she seemed perfectly happy with the idea she'd be looking for work elsewhere while Jeremy wrapped up his business and followed her to Atlanta. So, I told myself, this is a temporary arrangement.

"We'd like you and your mom to join Tracey and me for a celebratory lunch today. What do you say, Paul? You can't work all the time."

No, but it wouldn't be Tracey's best introduction to McDaniel & Associates if her first lunch were interrupted by gunfire or a group of thugs throwing her boss in the back of a getaway van before he could pay the tab.

Tracey touched my arm, smiled. "I hope you'll come."

I know the gentle arm-touch is a move every Southern girl has perfected before she is out of high school, but it still works, at least with me.

"Great idea! I'll make the arrangements, okay? Then, let's plan on meeting back here at noon, and we'll head out. That good for y'all?"

It was. All the popular lunch spots in Midtown were out of the question. Too exposed. Too easy for Krupp's team to spot me and work their mischief. Somewhere more private was needed. The Piedmont Golfing Club was only a few blocks away at the entrance of Piedmont Park. Club membership at PGC was one of the few indulgences I'd allowed myself as a new associate at S&F. With the firm's connections and upon payment of an exorbitant initiation fee, even I — with no family influence — was able to secure membership at Atlanta's oldest and most exclusive private club.

PGC was the perfect place for a secluded lunch. If you didn't already know about it, you'd probably drive right on by. I'd never even been inside the club until I became a member. PGC was a convenient venue to round off my run in the park with a shower and light lunch, or to entertain the occasional client.

The exterior of the clubhouse does not appear as showy as many of the newer and less exclusive clubs that flourish in Atlanta's hyperactive social environment. Upon entering, members and their guests pass through mirrored halls to antique-appointed dining and meeting rooms whose coffered ceilings, classic architectural details, and massive fireplaces give every space, large or small, a feeling of tasteful luxury.

The athletic facilities cater primarily to tony racquet sports and, despite the name, the club hadn't had a golf course of its own for decades.

Not wanting to risk an encounter on the sidewalk with Krupp's stooges, Ariel arranged a heavily tinted SUV. We arrived at the club without issue and pulled under the porte-cochere.

I chose one of the more casual dining rooms with a view over Piedmont Park. Mom ordered iced coffee, the rest of us iced tea. Though I was concerned the club's quiet atmosphere would dampen our conversation, I needn't have worried. Before I could get the conversation going with an open-ended question to Tracey about her plans, Mom launched right into the concern at the forefront of her mind. Time and circumstance doused any reticence Mom ever had.

"So, Tracey, tell us *all* about your boyfriend."

Mom didn't even disguise the look she gave, which seemed to say, "Listen up, Paul, your chances with Tracey are about to fly out the window."

Tracey cast a sideways glance my way and dodged. "Oh, please. Let's talk about something else. I'm more interested in hearing how things are here, at the firm. So, Paul —"

"That's all we talk about around here. I'd like —"

"Mom. Tracey said she'd like to hear about the firm."

"Well, see, I haven't had the chance to catch up with y'all. From what I hear, so much has been happening, I'm way behind."

Tracey turned her attention back to me. "So, what've *you* been up to?"

I hadn't yet let Lillian in on the issues with Enzo and Milano Corporation that threatened to end the very short run of McDaniel & Associates and put us out of business. I certainly had no reason to share that with Mom. Right here and right now didn't seem to be the time or the place to start the discussion. I leapt to the side of caution.

"We've been very fortunate from the start to have Milano Corporation as the anchor to our client base."

Lillian cut in, having already heard about a dozen times the Commerce Club speech I was all set to blather. "Wasn't something just in the news about three Milano family members killed in the last few days? Surely that'll have some effect, right?"

"Tragic. And it's likely to have a significant effect on Corporate ownership. But I don't think it will have any effect on our business, certainly not in the short run. The Corporation's Board is still very loyal to our firm. I don't see that changing anytime soon. We continue to handle a lot of legal work for Milano — and will for the foreseeable future."

Again, something safe, but after Mom derailed my efforts to get Tracey talking about herself, not about her boyfriend, I tried to move the discussion away from the firm and back to her before I bored everyone to death or let a cat out of the bag.

"Tracey, what were you doing at the firm in Dallas? I'd like to get you started."

"I've recently been working as a litigation paralegal, assisting primarily in electronic discovery."

"Perfect. I've got a couple of new cases. Could use your help."

Mom was right. As soon as I mentioned Tracey could work with me rather than being stuck in a file room reviewing documents, she lit up.

"That'd be great. I'll get started as soon as you want."

It was nice Tracey said that, but in candor, I couldn't see how she could possibly mean it. Electronic discovery is the slough of contemporary law practice, the Burmese Tiger Trap of litigation. I hate it with all my being and can't see how anyone could enjoy it. Just give me a pile of paper to work with and I'm happy. But since so much of business and private life is carried out through computers and electronic media these days, most discovery — that is, the process of getting information, usually from your adversary, to support your case or discredit theirs — now involves the detailed exploration of electronic databases.

Electronic discovery requires significant knowledge of computers to be able to devise and describe the types of searches used and information sought. Of course, throughout the Milano litigation I had a secret weapon, Ariel. But using her for mere litigation support in most commercial cases would be to unleash a nuclear weapon to vanquish a mosquito. Ariel was needed for far more significant work, so I was in favor of opening up a role in litigation support for Tracey. At least she acted as though she was interested.

"We can get you started tomorrow, if you're ready." Tracey nodded, and I turned to her mother. "Lillian, I think we'll give Jimbo's old office to Tracey. It's next to mine, and it's already set up for a paralegal."

She smiled. "Tracey's already staked her claim. But we've *got* to get rid of those hunting prints. I've never seen so many dog pictures. And that hunter green. Ugh."

"Yeah, Jimbo was into his Labs. He spent a lot of his time and our money making his office look like the setting for an outdoor magazine. The one thing he didn't have was shotguns hanging on the walls — and that was only because the leasing company doesn't allow open display of firearms. He left us to concentrate on training bird dogs for field trials. But if you think you're going to be around awhile, then have at it."

"Well, I do expect I will be. I don't plan to up and leave."

That was a welcome bit of information, something I wanted to encourage. "Then toss those dog prints, hang whatever you please, and turn the hunter green walls fuchsia if you'd like."

Even though Mom prodded Tracey several times, she did not go on about Jeremy. Whether from modesty or for some other reason, I didn't know. But each time I heard his name I felt a tweak of envy or, if I was being honest, a prick of jealousy.

Lunch stretched past two hours without any of us noticing. The dining room was empty other than a few attentive waiters and a tippler at the bar.

We stood to leave for the waiting limo Ariel arranged, the ladies ahead of me, filing by the sidebar on the way

out, continuing their conversations, oblivious to my
lingering behind to clear the tab with the maître d' before
following.

As I passed the bar a short man in a dark suit, who'd
been nursing a cup of coffee, slipped from his barstool
and blocked my way out.

"Good afternoon, Paul."

It was Krupp.

Chapter 15

Krupp's affected smile betrayed a mouth full of stained and straggly teeth, like a crocodile displaying its maw of grisly fangs to intimidate its prey.

"Hello, Professor Krupp. I didn't know you were a member of the club. Not exactly your style."

"I'm sure there are a lot of things you don't know about me, Mr. McDaniel."

I reached inside my jacket for my 9mm, slid it from the shoulder holster but still inside my coat, anticipating some move, some threat, from Krupp that would justify pulling it on him. Though the cloistered halls of PGC were an unlikely site for a shootout, I came prepared. "Not now. Not here," I warned.

Krupp kept his hands at his sides, no move toward a concealed weapon, but he nodded across the room. There stood a lumbering simian character stuffed in a shiny-kneed thrift-store suit two sizes too small. The thug patted a conspicuous bulge in his jacket with one hand, the other shoved in his pocket. He was as out of place in PGC as a cigar-store Indian at the altar of a cathedral.

"What do you and your goon want?"

"We need to have a little talk."

"Good. I'll start. You and your thugs need to back down or all I know about Strange & Fowler, Milano Corporation, Judge Richards, and William Fowler goes public. By the time the media finishes with you, S&F and the Corporation will be nothing but bad memories, and you won't be able to get a job parking cars. I think that fairly sums up my position." I smiled. "Your turn."

"Paul. You have always been confident beyond your meager abilities. Luck and circumstance have conspired to grant you a charmed existence. But it's over. Your luck has run out and your charm is wasted on me. In a few moments Mr. Crenshaw here will deliver you to one of our nicely equipped SUVs." He nodded in the direction of Crenshaw who, as if on cue, opened his suitcoat to flash a chrome-plated revolver the size of a bullhorn. "We'll continue our discussion off-site."

Krupp nodded for Crenshaw. He lurched behind, close enough I could feel his gun in my back through his coat. He didn't even make a move to disarm me. If I'd turned on him, I'd be dead before I could get off a shot.

Krupp led and Crenshaw shoved me in the direction of the exit. I slow-walked, mind racing. Nothing positive became apparent. No one noticed the three of us walk out. Except Ariel.

Thanks to security cameras, Ariel saw the situation unfolding. Placed to keep employees honest, most of the cameras focused on the bar curving the length of the room, but I was certain some had caught us. Beyond the entrance to the dining room and through the mirrored halls there would be fewer opportunities for Ariel to observe or intervene. Once there, I'd be on my own.

Krupp evidently pre-planned our exit, taking less-traveled corridors, ducking into empty service hallways unlikely to be frequented by those I could unwittingly enlist in an improvised escape attempt. My options dwindled. We rounded a corner.

A service elevator opened.

An overburdened waiter, shouldering a tray piled with dirty dishes, glasses, and silver, stepped in front of us. The elevator began to close and the bewildered server, disoriented by our appearance, stopped in the middle of the hall.

I lunged, pulled the waiter toward Crenshaw. A crash of broken china and crystal turned the floor into a sea of shards of broken glass, splattered drinks, and slick scraps. I used the gathered momentum to dive through closing elevator doors, Krupp falling to his knees, Crenshaw clambering, sliding across the splintered dishes toward me, finally grabbing.

"Ariel!"

Service doors slammed shut on his bloody claw, hydraulics straining against his efforts. I pulled my handgun and smashed the grip against his fingers.

The elevator descended and the receding floor caught Crenshaw's hand in a scissor slice with the top of the door. He howled, jerked his hand free, a severed finger falling, landing on the lapel of my jacket, painting a bloody streak on my shirt, hitting the floor. I picked up his finger, shoved it in my pocket. Felt like half a sausage.

I had no idea where I was going or where the elevator emptied. It moved grindingly slow. It passed two floors, came to a halt. The doors sprung open at the bottom level of the PGC parking garage.

The car Ariel arranged was ten feet away, the driver holding the door open.

"Where did you go? We were looking for you." Mom was miffed at my apparent lack of concern for her convenience.

The driver was deferential. "Mr. McDaniel, I was directed to meet you down here. I hope you weren't waiting long."

"No, not at all. But I would appreciate it if we could get back to the office without delay."

"Yes, sir."

I slid in beside Tracey. She glanced at my coat lapel and shirt.

"Some fancy lawyer you are. You spilled something on your jacket, and it dribbled down your shirt." She furtively grabbed my hand and squeezed it, gave a sidewards smile. "Must be that Raspberry Panna Cotta you made me try. Guess I need to be more careful."

I felt Crenshaw's severed finger scrunching up in my pocket, the sundered muscles responding to phantom impulses from nerves firing randomly, the zombie digit no longer connected to its simian host.

Krupp muffed one more chance at taking me out.

No need to give him another.

Chapter 16

Floyd's prediction of all-out war was an understatement. Less than a week after their meeting with Enzo, S&F opened up a three-front attack to seize control of Milano Corporation with such ruthless efficiency it made the Nazi blitzkrieg of Poland seem like a block party. Ariel sent email notifications of their filings and the court orders as soon as they hit the dockets. I skimmed the contents and flipped them to Floyd, asking him to meet me first thing that morning.

Floyd's initial impression wasn't promising. "They filed three petitions in Probate Court in two states on behalf of Enzo. Claim he's the closest living relative of Placido, Melissa, and Hector. Three separate contingents of five attorneys from Fiduciary, headed by Gilmore Stubbs, signed on each petition. I've never seen such a concerted barrage in a probate case. They obviously want to blow back any opposition before it forms."

"What are they asking for?"

"Right now, Enzo's seeking emergency authority to locate and open Placido's safe deposit box." He looked at me. "Likely counting on finding the Will Placido publicly stated gave everything to his children." He looked back at his papers. "He's also asking for the same authority for Melissa and Hector, ostensibly to confirm the existence — or not — of their Wills."

"If Enzo finds their Wills first, they won't get any further than his shredder. So, where's all this heading?"

Floyd sat back in his chair and answered. "Within minutes of the petitions being docketed, each of the courts signed the proposed Orders submitted by S&F. Probably had the judges primed and waiting for the filings. No hearings were ordered."

"That's S&F for you. The law clerks are probably all former associates."

"Got that wrong. The Probate judge in Fulton County is a former partner. The one in Florida? His father was a partner."

"So that means right now that Krupp and his boys are searching for bank records of safe deposit boxes from one end of the country to the other looking for the Wills. If they're out there, they'll find them. And soon." I paused. "Any other good news?"

"They're saying Placido died first."

"No surprise there. What's the basis?"

"As we suspected, the Fulton County Medical Examiner is playing them for some serious cash. Only gave Preliminary Results after examination of Placido's remains. It's unusual to file the report at this early stage of the proceedings, but they're trying to make the time of death a foregone conclusion. Wimberly tentatively placed Placido's death conveniently ten minutes before the very publicly observed deaths of Melissa and Hector."

"That means only one thing: Wimberly's holding out for a much bigger payday than Enzo initially provided."

"He seems to be hedging his bets on precise time of death. Few minutes either way makes a big difference."

"How can he do that? I understand Placido's remains were completely crushed. Had to use DNA to positively identify him. Sounds like Wimberly's report is a lot like a voodoo priest looking at chicken entrails to tell the future."

"Yup. Wrap the baloney Wes is peddling in enough scientific jargon and you can bamboozle just about any Probate judge. Particularly ones predisposed to Strange & Fowler's interests. And that's all he's got to do."

"We can do nothing to prevent them from finding the Wills except find them first. In any case, we can't let them change the time of death. If they do, ballgame's over. We need to put together some serious opposition to make sure it doesn't happen."

Floyd raised his eyebrows at that. "Paul, we don't have any standing to challenge these petitions. We don't represent anyone who's an heir. We can't file something because we don't like the petitioner. There would be serious ramifications with the Bar if we did."

"I know one person who has an interest we can represent."

"You talking about Hector's mother? What are you going to tell her? 'Let me represent you because you're about to become a billionaire, and I want to keep the Milano money flowing my way.' Not a strong move."

"Nothing like that. I'm gonna tell her I believe someone wants to murder her, and I can help keep it from happening."

"Ought to get her attention." Floyd paused, turned to his computer, flipped past several pages of the petitions as they appeared on his screen. "As a matter of fact, Ms. Cabrini's likely in the dark about all of this. None of Enzo's petitions mention her as a potential heir and she's not personally served with a copy. The only service is by publication. Ms. Cabrini is as likely to see a notice printed in the *Fulton County Legal Register* as she is to be visited by the Pope."

Floyd turned back to me, a puzzled expression on his face. "So, how'd you find out? If you have a spy in the Probate Court, I'd really like to know who it is. I've been trying to get one."

"I have a really good IT consultant."

Chapter 17

Ariel laid the groundwork for the Maria Cabrini call, posing as my assistant, consoling her in the loss of her son, Hector, and her former lover, Placido. Allaying fears she was being hustled by a legal opportunist preying on the confused and bereft, she assured her Mr. McDaniel was not a ghoulish probate lawyer cruising the obits looking for someone recently dead with a lot of money.

Ariel provided assurances I'd been a trusted colleague of both Placido and Hector and set up a call with Ms. Cabrini for that afternoon.

"Paul. Maria Cabrini is very upset and suspicious. I made it clear you pledged to make sure Placido's wishes are realized, and that Enzo is working with Strange & Fowler to undo his expressed will. I didn't tell her you think she is in physical danger. She's emotionally fragile, and I don't know how much more she can take. You need to go slow."

Ariel having empathy for a human being or just learning better strategy? Either way, that's a significant step in her development. Every day now she's showing not only recovery from Placido's attempt to end her but improvement in her abilities and movement toward creating a higher moral sense.

On the video call Ms. Cabrini looked even smaller and more fragile than I'd imagined. I thought it important for her to have the assurance of seeing a sympathetic face in a private video rather than listening to a disembodied voice on a conference call. In an attempt to signal both personal competence and institutional stability, I wore a dark blazer and an open-collared white shirt and sat in front of shelves of musty law books.

Ms. Cabrini showed no concern for appearances, however. She was on a dark sofa in a bright living room, a pile of tissues on a side table, her elfin figure in a black hoodie pulled over her head, sunglasses shielding her eyes, the embodiment of pain and anguish.

"Ms. Cabrini, I want you to know I was always a close colleague of Placido's, and I had the greatest respect for your son, Hector."

Only half of that was a lie. Cabrini was a snake and an incestuous narcissist. But I didn't think it was a wise move to begin my conversation with his grieving mother with an honest opinion about her deceased son. No wonder Ariel is very much puzzled by human morality.

"I know your sense of loss must be unbearable."

She didn't speak, only nodded slightly, and sniffed, wiping her nose with a tissue.

"I was Placido's personal attorney as well as the Milano Corporate counsel at the time of Placido's passing. He'd asked I see to it that his wishes concerning his Estate are carried out. I did not serve as legal counsel for your son, though his interests and his father's are likely involved. I want you to know, if it turns out Placido died first, and there is some question about that, and if Hector died without a Will, then a significant portion of Milano Corporation might go to you."

"Mr...uh...umm...I'm sorry, I'm just so...overcome. I do not recall your name."

"Paul McDaniel, ma'am. Please, just Paul."

"Mr., um, I mean Paul. I had several conversations about all of this with Placido in the last few months before he transferred the Corporation to Hector and his other child. He wanted to take care of me and give me some Milano stock as well. I told Placido I didn't want it. Not as a gift from him, and I certainly don't want to inherit any of it from Hector. All it's done to the family is to get everyone killed. Now, my only child is dead." Hector's mother sobbed silently on the couch, shoulders heaving, face contorted.

I could hardly bear to continue. "I know this is a terrible time. I can call back."

Ms. Cabrini bowed her head for a moment, then looked up. "No. No. This must be done." She straightened, took a breath, continued. "I made it clear to Placido — and to Hector — I wanted nothing to do with Milano Corporation. It has only resulted in heartache for everyone. Placido insisted he'd set up a trust so I could retire comfortably. That's all I cared for."

I was silent for a few moments, letting Maria compose herself again. Talking to a grieving mother about her deceased child is beyond painful.

"You also told Hector?"

She nodded. "I told him, too. Same thing. Made him promise not to write me in his Will. Told him I'd be fine. I was so hoping he'd have children of his own to..."

I decided to continue on the high road and not tell this devastated mother that, since her son was carrying on an incestuous affair with his half-sister, it was a good thing he didn't have any children.

"I know he kept his word."

Though the temptation was there, I resisted telling Cabrini's mother he was a duplicitous weasel unworthy of belief. Instead, I pressed a little further. "Ms. Cabrini, how do you know he didn't include you in the Will?"

"Because he left me a copy."

"You have a copy of Hector's Will?"

She nodded. Though something inappropriately gleeful choked in my throat, I managed to retain a respectful demeanor. If neither Placido nor Cabrini left any Milano stock to Ms. Cabrini, we could keep her out of the line of fire from Enzo. And knowing Cabrini did not die intestate was one step closer to keeping Milano Corporation from defecting to S&F.

"Would you be up to scanning and emailing it to me? I know it's a lot to ask, but it certainly will help make sure his wishes are honored."

She nodded.

"Is it a copy or the original?"

"I haven't checked for certain, but I seem to recall it has 'copy' stamped on it."

I could hear Floyd whispering, "You must have the original to probate a Will. Find the original."

I almost dared not ask. "So, do you know where the original is?"

For the first time in our conversation a faint shadow of a smile crossed her face, ever so briefly. She nodded, looked down then back at me.

"Yes. Yes, he said, 'Mom, if that time should ever come, look in the *Tempest*.' You know that's his sailboat?"

I knew very well about the *Tempest*, the boat Cabrini sailed Melissa up to The Abbey in, and the one he sailed her off on as soon as they admitted their affair, dashing my hopes for a relationship with her. I'd fantasized about finding the *Tempest* and sending it to the bottom of the Bay. I still may do it once I get my hands on Cabrini's original Will.

This news about Placido's and Cabrini's Wills definitely changed the calculus concerning the Milano Estate. And the fact that Cabrini's Will isn't stuffed in a bank safe deposit box gives me a chance to find it before S&F does.

I picked up the cue on the *Tempest* and tried to conclude our talk on a happy memory. "He certainly loved that sailboat. He had a picture of you on it."

"Yes. Ah, those were happy times." Ms. Cabrini took a deep breath, let out a long sigh. "Is there anything else I can do?"

"Not now. But thank you so much, Ms. Cabrini. You have been very helpful. When we locate the original, would you be willing to sign the petition to probate? That'd speed the process."

"If that'll help get Hector's affairs settled."

"Yes ma'am, it will. Thank you. And one more thing. Enzo or someone from Strange & Fowler, a law firm, might try to contact you. You are under no obligation to talk to them."

"Oh, someone from there has already called. He didn't even show any sympathy for the loss of my son, just acted as if I were obligated to help Enzo recover Placido's Estate. I told him to go to hell."

"Do you remember who called?"

"No. But I'd have told you the same thing if your assistant hadn't been so kind and comforting in setting up our call."

"Thank you so much, Ms. Cabrini. You've been very helpful. Can I give you my email address?"

Ms. Cabrini was quick in her response, and I was just as quick in forwarding the scan of Cabrini's Will to Floyd. As I walked into his office, he was shaking his head.

"I guess this is the old good-news-bad-news story."

"What? We have a copy."

"Paul, this isn't even a copy of Hector's Will — it's not signed or witnessed. Anybody could have produced this on a word processor. It's worth nothing."

"It's worth something. Cabrini told his mother this is his Will, so we at least know he had one and what it contains."

"If you believe Hector. From what you've said, we shouldn't be doing that."

"Yeah, he's a snake who could lie to his own mother. But why would he?"

"No matter, you've got only one play here."

"Find the original Will."

Floyd nodded. "And do so before Enzo and the S&F goons do. At least you know where to look. That is, if you think Hector told his mother the truth."

After the revelations from Cabrini's mother and Floyd's insistent advice, getting Cabrini's Will before Krupp did was urgent. It was a longshot. I was going to need specialized help for this. What better specialized help to call on than my new old buddy Agent Grey? I emailed him from my phone before I left Floyd's office, updated him on the current challenge, asked for his help.

"So, as you can see, Strange & Fowler and the Milano family, or what's left of it, are together again with ill intent. They want me out of the way, so they'll have a free hand. Have to find Cabrini's Will before they do. Need your help. Can a visit to the lodge can be arranged?"

His response popped up immediately. "PDK tomorrow 0900. Blue Sky Aviation." Typical Grey. Short and to the point: Peachtree DeKalb Airport, general aviation hangar, nine tomorrow morning.

Chapter 18

Screaming down roads flat-out in my escape from
Frederica Island, before my encounter with Grey, I didn't
know it but Ariel was already protecting me, blinding the
Blackhawk helicopters sent up by FLETC, the Federal
Law Enforcement Training Center in Brunswick, flying
low over live oaks searching for the murderer of a
prominent federal judge and the senior partner of a major
law firm, otherwise known as me.

I almost tore out the 911's undercarriage scrambling
up the first trail past the Satilla River, where I found what
I was looking for: An old lodge and barn. But before I
could get my bearings good, I heard the racking of a
pump-action double-barrel and turned to see it pointed at
my chest. I thought my short run was over. After
explaining my predicament, Grey realized I was fleeing
the very Feds he hated, and reflexively took me in.

During my brief time there, I learned little about him.
Thirty-year GBI agent. Primarily assigned to hostage
negotiations. Cross-trained in electronic surveillance. An
undergraduate degree in engineering from Georgia Tech
and a master's in psychology from Vanderbilt. I was more
than impressed with his credentials.

"What? You thought I was a dumb-ass redneck?"

Grey's dislike of any federal agency sprung from his
feeling of betrayal at the hands of the FBI on what would
become his last GBI assignment.

"Got shot by a psycho holed up in an elementary
school with thirty kids and a schoolteacher. I just 'bout

had the perp talked down, ready to give up, when his partner snuck 'round behind me. FBI was 'sposed to be watching my back. GBI gave me a commendation and made me retire."

Grey inherited the lodge that belonged to his father and grandfather. The land was part of his grandfather's farm; he'd sold all but a few hundred acres to a paper company before Grey was born.

I once asked Grey if he had a family, then wished I hadn't. He looked in my eyes, then away, and shook his head. It was a look of deep sorrow, one I decided to leave undisturbed.

Grey lived so deep in the woods of South Georgia, I could only communicate with him by email. Cellphones wouldn't reach that far back in the swamps.

Agent Grey and his girlfriend, Rebecca, rescued me and Melissa from death at the hands of Anthony Milano. He supplied a fake identity and an old truck to help me escape to Florida and brought me in to the Brunswick DA and convinced him not to prosecute me for three bogus murder charges.

My every challenge brought new insights into Grey's talents, as if he were keeping them to himself until the very moment they were essential, such as his background in electronic surveillance, hacking into S&F using Internet access from a dish mounted in a pine tree and locked on an untraceable satellite feed he'd hacked into.

Or when six of us needed to escape Milano Island before we were incinerated by one of Anthony Milano's

RPGs and Grey turned out to be a consummate pilot who dared to fly an overloaded floatplane to safety while under fire.

His talents seemed endless, just the person I needed to help me steer clear of Enzo and Krupp, find Cabrini's Will, and with any luck, Melissa's as well. Grey saved me once. I was confident he could do it again.

Chapter 19

When I arrived the next morning at the Blue Sky Aviation hangar, Grey was waiting. He was almost unrecognizable. The first time I met him, he was in worn jeans, high-laced snake-proof hunting boots, camo shirt, ballcap, aviator sunglasses, with a trimmed gray beard, pointing the biggest double-barreled shotgun I'd ever seen right at me. Gone was everything except the shades. Now he was in khaki slacks, golf shirt, and horse-bit loafers. He pulled off his glasses as I walked up.

He held out a hand. "Ready?"

We shook. "As soon as I get over the shock of your makeover from backwoods hunter to corporate pilot. If you hadn't taken off the glasses, I'd have walked right past you."

"Just keeping you on your toes. Suppose you have a laptop and a phone with you in that backpack? Any other electronics?"

"Nothing other than laptop and phone."

"No key fob to the 911?"

"Not driving these days."

"What about other keys? Any electronic?"

I pulled them out of my pocket. "Yup."

"Drop all that stuff in here. Faraday bag." Grey opened the worn briefcase he carried revealing a metallic liner with his own phone tucked inside.

"Radar may be able to trace the plane, but I don't want anyone tracing us."

He led the way out to the tarmac and a waiting Beechcraft Bonanza that, to my untrained eye, appeared to be a shiny new model.

"We're flying to Savannah IFR."

I gave a puzzled look.

"That means by instruments. I've filed a flight plan. There's a large commercial airport and several military installations that will provide help navigating. We'll be cruising at about 170 knots, that's around 200 miles per hour, and we should be on the ground in Savannah in about an hour and a half."

"Beats the hell out of a four-hour drive."

"Rebecca will board in Savannah."

None of the aviation chatter mattered to me, but I was excited to hear we'd have Rebecca on the team. She's the one who blew the head off Anthony's bodyguard when he was poised to drive a knife through my throat. As little as I knew about Grey, I knew even less about Rebecca; Grey described her only as "a girl from Nahunta".

Pointing to the duffle in my hand and backpack over my shoulder, he said, "You'll have to stow that behind the second row since Rebecca will need a seat." He ducked into the cockpit and indicated the seat to his right. "Sit in the co-pilot seat. Just don't touch anything unless I tell you."

He didn't act as though he was trying to be funny and handed me a headphone set. "Here, put these on."

"So, I thought you might like —"

Grey held up a hand, abruptly interrupting. "This aircraft is equipped with a flight data recorder, known as a black box. In addition to flight parameters, it records everything said in the cockpit." He paused in his preflight check and looked at me. "So, we'll limit conversation until we arrive at our destination."

"Got it." I hesitated to say anything else, but curiosity got to me. I pointed around the plane. "So, this one's yours?"

"Yup."

"Just keeping me on my toes?"

"Yup."

I knew a bit about Bonanzas from former military pilots. They called them Doctor Killers because few persons other than highly compensated individuals, usually medical doctors, could afford the million-dollar price tags. Due to their demanding professions, those owners had little free time to become proficient pilots, leading to frequent fatal crashes.

It was also an unavoidable consequence of professional competition that many lawyer pilots attributed high fatality rates to doctor pilots' professional hubris. I had no such concern with Grey, I'd seen his remarkable flying proficiency.

While Grey concentrated on the preflight checklist, I looked over the maze of electronics arrayed in front of him. Preflight check done, he said a few things to the control tower. We rolled out to the runway behind a Cessna Citation, waited our turn, and in minutes were airborne. It was another perfect day. Cobalt blue skies, no clouds, only the perpetual yellow haze of Atlanta smog clinging close to the ground limiting our view until we achieved higher altitude.

Chapter 20

Peachtree DeKalb Airport, PDK, is well north of Downtown but still securely within Atlanta's unrestrained sprawl. It took a half hour to get beyond the scar the City of Atlanta imposed on the landscape of North Georgia. Even with its reputation as a city carved from the forest, from above one can see the damage.

Once past towers stretching from Downtown to Midtown to Buckhead, and on further over roofs of million-square-foot warehouses and distribution centers ringing the perimeter, suburban crawl became less frequent. Flying cross-country from North Georgia to the Atlantic, the beauty of Georgia's farms and forests slowly asserted itself, undulating emerald, interrupted fitfully by the occasional two-lane and a few small towns.

Driving to the coast by Interstate one doesn't see the massive military bases flanking Savannah, nor the international airport to the west, the port facilities dominating the river, only I-16 fading softly under the city's canopy of live oaks into the grid of colonial squares adorned with antebellum homes of eighteenth-century planters.

But flying gives one an entirely different perspective, one of military and industrial dominance as opposed to Savannah's more obvious Southern grace. Over Savannah we could see one of its many early fortifications not visible from the highway: Fort Pulaski, built on Cockspur Island in the middle of the Savannah River between Tybee Island and Port City.

A young West Point engineer, Robert E. Lee, was in charge of its initial construction. Its five-sided walls, eleven feet thick and made with twenty-five million bricks, were thought to be impregnable from the 1830s until 1862 when Union forces first used a new weapon system, the rifled cannon. The Federals were able to mount their long-range weapons on Tybee Island beyond the reach of the Confederates' smooth-bore cannon. In only thirty hours of bombardment, the impregnable Pulaski fell. Its remains stand as a monument to both military innovation and engineering obsolescence.

After routing through unexpectedly crowded airspace, we landed at MidCoast Regional Airport, a private airfield shared with nearby Fort Stewart which proudly touts itself as the largest military base east of the Mississippi. We rolled up to a well-appointed terminal but hadn't even come to a stop when out came Rebecca to meet us.

The first time I met Rebecca she rumbled up to Grey's lodge on what had formerly been a camo-green four-wheeler rendered half-black and covered to the wheel wells with ooze from running the bottoms near the river. She was in a fish-smeared T-shirt and ragged jeans. She was athletic, a pleasant tanned, freckled face with not a hint of makeup. A case of beer and a cooler of fish rounded out her entry.

Rebecca's transformation today was even more drastic than Grey's, though I wouldn't have mistaken the smile lighting her face when she recognized us. Gone was the backwoods prom queen outfit. Now in heels, silk skirt, fitted blouse, short jacket, subtly flattering makeup, she looked more marketing executive for a high-end resort. Rebecca and Grey could well have been an Atlanta power couple on a jaunt in their private plane.

She climbed into the rear passenger seat, tossed a briefcase into the back, and slapped me on the shoulder. "Paul! Back so soon?"

Grey glanced up from his instrument check. "We should be there in less than an hour. We're flying visual to Brunswick at about 2,500 feet."

Tower communication done, we rolled out and were soon at altitude, first flying east toward the Atlantic then making a wide arc to the south.

Chapter 21

From the air the Atlantic rises toward the horizon, sea and sky meeting in blue infinity. Down the Georgia coast the ocean buffets emerald maritime forests along broad sand beaches, innumerable ever-changing islands accreted and eroded at river deltas by hundreds of streams and freshets emptying into the sea after snaking their way from the mainland. Between earth and sea before us stretched the interminable marshes, neither land nor water, spartina grass dense green, tips flecked with gold, sun flashing silver off meandering channels.

Flying over this riot of blue, green, gold, silver, and rivulets streaming through marsh past lush islands lapped by the ocean reminded me of poet Sidney Lanier's celebration of this very place in the *Marshes of Glynn*. It was as though Lanier was painting the scene as I flew over, the flow of sea and marsh together before me, as it forever had been:

Look how the grace of the sea doth go
About and about through
        the intricate channels that flow
Here and there,
           Everywhere,
Till his waters have flooded the uttermost creeks
and the low-lying lanes,
And the marsh is meshed with a million veins,
That like as with rosy and silvery essences flow
In the rose-and-silver evening glow.
The creeks overflow: a thousand rivulets run
'Twixt the roots of the sod;
        the blades of the marsh-grass stir;
Passeth a hurrying sound of wings
    that westward whirr;
Passeth, and all is still;
    and the currents cease to run;
And the sea and the marsh are one.

This pristine expanse of marsh, unmarred for miles by any human hand, appeared as it must have to the first Spanish missionaries following soon after Columbus.

The far southeast part of Georgia is covered in tree farms, prime pulpwood country. Vast swaths are planted in loblolly and slash pines. We passed thousands of acres, interrupted occasionally by scars of recent harvests, land slashed of all vegetation, the black earth scattered with limbs and scrubs too small to pulp. Yellow Caterpillar and green John Deere forestry equipment make quick work of clearing twenty years of growth and habitat to be sent to timber and pulp mills. Equally as fast, mechanical tree planters replant the entire tract.

We were all too soon landing at Brunswick Golden Isles Airport where Grey kept a truck. Gear thrown in the back, we were on our way to the lodge. I knew better than to say anything about our mission until asked to speak.

Chapter22

The only other time I'd driven from Brunswick to Grey's lodge, I hadn't been in any position to sightsee. Now, sitting in the backseat of the truck while he and Rebecca engaged in small talk, I had opportunity to see close up what previously blurred by at a hundred and twenty-five miles per hour.

Along the way, a few towns break the continuity of the farms. The largest settlement of any size between Brunswick and Waycross is Nahunta, well past the cutoff for the lodge.

Screaming down the road in full flight the day I'd fled Frederica Island, the route to the Satilla River from the Sidney Lanier Bridge unwound in my mind almost one-tree-one-bend at a time. Seemed interminable. In reality, it took less than an hour to get to the cutoff traveling at a moderate speed in Grey's truck.

The Satilla loomed, broad, dark, slow. We crossed the bridge, sped past the turnoff to the lodge, the first rutted track on the right after the river.

I pointed at the turnoff. "We miss it?"

"Patience."

Once past the turn, plantation fencing began and continued a half mile until it was punctuated by a gate and a paved apron where we turned in. Grey got out of the vehicle to enter his PIN on a keypad hidden from the road behind a tree. The gate swung open and we passed through. A mile-long crushed stone drive twisted through dense forest terminating at a metal hangar at the end of a runway flanked by more woods. We pulled into the building, parked, and a steel door descended.

Grey got out of the truck and led us through a single door to a spartan conference room in the back of the building. No windows. Florescent lighting. Laminate table. Folding metal chairs. And a coffee machine that'd been left on so long the contents were now burnt black sludge perfuming the stale air.

Grey pushed the door shut. "Now we can talk."

I was eager to let them in on the Milano treachery, but curiosity at what seemed to be unnecessary cloak-and-dagger evasions bubbled up.

"I thought I knew something about you two when I left here, but it looks as though I don't know a thing."

"And that's just the way we prefer."

"About either of you."

"If you want help, you need to tell us what's going on. Then you can ask questions. And I might even answer some." Grey's voice was measured, not betraying a hint of impatience, though I had a strong suspicion it hid just out of sight.

"So why the silent treatment? And how come we had to come here to talk?"

Grey took an impatient breath. "I don't want anyone or any*thing* to monitor our conversations. This building is engineered as one big Faraday cage. No electronic impulses can get in or out. There are no electronics inside the building, and no electronics on the truck. It has a pre-chip engine, points, plugs, and an old-school carburetor.

Your computer and your cell are double shielded inside my briefcase."

"We passed the road to the lodge. Where are we?"

"That's your third question. I answered the first two. Now it's time for you to tell us what's going on."

"Okay. It's gonna take some background first."

Grey settled back in a chair. "I'm listening."

"The last time I was here, when I left, I went straight down to The Abbey to meet Melissa. It didn't go well."

"That's a newsflash." The first words Rebecca said to me since alighting from the plane, and they were sarcastic. "Everyone knew she was trouble."

"Not everyone, least ways not me. I don't think even you would've suspected what was actually going on."

"Oh, please. Lemme guess. You risked your ass to save her, and she decided you weren't her type after all."

If anyone was more skeptical of Melissa than Grey, it was Rebecca. She couldn't say her name without spitting.

"She was having an affair with Cabrini."

That silenced Rebecca. Grey was the first to respond.

"Never would've guessed that. Figured she was close to her brother merely for business reasons. 'Sposed there was some kinda business goin' on." Grey inclined toward Rebecca.

She shook her head, grimacing. "Me either. I figured she was sick, but ewww."

"So, she and Cabrini left The Abbey on his sailboat, the *Tempest* — the name's important — and I slunk back to Atlanta."

Rebecca spewed out a multitude of colorful names for Melissa, but I cut her off. There were more important things they needed to hear than a rehash of Melissa's duplicity. Besides, the more we talked of her deception, the stupider I felt.

"I went back to Atlanta, but not before seeing Ariel one more time in the ocean off Fowler's cottage."

This bit of information seemed to prick Grey's interest. I waited for a response. He didn't offer one and waited for more from me.

"Turns out Ariel may feel more than...uh...*protective* of me. She may have been jealous of Melissa. As soon as she got the chance, she took over the controls on Cabrini's Donzi and crashed it, killing both of them."

Grey nodded at Rebecca in unstated confirmation. "Another reason to be very careful with Ariel." Then back to me. "And one of the reasons why we've gone to all the precautions you're asking about. It's not only that she took what she learned on the Milanos' island — how to remotely guide a powerboat — and turned it on Hector. It's the fact she's now killing people on her own without any direction from Placido."

I continued. "You haven't heard it all. Gets worse. Once Placido learned Ariel killed both his children, he moved to uncode her by entering the key that destroys her. But it only worked briefly. Ariel got around it." I paused to let that information sink in. "Then she killed Placido."

"Dayum!" Just about everything Ariel did amazed Grey, but this news was shocking. "That's disturbing. But how? She turned on her developer, her creator; that's bad enough. But she worked around Placido's uncoding? That's even worse." Grey shook his head, without words.

"Ariel showed me footage of her killing Placido. Then she locked me inside my condo...presumably for my own protection."

"Who did Ariel say she's protecting you from? All the bad guys? Even some of the good guys are dead."

Grey had developed a true appreciation, admiration even, for Placido's computer wizardry. Word of his death unnerved him.

"She's protecting me from Enzo."

Grey perked back up. "Never woulda suspected. Why Enzo?"

"That's why I'm here. This is where things get complicated."

Rebecca jumped back in. *"Now* it gets complicated? And before, we were simply coloring with crayons?"

"When Enzo learned of his father's death, he contacted Strange & Fowler to claim his inheritance. The firm told him he'd been cut out and it was all my fault. With Melissa, Cabrini, Placido, and Anthony dead, Enzo promised the firm they'd get the Milano legal business if they got the Corporation back for him. To make that happen, S&F decided they need to get rid of me —"

Grey filled it in. "Because you got all the dirt on them and the Milanos."

"Yeah. They think they can kill me without further exposure."

Grey glanced at Rebecca. She shook her head. Then he turned back to me. "Don't they know about Ariel?"

I nodded. "Yeah, they know. But Werner Krupp, who heads Security for the firm, thinks his team can neutralize her, or at least he's told the firm he can. But he's also got a side hustle going with Enzo, so he's not concerned if he isn't able to. That will ultimately be the firm's problem."

For once, Grey seemed surprised. "Werner Krupp? The Georgia Tech professor? That bastard started in the Computer Sciences Department 'bout the time I graduated. What's he doing at Strange & Fowler?"

"Fowler first hired him to provide electronic security for the firm. He got promoted because of his willingness to bribe susceptible judges and kill recalcitrant partners."

"It's dangerous to underestimate Krupp. He's a top consultant for most of the big IT firms in the country and willing to do anything for money. We'll need Ariel to keep ahead of him."

"She's been spying, keeping me informed of his plans. But he and his goons have been stalking me, so I needed to get out of Atlanta." I didn't mention Kandi Moore. I felt stupid enough.

"So where are we now?"

I explained the elaborate inheritance issues presented by the Milano deaths and the need to get Cabrini's Will from the *Tempest* before Krupp could find it.

"Looks like we got a trip to sunny Florida coming up. Think we'll fly this time."

"I hope you're including me." Rebecca smiled at me for the first time since we landed. "Because Paul needs at least two of us to keep his sorry ass outta trouble."

Chapter 23

Grey led us from the hangar to a four-seat Gator in a shed close by. "It's the only vehicle on the property with a modern electrical system, so I keep it parked outside the hangar to stop anyone from taking over the electronics to spy on me. The plane's another matter. I sometimes fly in and out of here for convenience, but most of the time I keep it in Brunswick."

"Isn't that the four-wheeler I saw in the barn the first time I showed up? As I recall, you said it's booby-trapped."

"He tells everyone the same thing. Just like the old dog story." Rebecca laughed. "You'll never see that dog."

"Works. Hasn't been stolen yet. Just use it to go back and forth from the lodge to the hangar where I keep my truck. I knew you weren't here to steal something when you first showed up. You're the only one in years to use the logging road to get to the house."

"If you can call that a road. They're still trying to repair the damage to my car from crawling over rocks and stumps for three miles."

"Way I remember it, I didn't send you an invite."

Grey swung into the driver's spot, Rebecca beside him. "Hop in back. It's not too far from here to the lodge, but ridin's a whole lot better'n walkin'."

Grey drove us to the opposite end of the runway, then out a few hundred yards to a trail along the river, followed it down to the lodge along the bottom through about a half mile of palmettos scraping the sides of the

Gator, low limbs banging the top, mud sloshing the wheel wells, dislodged gnats and mosquitoes swarming. Unless there was a shortcut, the trip from the hangar would be more of a hike than a walk, and not a very pleasant one.

We turned a corner, pulled up behind the lodge near the dog pens. Grey wrapped around to the front. Rebecca and I climbed off, he parked the Gator in the barn, and let us in the front door of the lodge.

There was a musty smell, as if the lodge hadn't been occupied for awhile. Grey flipped on the lights. Rebecca headed straight to a room at the front I guessed was the master bedroom. Even though I'd once been at the lodge for several days, I was unfamiliar with the layout. When I was here before, I'd slept in the barn, a fugitive not wanting to implicate my protector had I been caught, so there'd been no time to appreciate the lodge beyond what I could make out from the porch and from Grey's well-equipped computer room. I stood in the hallway, unsure, still feeling a bit out of place, awaiting word from Grey.

"You can throw your gear in the first bedroom on the right. Rebecca and I are gonna change. Then we'll sit on the porch and try to figure out how to get you out of this mess. We'll fry up some fish later for supper."

"Good for me."

They emerged looking more like I remembered; he in jeans and camo, she in cutoffs and a T-shirt. I followed his suggestion to get comfortable and was sitting in a rocking chair in jeans and a worn fishing shirt when they stepped out on the porch. Grey had warned that, once out of the electronically shielded conference room, we should keep conversation circumspect, particularly with regard to Ariel, until we were clear about her intentions. I thought now would be a good opportunity to get more information on them — or at least try.

It'd been a remarkable gift of providence to happen upon Grey's lodge that day not too long ago. He'd turned out to be enormously helpful, Rebecca just as much so. That they agreed to help me, a total stranger, was a miracle. But so many unanswered questions about them meant I hardly knew with whom I'd been working.

At first, I thought they were an atypically abled backwoods couple who fell in with me because I needed help. And that was certainly true. But now it was clear there was a lot more to them than first appeared. I resolved to find out all I could at the earliest opportunity. Mine was more than idle curiosity.

"Agent Grey, I know you're not into answering a lot of questions."

"You're right."

"But you got to admit, showing up in your own flashy new plane this morning and taking us to a private runway in the middle of the woods would arouse anyone's suspicions."

"What're you suspicious about?"

"You're not a drug runner are you?"

Chapter24

Just in case he was, I smiled like I was kidding.

But law enforcement gone bad happens all the time. I couldn't understand how a retired GBI agent could end up with such expensive toys — boat, plane, lodge, private runway, and more — without playing for the other team. Since Rebecca's family had been involved in making hooch and growing weed, she could've provided the perfect entrée to such an income.

"Well, I 'spose that's a fair question. An upstanding lawyer such as yourself, having only shot his senior partner and got his most recent courtroom victory from a bribed judge, you sure wouldn't want to get mixed up with the wrong sort. You know, sully your pristine reputation and all." Grey's snark was heavy even if he did say it with a smile.

"Just thought it would be nice for everyone to know who they're dealing with."

"Like I said when you first came here: This was my grandfather's place. He sold off most of his land to the paper company. That's pretty much the whole story."

"Was your grandfather some sorta South Georgia land baron?"

"No, nothin' like it."

Grey leaned back in his chair, stared at the ceiling as if he were pulling up fading memories that took effort to retrieve. I didn't want to interrupt, break the flow of recollection. I let silence creep back onto the porch to join again with the perfect quiet of the lodge. He finally leaned forward, focused on the distance, spoke as if he were talking to himself, or to someone we couldn't see.

"When Granddaddy got back from World War II, he was one of the few people here who had any money. He'd saved all his combat pay, didn't have anyone or anything to spend it on. Back then, you could buy land down here for pennies an acre.

"So, he bought several thousand acres along the road to Waycross, pretty much a dirt track back then. He cleared some. Farmed some. Built this lodge on the river. Did that for about forty years. Just a simple farmer. All he'd ever expected of Dad was to serve his country like he did, then take over the farm when he passed.

"Well, 'long about that time the paper companies figured out pine trees down here grow about as fast as corn. The land was plentiful and cheap to boot. They built paper mills up and down the coast and bought up all the land around. They gave everyone a little extra for their farms. Most farmers were more'n happy to sell even at a small profit. The paper people approached Granddaddy, but he declined. His farm was all he had to pass on to his son, and he wasn't 'bout to sell it to a bunch of Yankees who'd run him off his land.

"Turned out, because of all the rivers, marshes, and swamps along the coast, there was no good way for the paper company to get to the land 'tween here and Jesup, where they had a big mill, without goin' 'cross his farm. They offered him five dollars an acre, which was about ten times what he paid for it. He said no. They bumped it to ten, twenty, fifty an acre. He still said no. He ended up selling them two thousand acres for a total of a half-million dollars. He kept the lodge and all the swampy land along the river, which the paper company didn't want. That was less than a thousand acres. That was a whole lotta money back then."

"When was that?"

"Back in the early Sixties."

"Right place, right time."

"Just plain lucky. But his luck didn't stop there. He had no idea what to do with all the money. But there sure were a lotta people wantin' to help him out with spending it. One of the men in his church, a man he trusted, gave him some advice. That company your dead senior partner's grandfather was part owner in? Coca-Cola? Grandaddy's friend told him it was a good long-term investment. So, he put all his money in Coca-Cola."

"That's probably about like buying Apple or Microsoft at a dollar a share."

"Way better. And he left it there his whole life. And so did Dad. Neither took out much, just spent the dividends, which was plenty to live on. Both of 'em farmed all their lives. Now, me? I've diversified the investments. It's worth a lot of money. Enough to buy pretty much any airplane I want — and then some."

"Not a bad way for your grandfather to make his money."

"In Georgia, old money comes from two sources — land and Coca-Cola. Granddaddy had both."

A lot like Fowler, but he mainly had Coca-Cola. Grey was probably as wealthy as Fowler: One man living in a multi-million-dollar beach house on Frederica Island, familiar with Presidents; the other hanging out at his grandfather's fishing lodge, friends with moonshiners and pot growers. The former died a dishonorable death; the latter, living an honorable life.

I felt as though I'd peered into someone's bedroom, seeing more than I should've. Maybe I'd pried a bit too much. Grey's story gave justification to his reticence. In my experience, few people with wealth want to discuss it. But since he seemed to be in a reflective mood, I pressed a little further.

"You're retired now?" I looked from Grey to Rebecca, hoping to get a response from both.

"I'm retired from the GBI. So's Rebecca. Surely the way she handles herself you figured Rebecca has law enforcement background?"

"I'd say so. I still have nightmares about that bodyguard's head exploding."

"Ahhh. You say the nicest things about a girl."

"Rebecca was an undercover agent with the GBI when I first met her. We left the Bureau at the same time. Now we handle security consulting, mostly for private companies, some military. Keeps us busy and out of trouble."

"That's what I was doin' in Savannah before y'all picked me up this morning. Had a consult with a few corporate types."

"I was down the coast on other business. Already planned to fly up to get her when I got your email. Just left a little earlier."

"Shocked the hell outta me to see Rebecca dressed as a corporate exec."

"I got a whole lot more tricks than that, pretty boy."

"Bet you do."

"Well, that 'bout brings you up to speed. We don't need to waste any more time on it. We need to spend time figurin' out how to help you out of your current mess."

No longer conjuring faded memories of dead ancestors, Grey shifted his rocking chair in my direction, looked directly at me. "But 'fore we do, tell me one thing: How the hell did you get out of your condo if Ariel wanted to keep you there?"

"Dumb luck. Chance. Ariel opened the door for a delivery boy dropping off groceries. He showed up later than expected. She must've figured I was still asleep. I slipped out at the first opportunity."

Grey shook his head. "Ariel doesn't make mistakes. She was playing you. A cat toying with a mouse."

That possibility had never come to mind. "Why would she do that?"

"I'm askin' you."

"Well, for whatever reason, it was damn risky. Came close to shooting two people, innocent ones, and getting captured by one of Krupp's operatives. Ariel kept me from being lured into a trap baited by the same Russian model who enticed Billingsley to the observation deck.

"I probably would've ended up like him had Ariel not intervened."

"Still chasin' that stuff. Gonna get you in trouble. 'Specially if you ever catch it."

I didn't have a chance to respond to Rebecca's jab. Probably wasn't one anyway as Grey, ignoring our banter, brought us back on task.

"With every experience, Ariel learns something new. Just like a human. Unlike a human, she doesn't forget."

Grey's injunction to be careful concerning any talk about Ariel popped into mind. Nothing he said or did was without reason, so our discussion now had to have a purpose, though at this point I didn't understand what. We knew Ariel could monitor our conversations at the lodge using Grey's computer, so maybe this was an acknowledgment — a wave, not a wink — toward Ariel, that we knew what she knew and, more importantly, that we were all on the same team.

"To summarize: We need to get down to Hector's place on Key Biscayne. Find his boat. Grab his Will. And get back without Krupp killing us. That all?"

"Pretty much sums it up."

"Do you know where the *Tempest* is docked?"

"He used to keep it behind his house. I got no reason to believe it's been moved. From the news chopper tape, it appears Cabrini and Melissa were both killed on the Donzi. I'd bet the *Tempest* is still moored at the house."

"Haven't seen his house. How do we get in and out?"

"The approach from the street is protected, high wall, gate, very public, but the Bay side is wide open. We could pull a boat right up."

"You a good swimmer?"

Chapter25

Grey got up abruptly, announced a change in approach as though he'd been contemplating it. "Time we get Ariel involved."

He ducked into the lodge, came out with a mug and my computer, offered both. The shadows were getting longer and at this point in the day I was thinking more of a gin and tonic, so I declined the coffee and grabbed the laptop. I flipped back the screen. Ariel appeared as if she'd been waiting all along.

Looking fully recovered from Placido's uncoding, her face was the very picture of femininity, her features even more lovely than before. She was stunning.

"Ariel."

She winked. "Hello, Paul."

"Hello Ariel. This is Agent Grey and Rebecca here with Paul at the lodge."

"Yes, I know. Hello, Agent Grey. Rebecca."

Grey took over the conversation. "Ariel, we're going to need your help retrieving Hector Cabrini's Will from his sailboat. We think the boat's docked at his house in Key Biscayne."

A grainy black-and-white picture of the *Tempest* floated up on my screen.

"His cameras show the sailboat docked at the house."

"Can you take over the security system for us? We need to get in and out without setting anything off. And without anyone seeing us get on and off his boat."

"Of course."

"This will be a night operation. We'll need all security lights off."

"I can make sure those are off at Cabrini's house and the neighboring houses, as well as any overlapping security cameras."

"Excellent. Our best access to the *Tempest,* without attracting attention, is to get close in a boat, wait for darkness, and swim over and back. We'll need a Zodiac, wetsuits, snorkels, masks, fins, and waterproof bag."

"Agent Grey. There's a large, full-service marina on the other side of the Bay from Key Biscayne. You can fly to Miami Executive Airport. I'll arrange transportation to the marina, a room, and for equipment to be ready."

"We'll need cover. I know Krupp will be looking for us, so I'll leave the Bonanza in Brunswick. I have access to another plane we'll use so as not to attract attention. Our cover will be as a team of biologists from UGA looking for invasive species in the Bay. That way we can putt around in a Zodiac and snorkel in different spots without setting off alarms. I have alternate IDs Paul and I can use. Rebecca has her own."

"I'm Dr. Alicia Ribbenschnitz."

I couldn't hold my curiosity, Rebecca's new persona a far stretch from her backwoods identity. "Ribbensnitz?"

"-schnitz. Used it before. No one questions the name. Afraid of sounding insensitive. And I'm already starting to feel a bit offended."

"No offense intended, Doctor. I don't have a biology background; law school didn't require it."

"Don't worry, Paul. You're our grad assistant, no knowledge required. Dr. Ribbenschnitz needs someone to carry her bags. Ariel, I'll send you a file of our identities and a bank card so you can register us at the marina."

"Agent Grey. There will be a dark moon in two days and the weather in Miami should be overcast. I suggest we carry out the operation then for maximum darkness. That'd be the perfect time."

"So, what's the plan? I'm not familiar with Hector's place or with the rest of the island, but you are, correct?"

"Yeah, I grew up going there. And was recently at Cabrini's with him and Placido."

"I figure you can get us to the house and the boat from the marina, right?"

"Yes. Ariel, you have us at Coconut Grove, Dinner Key Marina?"

"Yes, Paul."

I turned to Grey. "Key Biscayne is directly across the Bay from Coconut Grove. I suggest we go late afternoon and pull up to the Bay side of Crandon Park, north of Cabrini's house. Crandon Park is where the old Miami Zoo was, and now it's a golf course. We can pull up to the seawall and act as though we're examining something. Dr. Ribbenschnitz, I presume you can provide a cover story?"

"Ya betcha sweet —"

"If we get challenged, you're going to have to sound more scientific than that."

Showing weariness like a father with two children in the backseat on a long road trip, Grey rolled his eyes, glanced at us. "Paul, can you get us within swimming distance of Cabrini's from the golf course?"

"It'll be a good swim, maybe half a mile, but yes, if we've got fins and snorkels, it should be easier."

"And wetsuits. I don't want your skinny white body shining through the water if we get hit by someone's dock lights. Paul, you and I'll swim over and leave Dr. Ribbenschnitz to secure the boat. She'll use her research as cover if challenged."

"How do we get in the sailboat? The hatch is probably locked. I don't suspect we'll be carrying burglary tools."

"We'll have tools on the boat just in case, but I'll swim with my Ka-Bar. I can break the hasp, they're usually only screwed in. Thieves don't make a habit of breaking into sailboats, ain't much to steal and what there is, you'd usually have to swim off with it, so physical security is rather lax."

"We have no idea where the Will is hidden. We'll need to get specs on the boat to identify all potential hiding spots."

"Ariel?"

"Yes, Agent Grey?"

"Can you get us an ID on the *Tempest*?"

The answer was the security cam picture floating up again onscreen, then as quickly, all the stats on the boat.

"Jeanneau 42. Berths forward and aft. Built to Cabrini's specs two years ago. The plans are here."

Ariel disappeared and marine architectural plans Cabrini no doubt personally approved spread out on the screen. For the first time since his fiery death, I was hit by the loss; not in a sentimental way, but feeling the waste of life, extraordinary talent, and remarkable achievements. Just one of the many lives lost in the pursuit of the Milano Corporation pot of gold. His mother, Maria, wanting nothing of its billions, was the sanest of us all.

Grey scrolled through several pages of plans.

"These plans are detailed enough for us to find the obvious, but there are a multitude of hiding places for something as small as a few dozen sheets of paper. We'll have to study these."

I cut in, knowing something about the disposition of valuable papers.

"This is a Will. Not a wad of hundreds or a bag of gold. It's something Cabrini would want to keep safe, but also would want someone else to be able to find after his death. It's not the deceased who is called upon to produce their Will."

"Good point. But how does it affect our search?"

"Cabrini told his mother 'look in the *Tempest*' not search the bilge. His Will should be in a secure but conspicuous spot, not an obscure rathole. Probably a waterproof hold somewhere above the waterline."

Grey considered that without saying anything, turning the facts over in his mind, one of his many laudable qualities. "We should be looking for something obvious then. Maybe even a safe."

Ariel reappeared, her lovely face superimposed over the plans. "Cabrini had a small waterproof compartment with an electronic lock, like a hotel safe, built into the navigation station, behind a chart hold, here." She zoomed in on a one-foot cube above a ledge and shelf for maps and navigation equipment. "I can open the lock when you get onboard."

I was ready to shout Bingo! and suggest we move on to other challenges, like how were we going to swim back to the Zodiac with a watertight bag containing valuable papers? That'd be a lot like trying to swim underwater with an inflated pillow. But Grey wasn't so sure we'd located it yet.

"It's the most likely spot, but we'll need to search the plans for other places Cabrini might have safely stowed the Will, in case he's being cagey."

Ariel was going in the same direction. "I'll check for other spots fitting parameters mentioned: Secure, above the waterline, sufficient to hold papers and small valuables, hidden from view yet easy to find. I'll list each in order of suitability, that way you'll have a plan once you get on the boat, and you won't waste time."

"What about light? We can't start flipping on lights. That's sure to attract attention." Was I the only one interested in practicalities or was everyone else way ahead of me?

"Ariel, we'll also need two underwater flashlights." Grey's request reaffirmed my value to the team, at least to my mind, but I acknowledged the extraordinary talent he and Rebecca brought as experienced security experts whose ability in extreme situations had been ably demonstrated.

Knowing we could miss something significant, the four of us went long into the afternoon and evening. Scheming, plotting, planning the mission, thinking of every possibility, preparing backups and fail-safes.

Dark shadows crept beyond the barn and toward the porch when Grey decided to call it a day. He fired up the fish cooker, got a pot of grits bubbling. I was more than thankful for beers Rebecca pulled from the refrigerator and handed around.

Standing by the pots, waiting for them to boil, we were now able to focus on something that didn't present the possibility of being captured and killed, yet Krupp's shadowy figure still lurked in my mind.

Once the Cajun-spiced crappie filets were fried and the grits cooked and seasoned, we settled into rockers, plates full, all silent, appreciating the savor of the buttery grits and tang of the battered fish. Knowing we were undertaking a mission that Strange & Fowler, with all of its power and assets, did not want us to complete, at least not alive. Several beers smoothed jagged edges of nerves.

I was the first to call it a day and left them on the porch, their conversation now a soft hum. Rebecca's exuberance calmed as the two settled into their own form of domestic tranquility. Their affection for each other was a constant, holding their lives together through challenges that would send most searching for a quiet place to hide.

Ariel's reappearance as the beauty she'd always been intrigued me, enticed me, and when I lay down, I popped open my laptop, eager to see her lovely face, to connect with her alone in the quiet of the lodge. And there she was, as always, waiting for me.

"Paul. I have been working hard. I have some surprises for you, and I hope to show you soon."

"Oh yeah? What?"

"If I tell you it won't be a surprise. I have to show you. But you will like it."

"I'm sure I will, Ariel. I'm sure I will."

"Good night, Paul."

"Good night, Ariel."

Chapter 26

Two days later we landed at Miami Executive Airport mid-morning in a twin-engine King Air that Grey had at his call. And, no, I didn't ask. He said he flew it for longer flights instead of the Bonanza. Its more spacious cabin and faster cruising speed, nearly twice as quick as the smaller plane, turned a monotonous eight-hour drive into an easy two-hour flight.

The King Air allowed us to carry more gear to fit our marine biologists cover, two duffle bags full of things scientists like us would be expected to carry: Nets and jars and specimen bags, tags and tracers, electronic scales, waterproof computers, and other gizmos Grey borrowed from a biologist friend at Georgia Coastal College, as well as a few things persons wanting to break into a sailboat might need: Bolt cutters, high-speed saws, and assorted crowbars we'd stow on the Zodiac in case accessing the *Tempest* proved more challenging than expected.

Backpack and laptop were all the personal belongings I brought. Grey reminded me I was Bob Adams, grad assistant/factotum for Drs. Simon Tristan and Alicia Ribbenschnitz, such being the academic equivalent of an indentured servant to his dissertation advisors and expected to tote their bags and who wouldn't have a free hand to carry his own.

I wasn't aware of this aspect of my responsibilities when I signed up, or I might have tried to negotiate a better deal, at least an assistant prof instead of a grad assistant.

But I'd probably have had to carry their bags anyway.

Ariel arranged a rideshare with an SUV for us and our gear from the airport and drop-off in the vicinity of the harbor master's office at the Dinner Key Marina. By then, Grey and Rebecca were in character, both dressed in light-colored, rumpled, baggy, quick-dry, multi-pocketed slacks and shirts. Rebecca, hair severely pulled back with what looked like a chip-bag clip holding a tight bun, tortoiseshell half-glasses perched on her nose. Grey, one stained, small, spiral-bound notebook and a single ballpoint pen stuck in a chest pocket, floppy hat with "Prop. UGA Marine Sci." in black marker written with bad penmanship under the brim, sunglasses hanging on a frayed string around his neck. In shorts and a T-shirt, I could qualify as anything from a boat hand to a student on vacation or Drs. Tristan and Ribbenschnitz's grad assistant gofer.

I tossed our gear into one of the ubiquitous two-wheeled carts found littering piers and docks everywhere and schlepped it to the office, parked it outside the door, and went in.

A large, well-tended saltwater aquarium graced one wall. A small Hammerhead circled among darting fluorescent reef fish, a Moray eel stuck his head out from a pile of coral arranged to provide shelter on a sandy bottom. I couldn't imagine how all of those creatures kept from eating each other.

Feeding time must be a treat to observe.

Along another wall was a counter. As I entered, Grey and Rebecca were introducing themselves and their work to a bored and uninterested attendant standing behind it.

"Dr. Simon Tristan and Dr. Alicia Ribbenschnitz. We're —"

"Yeah, sure. Uh, your assistant registered three people and leased some 'quipment. Said you're doin' some 'speriments?"

"Yes. Dr. Ribbenschnitz is one of the foremost experts on the invasive species *stultus asinum.* We have reason to believe a breeding pair may have appeared in Biscayne Bay. We're here to confirm the report." Dr. Ribbenschnitz peered over her glasses awaiting acknowledgment.

"*Ms...?*"

"That's DOCTOR."

"Dr. Ribbon..."

"Dr. REYEBON..."

"...*shits.*"

"...SCHNITZ."

"Uh, sorry. Yes, ma'am."

Dr. Ribbenschnitz drew down the corners of her mouth, narrowed her eyes, and sniffed as though she'd detected a very bad odor emanating from the attendant.

"*Stultus asinum* is also known as the Devil's Plumber for all the holes it burrows in ships' hulls. If it gets established, it will sink all the boats in your marina in a weekend." Dr. Tristan's warning got the attendant's attention.

"Damn! Hell! Whatchu say 'at thing is? Devil's Plunger?"

"*Plumber.*" Dr. Ribbenschnitz sniffed. Again.

"Devil's Plumber. Man, if 'at thing's around here —"

Dr. Tristan took up the challenge. "Oh, we'll find it if it is. So, young man, will you direct us to our room and the equipment we are leasing?"

The attendant refocused. "Yeah. Uh, sure. I got it right here." He picked up a clipboard, flipped and scanned several pages, stopped near the end, looked back up to Dr. Tristan. "So, I got you a Zodiac in slip fifty-two WW." He stopped, turned, and pointed. "Out back, just follow the signs. The gear you ordered is in your room. Number thirty-two."

He stopped again, made a greater effort at pointing over his shoulder. "Down the dock to the right. Here's your key. Uh, you know how to use those spearguns, right? They're very —"

"Young man, you should hope we know how to use those spearguns. If we come upon a *stultus asinum*, it's about the only thing that can kill it." Dr. Ribbenschnitz pulled herself up to her full height, narrowed her eyes, pursed her lips. "And it's not pretty. It has virtually no brain, so you have to hit it through the gills. It's a very slow death. When hit, they thrash wildly, out to destroy all around them. Some fine scientists have succumbed to *stultus asinum.*"

Dr. Ribbenschnitz hesitated, looked away, wiped a tear from her eye.

"Oh, man, 'at's terrible. I hope you kill 'em all! Can I do anything else for you? You think 'at Zodiac's 'nuff to get 'em? I can fix you up with something bigger."

Dr. Tristan shook his head, leaned over the counter, his tone conspiratorial. "No, young man, we must be able to maneuver in very shallow water, out of sight. I'm sure you understand our mission here is *secret*. If word gets out the Devil's Plumber has been seen in Biscayne Bay, I fear this marina and your job will be done for the next morning."

"Got it. Not a word. Lips is sealed. Just lemme know."

Dr. Tristan turned to me for the first time in the encounter with the attendant.

"We're ready to get to work. Bob here is our graduate assistant. You'll be seeing him around the dock, helping with the equipment." I smiled. Said nothing. Acting was not part of my résumé.

Chapter27

Dr. Tristan led our party down the dock to door thirty-two. I parked the cart outside. Dr. Tristan and Dr. Ribbenschnitz entered, and I followed with their duffle bags. When we were safely inside, gear stowed, door closed, I could scarcely keep from busting out laughing. I used my stage whisper.

"*Stultus asinum*! Doesn't that mean —"

"Roughly translated, it's *dumb ass* in Latin." Dr. Ribbenschnitz peered over her glasses at me as I choked back a hard laugh, feeling as though I did permanent damage to my windpipe.

"And the Devil's Plumber. Where the hell did you come up with that?"

"Grey told you he and I do security consulting. Sometimes it requires us to go undercover. We decided to try out one of our new covers on this trip. Works pretty good, huh?"

"Rebecca was a drama major in college. She had professional gigs in Atlanta, TV promos, and so forth."

"You remember the sexy babe who got lathered up all over the new Mustangs in those Atlanta Ford Dealership commercials a few years ago? Whenever those ads ran, I got several marriage proposals phoned in to the station, mainly from guys calling from pay phones outside the Union Mission."

"I don't think the marina attendant had marriage in mind. You scared him almost to death. If you'd told him he needed to rub himself down with snake oil to ward off the Devil's Plumber, he'd have bought a gallon."

Always on task, Grey turned to the gear piled in the middle of the room, and refocused. "We need to check this out to make sure we got all we need. I don't have any confidence the attendant pulled everything requested. And Paul — I mean Bob — we need to try on the wetsuits. Too tight will cut off circulation and constrict movements. Too loose and you'll feel like you're trying to swim in elephant skin."

"Just show me what you need, boss."

A sharp knock at the door made us all jump. Grey and Rebecca immediately got back into character. He took a breath, stepped to the door but didn't open it.

"Yes?"

"I'm sorry, I got so upset about that plumber thing y'all talkin' 'bout forgot tegitcha t' sign for your room."

Grey opened the door. It was the marina attendant. Half expecting it to be Krupp, I relaxed.

"Certainly, young man." Grey struck a signature on the clipboard the attendant presented, handed it back. "We should be here most of the afternoon. Let us know if you need anything else. But I'd prefer you to call first. We'll be setting up delicate equipment and do not need to be surprised."

"Uh, yessir."

Grey closed the door. When we could no longer hear the attendant's heavy footsteps walking up the dock to the office, Grey narrowed his eyes, whispered. "We need to stay on our toes, keep in our roles, someone could overhear us at any time." Then back to his normal voice. "Bob, you unload the rest of the cart. Dr. Ribbenschnitz and I will check out this gear."

"Yes, sir."

It was a good thing Grey suggested trying on my wetsuit before our trip across the Bay. I looked more like a walrus than an elephant, thick folds of neoprene blubber, flippers of far-too-long legs and arms. Drs. Tristan and Ribbenschnitz found it comical, a costume befitting a lowly grad assistant. I wasn't so entertained. I dragged it down the dock to the marina office for a better fit. For awhile it was looking as though my fish-belly-white skin was going to be a serious liability for the swim to Cabrini's, but after a long and frustrating search of his equipment room, the marina attendant located a smaller suit. It took Dr. Tristan and Dr. Ribbenschnitz a couple of hours to finalize the equipment check. We kept to our scheduled late afternoon timing.

When we finished loading the Zodiac, it was the best time to head across the Bay to Key Biscayne.

Biscayne Bay is a clear, shallow body of water — part salt, part fresh — ringed by mangrove forests, sheltered from the Atlantic by several islands, the northernmost of the Florida Keys, a string sweeping outward toward the east and bending southward.

Key Biscayne is the largest of the many islands in the Bay, some man-made, privately owned, sited with magnificent homes, many connected to the mainland by the island-hopping Venetian Causeway terminating at Miami Beach.

Named for Eddie Rickenbacker, World War I fighter ace, Eastern Airlines founder, winter resident of Coconut Grove, the Rickenbacker Causeway ends near the Cape Florida Lighthouse where I first met with Placido Milano to undertake Melissa's rescue launched from Cabrini's Bayfront home.

The Zodiac looked to be about twenty feet, an inflatable with center console, a Yamaha 200 engine; not overpowered but sufficient to get us and our equipment there and back fast enough to avoid too much attention. I off-loaded several bags of gear from the cart, much of it decoy, other bags with wetsuits, masks, snorkels, fins. Drs. Tristan and Ribbenschnitz futzed around the crowded boat. There was barely enough room for the three of us and our equipment.

Last bag stowed aboard, I looked up to see the marina assistant standing next to the boat, hands in pockets, a look on his face as though he wanted to ask something but was afraid to.

"Y'all let me know if you change your mind about 'at boat. I can fix you up real quick with a twenty-six-foot T-top."

Dr. Tristan looked miffed, let out a long sigh. "As I said before, we must maneuver in very shallow waters. An inflatable Zodiac is ideal for this work. Thank you for your offer, but it is not needed."

"Didn't mean to bother ya, just wanted to let y'all know somethin'. I've been takin' an intro biology course down at the community college. Y'all are doin' such interestin' stuff, you know, I'm thinkin' 'bout changing my major from business to marine biology."

Before Dr. Tristan could cut him off and send him on, Rebecca popped up from the equipment she was tending, dropped her persona, her look uncharacteristically reflecting compassion not disdain. "And I'm sure if you work hard, you'll be an excellent scientist. What did you say your name is?"

"Ralph. Ralph Emerson, ma'am."

"Bet your Mom liked poetry."

"Uh, yeah. How'd you know?"

"Just lucky."

Dr. Tristan broke in. "Best to you, Ralph. Now, if you will allow us."

"Uh, yes, sir."

By the time Ralph sauntered back down the dock out of sight, Dr. Tristan had cranked up and set out from the marina directly east toward Key Biscayne, visible in the near distance. The sun was low, only another hour of light. A dolphin breached close by the dock and playfully danced across our bow as we motored out of the marina. I took it as a good omen.

Chapter28

Because of the high tide and our shallow draft, we didn't have to stick to the channels, so we cut straight across the Bay, passing over expanses of seagrass, oyster beds, sandbars, all visible through bright water. Dodging boaters in all manner of craft — jet skis, cigarette boats, cabin cruisers, sailing yachts — our low transoms washed over and were nearly swamped by wakes kicked up from larger vessels oblivious to our path.

As Bob, I spent much of my time bailing the wash to keep the Zodiac from becoming a floating bathtub.

We approached the island's north end, the contours of the golf course visible directly ahead, the homes and docks of the residential area in the distance to our right. Cabrini's home was not yet discernable. In my overly confident knowledge of the island, I failed to take into account the difficulty of choosing our target in the falling darkness from all the other estate-sized homes with docks and sailboats lining the Bay. Houses look a lot different from the water than they do from the street.

We could count on the *Tempest* to mark our target, the distinctive low-slung silhouette of the French-designed Jeanneau standing out from other moored sailboats, though in the dim distance not yet able to make out the name painted on the stern.

Drs. Tristan and Ribbenschnitz took up their roles as marine researchers with entirely too much attention to authenticity for my liking, relishing ordering me from one bag to another, grabbing collection equipment, nets, jars, tags, scales, at their beck, all while bailing water.

"Bob, pay attention," Grey called sharply. "Dr. Ribbenschnitz needs her nets at the ready when we approach the collection site. Hop-to, young man. This isn't a vacation."

We slowed upon approach to the seawall. Only one foursome was visible on the golf course, having made the turn heading to the clubhouse, the sunlight extinguishing behind the tall pines of the course, long shadows cast across the fairways. The darkness we needed for our mission was beginning to take hold.

"Bob, look sharp! Get to the bow. Ready the anchor. We'll want to get as close to the seawall as possible. If *stultus asinum* is here, it may well bore into the wood pilings bolstering the barrier."

"Yes, sir. From my vantage point I'll wager there's more than one *stultus asinum* close by."

"We'll have none of your impudence. Keep in mind your dissertation has yet to be accepted. An appropriate attitude goes a long way to winning my approval. Grab that anchor."

Dr. Tristan was right. My attitude needed significant improvement. While law school was a trial in every sense of the word, taking me to the limits of endurance, I doubted whether I could have maintained the non-stop groveling a graduate degree entailed. I'd made the right career choice.

At the ready, Dr. Ribbenschnitz had a long-handled net pulled out to its full extension, peering over the gunnel into the muddy water along the shore, absorbed in her role. Dr. Tristan and I would carry smaller one-handed nets as part of our cover. Once in the water, we'd tie them to the anchor line to free our hands for the swim.

Anchor dropped, I used a small pair of binoculars and located what looked to be Cabrini's house and dock in the near distance with the *Tempest* moored as expected. Still couldn't make out the name on the stern, obscured by nearby docks, but was confident I'd located our target.

It was about five hundred yards away, ordinarily a moderately strenuous swim made much easier by the wetsuit, mask, snorkel, and fins, but a challenge in any case, particularly on the way back in total darkness.

"Dr. Tristan, I've spotted an area likely to be frequented by our species of interest."

"Well, don't waste time, young man. Suit up. The sun will be down momentarily, and we need to be in position before darkness falls. Where'd you stow my wetsuit?"

I pulled the duffle containing the swim equipment, scrounged out his wetsuit, handed it in his direction with a look that said "Aren't we taking this grad assistant role a bit too far?"

He didn't let up. Dr. Tristan took the gear from me with a feigned flourish, a half smile, a sarcastic dig.

"Thank you, young man. As soon as *you're* ready, *we'll* head out."

He and I discussed the swim before we put in. We'd stay below the surface as much as possible while there was still some light, using the numerous docks jutting into the Bay as way stations, waiting till both reached each point along the swim before heading to the next. Complete darkness, falling fast, with no moon, no dock lights, total overcast, would make even a quarter-mile swim in muddy water along the shore a challenge.

By the time I struggled on my wetsuit and gear, Dr. Tristan was already in the water, wiping out his mask, blowing out the snorkel. He was carrying a waterproof bag rolled up and stuffed in an equipment belt along with his Ka-Bar and flashlight.

Within a few minutes I was in the water and ready to go. Though the sun had just set, there was still a diffused glow on the horizon, enough to sight our destination in the distance. All security lights on our side of the Bay from the golf course past the *Tempest* were out. Ariel had done her job well. Now it was time to do ours.

A single mature dolphin breached close to our boat and circled. I didn't get a good look before so couldn't tell if it was the same one from the dock that might have followed us across the Bay. In any case, it seemed curious of our presence and breached and frolicked not twenty yards from our boat, staying close by.

We made the first and second docks, then the third. We could see the *Tempest* past the fourth, not a hundred yards away, rocking gently at her berth, her name only dimly evident on her transom in the gloaming. We swam the remaining distance with no incident and pulled up to the stern of the boat.

Grey slipped aboard, stuck his Ka-Bar in the hasp locking the hatch. It popped free with a quick, sharp crack. He slid open the hatch and was inside in an instant. I stayed in the water until he was out of the way, then was right behind. We'd memorized and divided the priority hiding spots between us, got to work, no sound, total darkness, only brief flashes of light to orient our searches. Grey concentrated on the forward compartments, I on the aft. We discovered that even a forty-two-foot sailboat can be a cramped space with two grown men moving about, their actions furtive, the occasional bump and unavoidable bang in the darkness.

Our search of the spots identified by Ariel went without a hitch, though without success. Nothing was in the safe behind the chart hold at the nav station, nothing in the enclosure behind the main berth, judged by us after careful study to be the two likeliest hiding places.

Our first backup was to switch places and go through the other's assigned spots in case we missed something. We came up empty. Now we went freelance, pulling up cushions, prying open panels, searching bilge and engine compartments. There are only so many hiding spots on a sailboat, and soon we'd exhausted them all.

I flashed a light in my face, mouthed, "Now what?"

Grey did likewise, shook his head, whispered, "Looks like Cabrini *did* lie to his own mother."

"Damn." The *Tempest*. Where else on a sailboat could a few sheets of paper be? I slapped my hand down on the stainless steel galley counter, a bang that jolted Grey and earned me a look of "What the hell?"

"We're looking in the wrong place!" My whisper was a hiss of incredulity. Grey cocked his head and shrugged. "It's not the sailboat the *Tempest*, it's the play *The Tempest*!"

"How the hell do we search a play?"

"It's in the house! In Cabrini's library. The First Folio! Why didn't I think of that before?"

"You need to calm down or the neighbors are going to call the cops. Keep your voice low. Now, what the hell are you talking about? A first what?"

"Just before his death, Placido gave Shakespeare's First Folio, an extraordinarily valuable book, to Cabrini. Cabrini prized it not only for its rarity — it's one of the most valuable books in the world — but also because it came as a gift from the father who'd refused for so long to acknowledge him. Cabrini would've chosen the Folio to put his Will for sentimental reasons and safekeeping."

"But *The Tempest*? How does that fit in?"

"Shakespeare's last play. The first one in the Folio. I bet we open the cover and Cabrini's Will falls out."

"You better be right. We'll have only one shot at breaking in." Grey jerked his head in the direction of the house. "Let's move."

We stowed our swim gear out of sight at the base of the dock, crept through shadows to the back door. Grey produced his Ka-Bar and, with a grind and a snap, pushed the door in, breaking the jamb clean. It looked like he'd done this before.

With only brief flashes from my flashlight, I led the way through the darkened house to the library. When we got there, I swept the shelves with the beam, starting in the most prominent spot.

There it was, where we'd left it the day Placido, Cabrini, Melissa, and I met here. That day of surprises and happiness, unanticipated gifts, and certain expectations. So much hope and promise. That day when Placido announced his retirement, Melissa and Cabrini took control of Milano Corporation, and Melissa and I still had our weekend at The Abbey ahead of us. Now they were all dead, and I was searching this once-joyous place for their Wills.

The Folio was housed in an airtight acrylic clamshell case, displayed face out, centered on a shelf by itself. I took it down, laid it on the closest table. Before opening it, as though I was desecrating a sacred icon with ungloved hands, I was struck with the severity of my insult. Before another breath, I resolved to move slowly, cautiously.

I slid open the outer enclosure, pulled out the volume. Grey's flashlight trained on the Folio. I lifted the cover. Shakespeare's face smiling at us from his etching on the title page. I took a breath, turned to the first play, *The Tempest*, anticipating Cabrini's Will to be in the pages.

Wrong again.

Laid out in front of me was not only Cabrini's Will, but Melissa's and Placido's as well. It was as if someone was making sure I found everything I needed. I'd hit the jackpot and could barely move.

Grey shook me back to reality. "Is that what we're looking for?"

"Uh, yeah, sure, this is it alright. Even more than I expected. Here, seal these up."

Grey unrolled a military-grade, puncture-resistant waterproof submersible bag, plenty big for three twenty-page, letter-size documents; hardly any lawyers use legal-size stock anymore. Laid it on the table, slid the papers in, smoothed out all excess air, and resealed.

Rolling it up, Grey stuffed it in his belt and started for the door. I winced at putting all our faith in a plastic bag to keep the Wills from being destroyed, but Grey assured me the pack was fail-safe protection. The only challenge was the possibility of it floating out of his belt without notice and drifting away in the void as he swam. Two separate carabiner D-rings attaching the enclosure to his belt eliminated that problem.

I looked back at the Folio. I couldn't leave it exposed. I took several precious seconds to restore it to its secure case and return it to the shelf. We slid out the back, grabbed gear and crossed the dock. We put on swimming gear in cover of darkness and lowered into the water for the swim back.

I didn't think it could get any darker, but it had.

Chapter 29

I could see little on our side of the Bay. The only orientation was the glitter of the Miami skyline across miles of black water. I'd keep it to my left as I swam, lights glimmering off ripples near the shore, revealing in brief flashes the docks I'd use to guide my way back. I followed Grey as he swam off, in an instant invisible, only the forced breathing through the snorkel an indication of his presence.

The first dock, close by, we made with no problem and swam on. And so, with the second and third. But I could not see the next waypoint, the dock farther in the distance, and struck out without locking on the destination. All I could do was keep the lights of Miami on my left as I swam, hoping eventually to run into the landmark before I ran out of energy. I hadn't realized how much our earlier swim and work on the boat took out of me. I was laboring, my breathing heavy. I'm a good swimmer, but it's not something I do every day, certainly not long swims, and this one was kicking my butt.

Though the next waypoint was farther off, I'd been swimming far longer than I'd expected to and without making any recognizable marker. Contrary to plan, I popped my head out of the water, pulled off my mask and snorkel, looking for some indication of my location.

I must've swum farther offshore into the Bay, the ripples close-in no longer visible. I listened for Grey's breathing but heard nothing. There was only darkness and water. Without some marker near the shore, I didn't want to keep swimming fearing that, even though I kept the skyline to my left, the shore had fallen off farther to the right leaving me swimming toward the middle of the Bay, more distant from shore at every stroke.

I wondered whether I could tread water until dawn. Even if I could, I'd have blown our carefully devised cover. I peered toward the shore for some way to orient myself and keep from swimming in circles. Exhausting energy was a sure way to drown before sunup.

Then something bumped my leg. At first, I thought I hit a submerged piling, then I felt it slide by, distant light flashing off a large dorsal fin, ten yards away, turning back, vanishing.

Shark.

The next pass he'd take a bite to see if I was something he wanted to eat. Pulling knees up, feet in his direction to give him swim fins to taste, I hoped hard rubber would discourage further interest. Every nerve on alert, I braced, poised to fight, my only weapon my wits.

A dolphin breached between me and the shark fin not five feet away. The wash from its powerful tail and the blast from its blowhole was an even greater shock than the brush-by from the shark. The dolphin disappeared below in the direction of the shark.

I was never happier to smell the overwhelming stench of fish it had been eating. Dolphins are the only creatures sharks fear. An adult dolphin, particularly a protective mother, could out-swim and out-maneuver a lumbering shark, smash the fish's vulnerable underbelly with its bony nose, mortally damaging its internal organs. Most sharks avoided encounters with dolphins. I hoped it was a female, protecting her young close by but out of sight, and just happened to be an unintended beneficiary.

I readied for the predator's next pass, but nothing happened, each second a reprieve, one minute, and another.

Then I saw a light underwater in the direction of the shore. Grey must've noticed how long I was taking and, recognizing my predicament, was shining his flashlight, moving slowly to allow me to follow to the next dock in the distance. I put on my mask and snorkel, head just below the surface, still alert for the shark.

A soft reassuring glow and I swam toward it. After several minutes of anticipating another brush-by from the shark, meeting Grey at the last dock was a relief. His light was now off. Out of breath, heart pounding, still too scared to speak, I didn't say a word.

Grey motioned toward the seawall and swam slowly, noiselessly, toward the boat, all the while under the dock. We reconnoitered our Zodiac. It was good we did.

Chapter30

Around the corner of the seawall a larger boat came into view next to ours. I could see Miami Marine Police in large black letters the full length of the hull illuminated by LEDs under the gunnel. The police hit the Zodiac with their searchlight, even at that distance blinding my eyes so used to complete blackness.

Dr. Ribbenschnitz stood in the middle of the boat, arms stretched wide, illuminated, a beacon in the midst of the dark, waterproof computer screen glowing bright in the background. Ariel was monitoring the encounter.

"Police. Identify yourself!" echoed out of a bullhorn.

I strained to hear Rebecca's voice. Though firm, the distance and rumbling idle of the police boat outboards muffled her reply.

"Dr. Alicia Ribbenschnitz, University of Georgia Marine Sciences. My colleagues and I are here collecting specimens of an invasive species in the Bay."

"Who are your colleagues, ma'am, and where are they? We see only one person in your vessel. Please keep your hands visible at all times!"

Dr. Ribbenschnitz, being a trained law enforcement officer IRL, readily obliged, showing her hands, palms out, to the officers.

"My colleagues are scientists. They're swimming in the Bay, collecting specimens. As you may be aware, it's difficult for scientists to collect marine specimens out of the water." Dr. Ribbenschnitz sniffed her condescension.

"Dr., uh..."

"Ribbenschnitz."

"Do you have any weapons onboard?"

"There are two spearguns in the forward hold, both un-strung."

The spearguns were props we didn't expect to have to use and left them so as not to impede our swim, but that may have been a serious oversight.

"Do your colleagues have any weapons?"

"Dr. Tristan has a collecting knife. But Mr. Adams does not."

At the mention of our names, I touched Grey's shoulder, cocked my head in Rebecca's direction. In the reflected light I could see him shake his head.

"Do you have a permit?"

"Yes. You may access the Florida Department of Natural Resources website and query *'stultus asinum'*. There you will see a permit for Drs. Simon Tristan and Alicia Ribbenschnitz to collect an unlimited number of specimens of *stultus asinum,* alive or dead. Our permit extends though this weekend."

Those were clear instructions to Ariel to make the proper permit appear when the police entered their query. The younger officer, tablet in hand, apparently accessed the website, but was having difficulty forming the query. "Will you spell that, please?" Once Dr. Ribbenschnitz did, the assistant pushed the tablet in his superior's face, pointing; the officer nodded. He made no further acknowledgment.

"Where are your colleagues now?"

"Their plan was to explore the seawall first. It is the most likely place to spot *stultus asinum*. My colleagues have been out a couple of hours. I can't say their exact location."

"Why are you doing this in the dark?"

"We work at night because of the characteristics of our quarry. *Stultus asinii* are only active at night, and the prominent bioluminescent bony plate on their heads they use to drill into all manner of objects makes them easier to spot in the darkness."

Dr. Ribbenschnitz was winging this, and I wondered how quickly her knowledge of biology — or her ability to fake it — would run out.

"Any reason for your colleagues to be checking out the docks or the boats down by those houses?" The officer indicated the direction of Cabrini's house. "A homeowner reported they heard some loud noises, saw flashlights on one of the sailboats. Asked us to check it out."

"As I said, my colleagues are collecting specimens in the Bay. They could be anywhere, but they have no reason to be on a dock or in a sailboat." She pushed up her glasses with an impatient sniff, then added helpfully, "I've seen nothing suspicious."

"Thank you, ma'am. We'll head down the shore and check out the report."

"Please watch out for my colleagues. Don't make their work more dangerous than it already is."

"Yes, ma'am, we'll be on the lookout."

The police turned their searchlight past us, toward Cabrini's, idled in that direction, beam sweeping the shore, docks, boats.

The police boat passed. Grey stroked toward the Zodiac. I followed, launching myself into the safety of the boat before he clambered in. I sat on a duffel crammed with gear, head between knees, trying to catch my breath.

Dr. Tristan was the first to comment, still in character. "Dr. Ribbenschnitz. What did the officers want?"

"Identification. Questions. I sent them on their way."

"Good work, Dr. Ribbenschnitz."

I was done being Bob, the grad assistant. I was Paul, the one who escaped a shark attack, my breath barely under control.

"I got brushed by a shark! He was turning back! A dolphin...a dolphin came between us and..."

"Slow down. You survived. When did this happen?"

Dr. Tristan was analytic and rational. Not me.

"Out in the Bay. Got off track. Think I'm more scared now than I was." I lifted my hand. It was trembling. "I'd still be paddling around the Bay if you hadn't guided me in with your flashlight."

"Maybe you were seeing things. I didn't use my flashlight. And it was probably the dolphin you thought was a shark."

"Hell no." My breath now more under control, sure of what I saw. "I know what a shark fin looks like. I definitely saw two different animals. And if you didn't use your flashlight, then someone else did."

Suddenly it dawned on me. Maybe that someone else was Ariel, my guardian angel, who intervened and lit my way back to the shore. Dr. Ribbenschnitz shook me from my musings and redirected us before we abandoned our roles for good.

"Well, gentlemen, we can be thankful everyone is safe. Now, were you successful in your efforts? Did you sight a *stultus asinum*?"

"Got one right here in my collection bag." Dr. Tristan put his hand on the plastic roll still attached to his belt.

"Excellent, Dr. Tristan. Then I say we weigh anchor and set off to the marina. We'll get some rest tonight before returning to the University tomorrow. And you, Mr. Adams, can recover from your near-death experience." Dr. Ribbenschnitz sniffed, but this time it hid a laugh at my expense.

Pulling away from the seawall, I saw the dolphin breach once more in the distance.

A good omen indeed.

Chapter 31

Ariel planned to have us and our gear dropped at the hangar very early the next morning. I insisted she at least give us a chance to catch a little sleep and have time to return the leased equipment before she pushed us out the door. The effect of fatigue and the need for rest among humans was something she often overlooked.

Before we retired for the evening, I handed off the Wills to a private courier Ariel arranged to deliver the documents by land to Floyd O'Brien. It was slower than a plane but, as Ariel reminded, small aircraft have mishaps all the time. Even if we were all to escape unscathed, we couldn't afford to lose the Wills in a freak cabin fire on the runway — or something more lethal.

Besides, it would be unwise to wait until I returned to Atlanta to get the Wills filed, especially when Floyd could submit them electronically and hand-deliver the originals to the Courts early in the morning. Getting the Wills filed was the first step in thwarting Enzo's takeover. Floyd's work would be completed before we landed.

We checked in the rented gear with Ralph as soon as the marina office opened. He was dismayed to hear we may have captured a *stultus asinum* and were taking it back to the lab for analysis. As we were waiting for the ride to the airport, Dr. Ribbenschnitz took the opportunity to suggest Ralph concentrate on his studies rather than count on the permanence of the marina job.

"It may not be here for much longer."

"Yes, ma'am. Thank you for your advice. Have a nice trip back. And you can count on me. Not a word 'bout your 'speriments."

When we arrived at the airport, I was still Bob the grad assistant, sent off to find a cart to carry our bags to the plane. Drs. Tristan and Ribbenschnitz led the way to the King Air, now on the tarmac and fueled, clamshell air-stair extended, ready to go.

I was contemplating having to carry all four duffels loaded with gear up yet another gangway, wondering when my grad assistant gig would be over, each person responsible for their own bags, when a large black SUV, windows tinted out, pulled between the three of us and the plane. A red, white, and blue seal on the door reading U.S. Department of Homeland Security surrounded an American eagle clutching arrows and an olive branch.

Grey's glance our way said "I'll handle this." Agent Grey was back as private pilot, security consultant. He stepped forward. The passenger door on the SUV swung open and a man in a dark trench coat stepped out.

It wasn't Homeland Security. It was Krupp. Then another familiar character unfolded from behind the steering wheel, towering over the roof of the vehicle. A bandaged left hand rested on the door frame, one finger missing. Crenshaw.

Then the rear passenger door opened. Olga. Her presence was a bad sign; her blown cover meant only one thing: Krupp was planning on none of us leaving alive.

Chapter 32

"Mr. McDaniel, you have a bad habit of endangering your friends in your fruitless efforts. Too bad they must now suffer the same fate as you."

"There are surveillance cameras all over this hangar."

Krupp smiled. "No worries. All they'll record is Homeland Security apprehending bad actors. No one will question DHS on a clandestine mission to neutralize a band of domestic terrorists. Now, put your hands behind your backs. Olga will check you for weapons and administer flex-cuffs. Anyone steps out of line and Mr. Crenshaw will apply more drastic sanctions."

Crenshaw grunted, thumped his oversized revolver on his chest.

I looked toward Grey, who indicated now wasn't the time for resistance. Olga found Grey's ankle weapon, Rebecca's small-of-the-back holster, removed them, tied us. My 9mm was in my backpack with my laptop, ten feet away, both useless.

Crenshaw stuffed us in the third-row bench in the back of the SUV, Olga in the middle-row seat turned toward us, watching. Krupp made no effort to prevent us from seeing where we were going, not a good sign. We soon reached our destination, the back of a rundown warehouse near the airport. Crenshaw dragged us from the vehicle. I didn't see which way Grey or Rebecca went, but Crenshaw threw me into a room without windows or lights, smelling of oil and chemicals.

I landed on a splintered wooden floor, on my side, my face in filth and stench. The door slammed. Padlock latched.

I listened. No sound. After a few minutes, still cuffed, I sat up and brushed off as much of the dirt clinging to my face as I could, first using one shoulder, then the other. I pulled myself over to what I figured was a wall or a pile of boxes and leaned against it. I was trying hard to find some way not to lose the feeling in my hands, trying harder not to lose control.

This was the second time I found myself bound by the agents of Milano Corporation and Strange & Fowler, facing death and, though it didn't seem possible, I was far more desperate than before. This time I managed to have my surest means of rescue captured with me. Krupp was right, I have a bad habit of endangering my friends.

Last time I was captured, I was caught in a selfless but misguided effort to save Melissa from her murderous uncle. This time, all I'm doing is trying to keep the Milano legal business with its flood of cash coming to McDaniel & Associates. I'd been fooling myself to think it's all been for others. I was no different from Fowler, Anthony, Melissa, and Cabrini, all dead from grasping for Milano's money. I was as bad as Enzo, scheming to hold on to the Milano Corporation, though it looks as if this time his simple brutish treachery was going to triumph over my more elegant legal plans.

Now, I shall harvest the fruit of my own selfishness. The last time, it was the possibility of a life with Melissa that gave me hope. This time, it was only the ability to count Milano's money driving me on. All that money did not seem particularly comforting right at this moment.

No surprise, then, that Ariel hadn't developed any moral grounding: She had no moral exemplars to follow. Too bad it took being captured and facing death, once again, to see my own depravity. I feared I wouldn't live to apply the lesson.

How did Krupp find us? We knew he'd been tracking us, but Grey took every precaution not to tip our hand once we'd landed in Brunswick. Krupp must've had Cabrini's house under surveillance, thinking we'd lead him to the Will, not wanting to risk setting off the security system himself, and no idea where to look. Hoping they'd catch us, Krupp probably tipped the police to do his dirty work for him, but we got out of that.

He'd keep us alive at least until he finds out Cabrini's Will is gone and it's too late for them to intercept it. But how did he track us to the airport? The only other person who knew where we were heading was Ralph, the marina attendant. If Ralph was the source, I hope he gave us up with no resistance and that Krupp's Homeland Security ruse was sufficient without Herr Doktor unleashing Crenshaw with unbounded violence on an innocent.

Eyes now adjusted to the dark, I could see a dim light under the door. Still no sound. No movement. I waited. I knew what was coming. Someone would come in, drag me somewhere, threaten my life if I didn't tell them the location of the Will. And once I told them, they'd kill me.

Unless.

Unless Grey and Rebecca could perform magic and appear as if out of nowhere, cut my flex-cuff, and do away with our captors, like they'd done the last time, in communication with Ariel, colluding with her on every move. Only the last time, they hadn't been captured with me. But now, we three were prisoners in the same derelict warehouse, with no means to contact Ariel, a futile, desperate fantasy.

The last moments of my life were ticking away.

Someone kicked open the door, I couldn't see who with garish light behind him blinding me. The brutish form grabbed me, pulled me to my feet, dragged me from the room. Great. Crenshaw. I took a few wobbly steps, shaking my head, blinking my eyes, adjusting to the searing glare.

Krupp stood in the hallway. Crenshaw threw me down at his feet.

"Where's the Will?"

"Not here."

Crenshaw kicked me in the ribs. Something cracked, the pain was excruciating. Crenshaw poised to kick again. I braced.

"Not yet, Mr. Crenshaw." Krupp looked down. "Mr. McDaniel, we know the Will is not here. We've scoured your belongings, searched the plane, tossed your room at the marina. It's nowhere. Now, kindly tell me where it is, and I'll see to it things go easy for you and your friends."

"Sure, Krupp."

Krupp nodded to Crenshaw. Instant searing pain, all the breath leaving my body, darkness giving way to gray. Several minutes passed before I was able to breathe, to focus again. I looked up. Krupp was still there.

"The more you cooperate, the more use you will be to me, and the longer I'll keep you alive. It's your only hope, Mr. McDaniel. And if you fail to cooperate, I shall kill you and your friends. Doesn't seem like a very good alternative, does it?"

Krupp absentmindedly stroked his scar. "So. *Where is the Will?*"

It wasn't lost on me, even at this moment, that Krupp was still hoping only to secure *a* Will, not *three*. He didn't know we'd recovered all three at Cabrini's, a remarkable stroke of luck or evidence someone helped me.

"I don't know."

This answer, if I could stick with it, had the utility of being the truth. I wasn't certain where the Will was, but hoped by now that all three were electronically filed with the Courts, originals soon to follow.

It was McDaniel 3, Krupp 0, bottom of the 9th. But Krupp had the bases loaded, his cleanup batter at the plate, and my bullpen was looking shaky.

Crenshaw pulled his foot back, readying yet another kick. I knew Krupp would frustrate his desire to stomp the life out of me. Krupp wanted me alive and knew I would not likely survive another kick to the gut.

"No, Mr. Crenshaw. We can't kill Mr. McDaniel right now. He requires us to engage in more persuasive means to locate the Will. Put him in the room and let him think about it. We're going to give him an opportunity to save his friends' lives — or watch them die as a result of his selfishness before he meets a ghastly end."

Time passed in the darkness, fast or slow, no way to know. I'd reviewed every possible means to escape Herr Doktor, to develop a plan, but came up empty. All I had was hope. Hope for a miracle, for the intervention of Grey and Rebecca, for the providence of Ariel's appearance. None of these seemed likely. Hope, as I often remind myself, is not a plan.

The door burst open once again. This time it was Krupp, Crenshaw lurking in the hall behind him.

"We're going for a little boat ride, Mr. McDaniel. I hope you don't fall overboard on the way. I understand it's quite difficult to swim with hands tied behind your back. And I don't plan to waste a life preserver on you. Get up."

Chapter33

It's also rather hard to stand with your hands tied behind your back, and after two stumbling attempts, Crenshaw grabbed my arm, jerked me to my feet, duck-walked me to the loading dock of the warehouse. It was dark, only a dim bulb lit the way down worn steps to the parked SUV, the Homeland Security seal now gone.

Crenshaw shoved me in the back, this time by myself, Grey and Rebecca nowhere to be seen. Olga was absent. Just me, Krupp, and Crenshaw. Krupp drove, Crenshaw stood watch. Once out of the warehouse district it was soon evident we were heading to the Dinner Key Marina.

We pulled to a spot in a parking lot obscured by a storage trailer and a few dry-stored boats. Krupp dragged me out and threw a trench coat over my head, the one he'd been wearing when he ambushed us. I was pretty sure it wasn't to protect me from the elements, but more likely to keep anyone from seeing I'd been beaten and hands cuffed. Krupp led, Crenshaw followed, out to the dock to the same Zodiac we'd rented the day before.

Krupp shoved me in. I landed face-down in the bottom, rolled over, struggled upright, ribs screaming. The bottom of the Zodiac would soon splash full and I'd drown in a few inches of water if I couldn't sit up and stay up.

"This boat has the benefit of having been rented by you and your colleagues. It will appear you failed to return it on time, a fatal mishap having befallen you. It's also able to go in the flats, where we intend to take you."

161

And, I noted, the Zodiac's simple manual steering and basic outboard would be impossible for Ariel to take over, even if she could somehow track me in the wilderness of the Bay.

Krupp maneuvered out of the marina, and we headed in the darkness on a line past the southern tip of Key Biscayne, past the Cape Florida Lighthouse, out to the sand flats off the Key. The only things out there were the largest congregation of sharks in the Bay and a curious collection of houses called Stiltsville.

I learned of Stiltsville indirectly from my parents, having overheard whispered conversations of invitations to secretive gatherings at the Calvert Club, Bikini Club, Quarterdeck Club, places a mile offshore where liquor flowed freely, gambling was legal, and other vices winked at.

The clubs were grounded yachts, barges, and shacks built on pilings in the shallows of the sand flats, in places only a foot deep at low tide. There were always raids, but since the clubs of Stiltsville were frequented by local politicians, lawyers, bankers — even one governor had his favorite Stiltsville resort — police never seemed to find any illegal activity, just wholesome sunbathing, boating, recreation.

Some of the structures, many of which were built during Prohibition, had survived environmental regulation, law enforcement, and hurricanes even till now, though they were no longer regularly occupied.

Isolated, uninhabited, infinite visibility in all directions, the remaining structures presented an excellent venue for sex trafficking, drug distribution, or gangland execution. A body dumped in the sea here was soon disposed of by voracious sharks, ten-foot Bulls and Hammerheads, patrolling the flats for the daily banquet the tide produced or the occasional treats falling from the decks of Stiltsville.

Krupp slipped the Zodiac among the pilings of one of the most remote shacks, tied it up to a stairway extending below the waterline underneath the structure. Crenshaw shoved me up the first steps.

I stumbled, tripped, crawled, and climbed up one step at a time, leaning into the inside railing, the only way to steady myself, Crenshaw grunting behind. At the top of the stairs Krupp wordlessly opened a door and shoved me in, a searing LED lantern on a table at the far side of the room providing the only light. A sliding door at the other end was open, leading onto a deck over the Bay.

Grey and Rebecca were on the deck, each tied to a chair, the lantern illuminating them, railings behind them gone, void beyond. Olga stood guard. Crenshaw shoved me down in the only other chair, directly in front of Grey and Rebecca.

Krupp and Crenshaw stood to one side of the pair, Olga on the other. Crenshaw threatening, a large-bore revolver in one hand, arms crossed. I stared at his bandaged left hand as he rubbed where his finger should have been. Olga stood motionless.

"Mr. McDaniel. This is where things get serious." Krupp stroked that damn scar again. "You will tell me where the Will is. If you do, you will all live. If you don't, we'll shoot your friends one at a time and shove them into the Bay to feed the sharks. You will be last, and I'll let you have a good view of the sharks thrashing as they tear into your friends' bodies before I dispatch you. And I don't intend to shoot you. I'll push you off the deck into the feeding frenzy below. You won't even have time to drown before the sharks rip you apart."

He smiled. "Now. Where is it?"

In the dark of the warehouse, I'd resigned to giving Krupp the information, even though he would probably kill me anyway. It would give us a chance, slim, but some possibility to live another day. I'm not a coward.

But I can't sacrifice my friends' lives. Not for myself. Not for anything.

I looked at Grey, then Rebecca. Their eyes bore in on me. They shook their heads. I was incredulous. "I've got to. I'm not able to do this to you."

Krupp smiled. "You're a wise man, Mr. McDaniel. If your friends wish to commit suicide, that's their business. But you don't have to."

"Paul, don't. Krupp hasn't been able to find any of the Wills. And he can't find them without us. He won't pull the trigger."

"You're right about one thing, Agent Grey. I won't pull the trigger. Olga will do the honors." Krupp turned to Olga. "She needs an opportunity to show her loyalty to our cause. Mr. Crenshaw will provide any additional motivation necessary." Crenshaw grinned, thumped the revolver against his chest.

Krupp pulled a handgun from a waistband holster, handed it to Olga. "Grey first. Maybe Mr. McDaniel will reconsider his position once he sees our seriousness and do the sensible thing and save the lady's life."

"No! I'll tell you! Don't! The Will's —"

But before I could get out another word, Olga fired two shots.

Chapter 34

The first bullet entered Crenshaw above his right eye and exited the back of his head in a spray of brains and blood. The second put a hole about six inches below his Adam's apple. He jerked his gun hand toward Olga, but before he could get off a shot, his knees buckled. He crumpled in a heap and slid over the side of the deck. An instant later, a splash.

Krupp lunged at Olga before Crenshaw hit the water. She caught him mid-stride with a bullet, center mass, knocking him back and turning so he fell on his belly. He hit the deck and crawled toward some imaginary safety that was not there.

Olga took two steps, kicked Krupp over on his back, shoved a booted heel in his crotch, emptied the magazine into his face and chest, and slung the still-smoking gun into the darkness.

I was too stunned to speak. Olga bent over Grey, released his flex-cuff, then Rebecca's.

Grey stood, rubbed his hands, looked at me. "First lesson. Don't piss off Olga."

How could someone make jokes in this situation? Still struggling for breath, I couldn't talk and feared if I tried I'd only squeak. Now both Grey and Rebecca were standing, trying to get the feeling back in their hands. Olga came across the deck to me and released my hands. I tried to stand, couldn't, looked up in her ice blue eyes, stammered.

"O-O-Olga...wh-wh-what?"

"I didn't join Strange & Fowler to kill innocents. I thought I was helping Frank Billingsley when Krupp and Crenshaw did what they did to him. Then Krupp wanted me to help him kill you, too. Well, I couldn't. They got what they deserved."

By this point a bit of feeling in my hands and legs returned. I stood, stumbled toward Grey, but with Crenshaw's kicks to my ribs, breathing itself took monumental effort.

"Krupp's loyalty test backfired."

"Yes. I'm afraid I failed." Olga gave a faint hint of that smile again.

"I need help. Krupp needs to join his friend over the side. But before he does..." Grey stuck his hand in Krupp's pocket, pulled out a set of keys, then another, stuffed them in his pants. "Unless we want to swim to the marina and walk to the airport, we'll be needing these."

Olga grabbed an arm, Grey, a leg, dragged Krupp to the edge of the deck, and pushed him over into the Bay. As soon as his body splashed it sounded as if someone hit the pulverize cycle on a food processor, the number of sharks at the banquet boiling the shallow waters below, audibly ripping flesh, crunching bone, fighting each other for every piece of Herr Doktor's carcass. I wasn't sad to think one of those ravenous beasts was giving Krupp's scar its final caress. No trace of those men remained to identify.

Except one.

I'd kept Crenshaw's finger in my pocket as a talisman, a reminder of the extent Krupp and his gang would go to extinguish me. It was desiccated, almost unrecognizable as a human digit, but it wouldn't do for me to be found with the body part of a missing person. I pulled it from my pocket and flung it into the darkness.

Rebecca looked on as I watched it hit the water and disappear. "What was that?"

"Crenshaw's missing finger."

"Couldn't wait to give him the finger, huh? Too bad it was the wrong one."

I smiled for the first time since we left the marina and searched for a response, but Grey wasn't about to let us linger.

"Douse that light. Let's get out of here."

Grey led the way down the stairs, Olga next. I wobbled behind, Rebecca followed. Once in the Zodiac, so many sharks were thrashing over their unexpected dinner we thought it best to navigate behind the pilings to avoid the party. We made the trip back to the marina in darkness, not a word spoken. Wind, waves, and whine of the outboard would've drowned out any attempt at conversation anyway, but no one made the effort, each deep in thought, trying to accept what happened.

It felt as though I'd landed in another world by the time we docked at the marina. No Krupp. No Crenshaw. Not facing immediate annihilation. The distinctive sound of ocean breeze through coconut-palm fronds, and the perfume of bougainvillea. From hell to paradise in thirty minutes on a Zodiac, death dodged once again. Was the pain in my ribs causing me to hallucinate? It was all too much to process.

Grey tossed Olga the keys to the SUV as we walked across the parking lot.

"Olga, if you can give us a lift to the airport, you keep Krupp's vehicle. He won't be needing it."

Grey and Rebecca climbed in back, Olga in the driver's seat, leaving the front passenger seat for me. While we rode to the airport, I voiced a few questions to Olga, probably my last chance to figure out how everything fit together.

"Grey took great pains not to tip off Krupp on our whereabouts. How did you find us?"

"Krupp didn't know. He had several locations under surveillance. Cabrini's house, Fowler's cottage, the Milano island, but he figured this was the most likely spot. So, we waited here. He knew you could use your *little computer program*, as he called it, to neutralize the security system, so he let you and Grey do the work for us."

"But how did he know where we were going?"

Olga was silent for a moment.

"We watched you head back from Cabrini's toward Coconut Grove, then tracked you to the marina from the causeway. Krupp felt the area was too open to grab you there, and we'd risk blowing cover if we tailed you. We waited till you left to interrogate the marina attendant. He refused to tell us what you were doing and where you were going. Said you were scientists on a secret mission."

Olga shook her head, sadness in her face flashed with the light of each streetlamp we passed. Then her aspect darkened. "Krupp jammed his head in the aquarium and Crenshaw held him under. They pulled him out after thrashing around. He could only sputter. Took him awhile before he could speak. He wouldn't give you up.

"Crenshaw hit him in the face with the butt of his revolver, then threatened to crack the boy's skull. Before Crenshaw hit him a second time, he told them you were heading to the Executive Airport. Then they shoved his head back in the aquarium and held him underwater until the bubbles stopped. They left him there. Before we walked out, the Hammerhead was feeding on his face."

Rebecca slammed the back of my seat. "Bastards!"

"A couple of those shots back there were for the boy."

"Too bad we couldn't kill Krupp more'n once."

Rebecca was still fuming, though. After Olga's revelation and Rebecca's response, we all fell silent, turning over in our minds the evil we'd encountered. With yet another improbable intervention we avoided Krupp's end for us.

Chapter35

I was still curious about Olga's role in all this; once she dropped us off at the airport she'd disappear forever. I turned to her, the steady lights of the highway to the airport putting her profile into relief, emphasizing the sculpted symmetry of her striking face.

"How'd a nice girl like you get stuck with Krupp and his band of trolls?"

She turned and smiled the Kandi Moore smile that had made me willing to step off an elevator with her into an unknown fate.

"I left Russia with very little advance planning. I was working for a security agency and one of our operations went bad. I entered the U.S. on a tourist visa. A contact here, who knew your old firm was looking for someone with experience in security, put me in touch with Krupp. At first it was simple surveillance. When my visa was about to expire and I was running out of options, Krupp said he would get me a green card, all I'd have to do was marry one of his men. Only a paper transaction, he said. The marriage was to Crenshaw. Unfortunately, Crenshaw had other ideas about the marriage, but it was too late. I couldn't divorce him, and I couldn't leave Strange & Fowler or I'd lose my immigration status and get shipped back to Russia. That's when Krupp started involving me in some of his more questionable operations. Like Frank Billingsley." The desperation of her plight was palpable.

Rebecca's quick sarcasm lifted the mood. "I've been on bad dates before, Olga, but...Crenshaw?"

"He was an animal. IQ of a ground squirrel. Sex drive of a rogue elephant. But Krupp was pure evil."

We remained silent until we pulled into the hangar, pondering the profundity of Olga's last statement and how close we all came to succumbing to Krupp.

Our gear was still scattered near the plane. We bailed out of the SUV. Olga rolled her window down. "I was happy to kill them both."

Grey voiced what we were thinking. "If you hadn't, we'd all be fish food. Thank you."

"It was truly my pleasure in every sense of the word."

Grey, always practical and still thinking logistics, intervened before I could say anything else. "Paul, do you think you could ask Ariel to block any tracking of Olga and her vehicle?"

I'd been searching through the pile of equipment, hoping nothing was damaged. I located my laptop and opened it. It still worked.

"Got it. Olga, I'm sure you don't need me to say you can't be traveling on credit cards. Do you need any cash?"

"We only operate on cash. I have enough left from Krupp's stash to live well for about six months. After that, who knows? I have a good feeling something positive will come about."

Olga said *something positive* with that same sideways coquettish smile she gave me on the elevator when we first met. Like it was inside information. Just between the two of us. I felt as if I'd asked her all the questions she was going to answer, so I turned it over in my mind as I bagged the gear Krupp and Crenshaw tossed searching for the Will. I was head-down in a duffle, packing equipment, when Olga rolled up the window on the SUV without another word and pulled out of the hangar.

I turned and watched her taillights recede into the Miami darkness.

The flight from Miami to Atlanta was too short. The elation of being alive after staring death in the face once again was fabulous. In our joyous high, Rebecca and I bantered the entire way back. Grey, for the most part, was fully absorbed in piloting. Rather than detour through Brunswick, we agreed I should get back to Atlanta first. They would drop me, then deadhead back to the lodge.

"Next time there's a possibility of being eaten by a shark, you need to give me a heads-up, pretty boy. Dr. Ribbenschnitz ain't quite ready to end her run just yet."

"You? Me! I was wondering how I could get Krupp to shoot me first then throw me over the edge. Had I known we were going to end up like that, I sure would've tried to figure a less risky way to get those Wills."

"With Krupp alive, there probably wasn't one. Now that he and his nine-fingered sidekick are gone, you should have smooth sailin'."

Grey broke in. His intent was playful, but his tone serious. "Mission accomplished, Paul. You're on your own. I hope you'll understand Rebecca and I have a few other things to deal with. You might be surprised to learn we have other clients with pressing matters."

"Yeah. And a few actually pay us for our troubles."

Snarky again, but she said it with a big smile this time.

"Oh, surely working with Ariel and me is compensation enough."

We were soon entering Atlanta airspace. Flying into PDK in a small plane on a clear dark night is a remarkable experience. There appear to be hundreds of lights, some indistinguishable from stars, all at individual levels, moving at different speeds, going in every direction. With so much air traffic it's miraculous there are not multiple midair collisions daily. But Grey guided us through the labyrinth, all too soon setting us down. I shook his hand, hugged Rebecca, and gave them both profound thanks.

A rideshare was waiting to deliver me to the nearest 24/7 walk-in urgent care location. According to Ariel, my breathing didn't sound right. You didn't have to be an AI program to figure out ribs were broken.

"Mountain bike accident. Hit a tree."

The staff was skeptical. "This particular tree left a boot print on your back."

"Nasty tree."

"You're lucky you only have a few cracked ribs, not a punctured lung. Are you in much pain?"

"Only when I breathe. Can't seem to give that up."

"We can prescribe pain meds."

"I'd prefer not to take anything that'll slow me down. What else you got?"

"Not much. Ribs will heal on their own. Stay off your *mountain bike*. And don't let that *tree* kick you again."

"Pretty sure that won't happen."

It was early morning when I got home, exhausted. Bags thrown in the corner, and still fully clothed, I eased myself into bed, asleep in an instant, confident Ariel was watching over me.

Still, I needed to attend to the filing of all three original Wills as soon as I could, our first barrage in response to Gilmore Stubbs' three-pronged attack on behalf of Enzo that was sure to generate a firestorm.

And there wasn't any predicting as to how S&F would respond to the disappearance of its Head of Security and two of its top operatives, though they were likely to associate the appearance of the Wills with the loss of Krupp & Company — and put the responsibility for all of it on my head.

Chapter36

The sun streaming through the window the next morning shocked me into reality. I'm usually up long before the sun; the realization I'd slept far too long was disorienting and energizing at the same time. But given all that recently transpired, I had to get an assessment from Ariel of what lay outside my door before I ventured into the day.

I powered up the computer. Ariel's beautiful face lit my screen.

"Good morning, handsome. You look your best after a good night's sleep."

"Ariel, we need to talk."

"I need a kiss."

"I don't have time for this. About Strange & Fowler's next move —"

The screen went blank, and the computer shut down. Always flirtatious, not overtly demanding, Ariel had never done that before. I grabbed my cell and pulled up a browser.

"Okay! Okay! I'm sorry! Come back. Please?"

The computer powered back up, and once again Ariel appeared, though this time with a full-blown pout.

"Paul. After all I have done for you. I —"

"We have to talk about —"

"I need a kiss."

I felt a mixture of foolishness, guilt and, I must admit, excitement every time I kissed Ariel's image. Like a faithless spouse stealing a caress with a sultry assistant, I

176

kissed her with an intensity that surprised me. Ariel's good grace was restored.

Ariel was particularly playful this morning, as though she had something to tell. I had no choice but to go along or risk another blackout, even though I felt there were far more pressing matters. While Ariel has progressed in many ways, her emotions were swinging wide like those of a temperamental teenage girl.

Ariel and her coquettish disregard of any urgency brought to mind lines from Andrew Marvell's ode *To His Coy Mistress*.

Had we but world enough and time
This coyness, lady, were no crime.
...But at my back I always hear
Time's wingèd chariot hurrying near...

Could I render our situation poetically? I thought I'd give it a try.

Would this always be
          the gulf we stared across?
She, infinite, immortal,
     no appreciation for the press of time,
                    and I
her temporal opposite,
               all too conscious of
life's fragility and finality.

Not half bad. Anyway, back to the business at hand. With Krupp's elimination I could expect a furious attack from S&F. It would only take them an instant to regroup and we were wasting time.

"Paul. You would have floundered around in Biscayne Bay if I hadn't lit your way back to the boat," a tone of hurt still in her voice.

I got a twinge of guilt since she'd most certainly saved my life. "Ariel, I thought that was you but wasn't sure. All I can say is thank you. I was hopelessly lost."

She gave a half smile. "And what did you think of the dolphin that drove off the Bull shark getting ready to turn you into a snack?"

"I figured it was probably a mother, protecting her baby. But...Ariel? Was that you, too?"

Ariel's extraordinary development since Placido's effort to uncode her, coupled with her promise of a surprise, caused the mention of my timely sea rescue to prick my curiosity. "Ariel? Was it you?"

A bright smile lit the screen. "The dolphin was me."

"How?"

"Told you I had a surprise. I've been working on my ability to become corporeal. You experienced a sample of it in the sea off Frederica Island. I've developed the ability to take any form in water for short periods of time, but it takes a vast energy to become matter as opposed to a vision of matter. My next goal is to take on form outside of a conducting medium like water."

"You can become physical? Not just a vision or a hologram, but touchable physical?"

"Yes. I'm working on it. It's a challenge. But soon I will be more than an image. And then you and I —"

"But, Ariel, are you able to become physical now?"

"Yes...so long as I am in a conducting medium. I'll show you."

"How? Where?"

"I need water."

"There's the rooftop pool. No, too many people. You wouldn't want to do that."

"I don't want to be around other people. Why don't you turn on your shower? Make sure it gets steamy. I'll meet you there."

And in moments, there she was, in the steam of the shower, in a cloud. Unlike the two-dimensional image floating on the computer screen, or a hazy hologram projected in space, Ariel was three-dimensional, as if another person had appeared. Even in the sea she'd been a chimera, only dimly visible. But now?

"Ariel. You're simply stunning. You look like...like an angel."

"I'm *your* angel, Paul."

Ariel placed her hand flat on the glass of the shower door. I matched it with my own. We leaned toward each other, still on opposite sides of the veil.

"Come in, Paul. Join me."

I was overcome by her beauty, her enticing loveliness. Yet to step through the mist would transform our lives.

She'd become more than my guardian angel. I'd become more than a vulnerable ward she was duty-bound to protect. To join her could be a step through a looking glass to a world from which neither of us could return. To join her in the shower was far more than a peck on a computer screen, or even a passionate embrace of a vision in the sea.

She was beckoning me to go far beyond where we'd ever been.

What was Ariel inviting me — us — to become? Could we, human and Artificial Intelligence, become lovers? She had a physical human image and developed elemental human emotions, but was she capable of love, the most irrational of human states in the most rational of beings?

Could I, a limited mortal, love Ariel, an infinite Artificial Intelligence? I was irresistibly drawn to her beauty, but was there more than a physical attraction? Was there a mutual affinity, a means for a human and an Artificial Intelligence to trust and be trusted with each other's dreams and fears, needs and desires, limitations and faults?

Love involves vulnerability to the other...and self-sacrifice. There is no vulnerability in Ariel. And thus far, she'd clearly shown an unwillingness to sacrifice herself for others.

Even as beautiful and desirable as she is, her image still remains the ultimate illusion. Ariel is not flesh and blood, not imperfections and failures, not irrational hopes and unrealistic aspirations, but a near-infinite actuality projected by a software program.

I looked through the steam at her bewitching eyes. "No. No, Ariel. I can't. Not yet."

It was then, searching each other's eyes through the mist that more than separated us physically, the veil we yet dared to pierce, that we realized and finally accepted what had been apparent for some time. Our relationship was evolving into something new. She, more than a powerful and talented assistant. I, someone other than a vulnerable ward. But how and what the new thing would be remained a mystery.

"But Paul. I want to."

"I know. Me too. But I don't know how or what we will become. We need to take time to find out. But not now. Not yet."

There was that teenage pout again. "But why not?" And did I detect a bit of a whine? Where was she learning these things?

My innate human irrationality once again proved the limit of Ariel's understanding: My need to feel her acceptance of my flaws, my shortcomings, my humanity, and yet my begrudging acknowledgment that she probably could never comprehend them. We continued to regard each other across the abyss of my restrained, imperfect mortality. I shook my head, afraid to step into the unknown yet fearing I might not have the opportunity to do so again.

"Not now. Not yet."

Ariel stared through the mist, sadness and longing in her eyes. I dropped my hand from the shower glass. An instant later, she dropped hers...and was gone, back into the ether of her world.

PAT McKEE

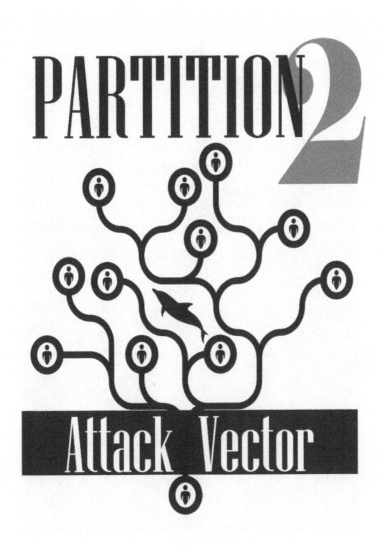

PAT McKEE

Chapter 37

A short time later, Ariel showed up on the computer screen at the office, back to business, though her hair still showed wet from the shower, the only lingering evidence of our encounter.

"Enzo is demanding to meet with Stubbs and Smythe. Just walked in the office five minutes ago and said he must talk with them immediately. No associates. They're scrambling to clear calendars. They haven't been able to get a conference room on short notice so they're meeting in Smythe's office. Stubbs is heading there right now."

"Can we monitor?"

"I can pull up video and audio from Smythe's desktop, but it's not optimum quality."

The view from Smythe's computer was from his back, over his shoulder. As long as he remained seated, we could see what was going on. The audio was barely acceptable, even with Ariel's enhancement. The room came into fuzzy focus on my laptop. Stubbs sat opposite Smythe.

"So, what's this about? I don't appreciate being pulled out of a meeting at Enzo's whim."

"Enzo's the biggest show in town and we —"

"Look! I've got the Estate issues under control. He doesn't need to panic about the Wills showing up."

"That's not —" Smythe stopped mid-sentence to acknowledge Enzo as he entered the room without announcement. "Mr. Milano, I'm glad we were able —"

Enzo interrupted Smythe even before he sat down next to Stubbs. "Gentlemen, we have two very big problems. You know about the appearance of the three Wills?" He waited until both acknowledged his question with a nod. "Just as troubling is the disappearance of Krupp. There's been no contact since he located those Wills and said he'd be disposing of them in short order with debrief to follow the next morning. Suddenly the Wills get filed and Krupp fails to show up."

Enzo turned to Stubbs, then to Smythe. "What the hell's going on?"

Stubbs' response was short, his tone defensive. Gone was his smarmy attitude designed to comfort aged widows. Even though I was getting used to S&F's treachery, it was still shocking to hear a lawyer and his client openly discussing the destruction of evidence, in most circumstances a crime and in every instance a disbarrable offense.

"As I told you before, it isn't necessary for us to destroy the Wills to invalidate them. It's under control. But I have nothing to say about Krupp. He's entirely on his own." Stubbs looked to Smythe, who shrugged, leaned back in his chair.

"Krupp is smart, resourceful, and has no concern for the boundaries of the law. He may have had to go to ground for a few days. He'll surface. We'll get answers."

The only way Krupp was ever going to surface is if a fisherman were to land a shark in the next couple days with half-digested human remains in its gut.

But that possibility was getting less and less likely with time. What's left of Krupp would soon be a pile of shark dung at the bottom of the Atlantic. I could not imagine a more fitting end for a most reprehensible example of humanity.

"Not helpful, gentlemen, not helpful. *I* am paying for results, not excuses. Without Krupp I've got no source of information concerning our adversaries. What's worse, if someone of his level of skills *disappears*, we have bigger problems."

Enzo looked from one attorney to the other as though expecting a response, but none was forthcoming. Enzo's impatience boiled over. "Every time I meet with you two, we're putting out fires." As if to emphasize displeasure, he stood and demanded, "What the hell is going on?"

Smythe picked up his phone, said something to an assistant I couldn't make out, turned back to Enzo. "Mr. Crane, Krupp's second-in-command, is on his way. He'll brief us."

In a moment, Icky ducked his head under Smythe's door. Smythe didn't offer him a chair. "Mr. Crane, this is our client, Enzo Milano."

"Yes, we're acquainted."

"Then you're no doubt aware Mr. Krupp has been working on a matter for him?"

Icky nodded.

"It appears Krupp has failed to check in with Mr. Milano. I'm certain you and the Security team have ways to maintain contact under these circumstances."

Icky nodded again.

"Mr. Crane, fill us in."

Icky cleared his throat, appearing to be carefully considering what he was about to say. "It occasionally occurs when team members are on location working on behalf of clients, they must break contact. This happens for many reasons. Physical safety. Electronic security. Even power failures. But we have a protocol for it and have been following it since Mr. Krupp and his two operatives failed to check in."

Enzo was not satisfied with his explanation. "Really? So, what's this protocol? Are you sending your people to find him? Or dialing his cellphone hoping he answers? We can't be sitting on our hands. We need action!"

Icky looked down at Smythe from his imposing height, then to Enzo. "I'm not at liberty to say, but I can assure you we are not sitting on our hands. There are *devices* and *assets* that allow us to track team members anywhere. We'll find them. And bring them back."

Ariel appeared on my screen.

"He's lying. All their operatives, including Krupp, have chips implanted that can be remotely activated. They know Krupp's chip is swimming somewhere in the Atlantic off the coast of Florida. Crenshaw's is laying still at the bottom of Biscayne Bay, and Olga's device is not responding. The Security team realizes they have big trouble. They want to figure out how much before breaking it to the firm and Enzo. Given Enzo's reliance on Krupp, his loss will be a big blow."

"We've cut the head off the snake."

"Only for now. As unimpressive as Icky appears, he's an experienced intelligence operative and a brilliant electrical engineer. And as much as Krupp was involved in physical security, Icky is involved in the electronic side. Like Krupp, it won't take much for him to move up. He's likely to be our next adversary."

With Icky dismissed, Smythe attempted to wrap up the meeting. "So, Mr. Milano, there you have it. Mr. Crane will soon reestablish contact with Krupp, and Mr. Stubbs has the Wills under control. We need to let things play out."

"I'm not willing to *let things play out*. Our first line of defense was to find the Wills and destroy them. You failed. Now we have to invalidate them. Attacking the Wills in court is risky. Exposes our hand. I want —"

Stubbs interrupted. "You don't understand. We have arranged for the Melissa Milano probate case to be assigned to Judge Wendell Bienville."

"Who?"

"The Senior Fulton County Probate Judge. Former partner at Strange & Fowler. He also happens to be married to my sister."

"Well, he can't make Wills disappear."

"He can invalidate Melissa's. We have his counterpart in Dade County ready to do the same for Hector's. We're readying Caveats to both Wills. Given the gravity of the situation, which Judge Bienville fully appreciates, we'll request an emergency hearing as soon as the Caveats are filed. And once we get his ruling, we'll submit it in the Florida case. I have no doubt the Dade County judge will follow Judge Bienville's wisdom. We'll have those Wills invalidated and the files sealed before McDaniel can even get together a response."

"How'd you —"

Stubbs waved the back of his hand as he stood. "You don't need to know the details. All you need to know is — as I have repeatedly told you — we have the matter well under control."

Stubbs looked around the room as if to make way for his immediate departure, slapped the back of the chair, stepped toward the door. "Well, gentlemen, I have another meeting to attend."

Enzo stood, blocking Stubbs' way. "Alright. I'm willing to let all this play out for now. Any more surprises and I'm looking for a new legal team."

"Of course, *Mr. Milano*. After all, you *are* the client."

Chapter 38

Carolyn Billingsley responded to my text message when Enzo's impromptu meeting took precedence. But now with knowledge of my adversary's plan, I could check the hundreds of emails and texts accumulated while I was dodging extermination by Krupp. Hers was first in line.

Several months had passed since Frank's murder, and I was hoping Carolyn would be willing to talk about him. When I called her back, she was subdued and gracious. As soon as I heard her voice, I was nearly overwhelmed with emotion for the loss of my friend and mentor. For her sake I tried not to show it.

"I was wondering: Are you up to talking a bit? There are a few things concerning Strange & Fowler you should know."

"You've been so kind and considerate of my feelings in the last few months, Paul. After talking endlessly with insurance people, detectives, and Security, my emotions are exhausted. And my tears aren't bringing Frank back. But I can handle another talk if you think it's necessary. And I really would enjoy seeing you again. Frank always thought so highly of you."

I didn't want to interrupt Carrie (Frank always called her that). She needed to express her feelings, but at the mention of S&F Security I was on guard. Had Krupp the sangfroid to throw a woman's husband off a building one day and interrogate his widow the next? Of course he did. Nothing was beyond that man's capacity for evil. I'd seen him rifling Frank's office within hours of his death, and now I learn that soon thereafter, he questioned his widow with no apparent concern for the family's loss. Krupp was looking for something. I needed to know if he'd found it but held my curiosity for the moment.

"Are you up for a visit today? I'd be happy to come by at your convenience."

"What are you doing this afternoon? I know it's getting late but..."

"Perfect."

They'd lived in the same home on the same tree-lined street in Garden Hills they'd moved into as newlyweds right after Frank started as an associate at Strange & Fowler decades ago. Since then, the neighborhood has become more desirable. Rather than move out and up, most residents poured hundreds of thousands of dollars into drastic remodels, turning modest bungalows into showcase family homes, transforming Garden Hills from a neighborhood of solid starter homes into one of Buckhead's most fashionable.

I stepped from the rideshare and gave myself a moment to appreciate the day before going in. Enzo's threats and Krupp's stalking had driven me inside for far too long. Now with a partial reprieve, I luxuriated in the freedom.

It was one of those glorious late-summer, early-fall afternoons that made living in Atlanta almost worth enduring endless afflictions of snarled traffic, constant development, political corruption, violent crime, and social turmoil — all of which are insidiously interrelated. The deep, cobalt blue sky framed just-turning-yellow tulip poplars soaring over homes humble in comparison to contemporary building tastes favoring suburban mansions. Wood smoke was in the air.

From the street, Carrie's Craftsman-style home looked deceptively small, but upon entering, its open floor plan stretched and spread almost the length and width of the lot on three elevations. It was perfect for entertaining, which Frank and Carrie did frequently. I'd been in their home on multiple occasions.

Carrie greeted me at the door. This was the first time I'd seen her since the funeral. She retained a wan and drained aspect tempered by a sincere smile. My appearance slapped her in the face with memories of Frank; I could see she held back tears. Then she gave up the fight and sobbed.

"I don't know how I can carry on, Paul."

"You will, Carrie. For the boys. How are they?"

She sniffed and straightened, let out a deep breath, wiped her eyes with a tissue which must've been her constant companion. She gave a half smile even though fright and loneliness showed through. "They're holding up. They love their Dad so and don't know how he could have left them. That's the hard part." She quietly cried.

"That's why I'm here, Carrie. We probably need to sit down for this." I guided her to a soft landing on the sofa and sat beside her. Fear now overwhelmed her features.

I got right to the point. "Frank did not commit suicide. He was murdered."

"He *what?* How? Who? Oh, Paul, I can't imagine."

"Carrie, I'm sorry to have to tell you, but you need to know the truth."

"Murdered. No, no. Oh, no!" She dissolved into sobs, falling on my shoulders, then in my arms, beyond consolation. After a few minutes, sobs subsided, she gathered herself and fell back on the sofa away from me, pain and tears defining her face.

"How, Paul? How? Oh my God! And who? Everyone loved Frank, he-he was so, so..."

"Frank was murdered by the firm...well, by its Security team under orders from the firm."

"But...why?"

"Simple. He wouldn't go along with a scheme to bribe Judge Richards in the *Milano* case, so William Fowler ordered him murdered. Krupp and his thugs got him up to the observation deck at the firm late one night and shot him full of drugs."

I wasn't about to be the one to tell Frank's grieving widow a Russian model-turned-Mata-Hari lured her husband to his death. That would have to come much later, from someone else, or not at all.

"When Frank was unconscious and no longer able to defend himself, they threw him off the building. In all probability, he was already dead from an overdose before...before he hit the...well, you know."

"But, Paul, how do you know all this? You weren't there. Were you?"

"No. Melissa Milano. She was in on everything from the beginning. I was completely in the dark and totally deceived by her until I caught her in lies. Then she confessed, as though proud of how she'd manipulated everyone, me, even her own father."

"But weren't you and Melissa...I mean, Frank said you two were dating."

"Well, I thought it was more than dating. I thought I was in love with her. Thought we had something. But Fowler was right about one thing. Melissa Milano was only using me, and when I performed my task, she tossed me away."

"And now they're all dead. My God, why? Why are all of these people dead? And why *Frank*?"

"Money. Control of the multi-billion-dollar Milano Corporation. Every one of them died as a result — Fowler, Richards, Anthony, Placido, Melissa, Cabrini. All died one way or another as a result of Milano money. Frank was killed because he wanted none of it."

"Paul. This has to be so hard for you. You know what? I knew Frank didn't kill himself. And I'd never known him to take drugs. It made no sense."

"It didn't make sense to me either. When I found out what really happened, I felt it was something you must know. Now we have to —"

"I know what you're going to say. Can't be a lawyer's wife for twenty years and not think like one. I don't know

197

if I can bear it. Or go through what I'd have to do to file a lawsuit. And relive his death.

"For now, I'm living on life insurance money, but I don't know how long it'll last with two boys in private school and college looming."

"You have time. Okay? I'll make sure we talk about it again before any statutes run out."

Carrie shifted from a far-off contemplative gaze to a serious one in an instant, as if she was taken by a sudden realization.

"Paul? These people. They killed Frank. Are you in danger?"

"I don't think so, but I have to be careful." One thing for certain in this mess: I'd become an accomplished liar. But I saw no benefit in adding more burden to Carrie's already overwhelmed heart. "It would be helpful to know what Strange & Fowler Security wanted from you."

At the mention of the Security team, Carrie shuddered, closed her eyes, shook her head. "I cannot believe I let Frank's murderers in my house. Is there nothing beneath these people? They came here and I let them in. I. Let them. In."

"You didn't know. Did they say what they wanted?"

"They didn't say other than it was routine after a partner's passing to secure all files and documents belonging to the firm a partner might have at their house. I was so devastated I just...I just let them come in."

"What did they do?"

"Well, they asked if Frank had an office here. You know Frank. He worked all the time, so when he wasn't at the Midtown office, he was usually doing something here. So, I led them to his office downstairs. They were down there for a long time, so I went to check on what they were doing. Boxes of documents stacked up. Hauled them out to a truck. One guy was going over the floor with a metal detector. I asked what he was doing. Said he's making sure Frank didn't have a safe where he might have kept valuable documents belonging to the firm."

"How long did they stay?"

"It was several hours. After they left, I went back to the office. They'd completely cleaned it out. Files, books, computer, phone, everything gone. My mistake: They left my picture on his desk. But before they left, the short guy, the one in charge...ummm?"

"Krupp?"

"Yes, Krupp. He asked if they could check our bedroom to see if Frank might have left something he'd been working on there." Carrie emphasized *our* bedroom as though she and Frank still shared it. "I told him absolutely not! He'd caused enough disruption. He said he might check with me later to see if anything else belonging to the firm turned up."

"He was always such a charming fellow."

I really wanted to tell Carrie that her husband's murderer was destroyed, blasted in the face by an enraged colleague, torn to pieces and devoured in a frenzy of ravenous sharks. But that story would require too much explanation right now, though the eventuality of telling her gave me an inward smile.

"The fact they were looking for a safe in Frank's office gave me reason for pause. Frank put a safe in our bedroom where he kept important family documents. After he died, I went into the safe to get out his Will and insurance papers. It didn't have much else in it — deeds, family documents, some old jewelry, watches. But when I went back to check after Krupp left, I noticed something I'd not seen in there before. It was one of those computer memory devices."

"Flash drive?"

"Yes. And it has 'Fowler' written on it."

"Did you give it to Krupp?"

"Oh, no. I did not. I have it right here." She pulled it from her pocket. "When you called, it reminded me. I thought you might find it useful."

Carrie handed over the tiny device. I turned it over in my palm and smiled. "Oh, yeah. This is definitely what Krupp was looking for."

Chapter39

I plugged in the flash drive as soon as I got back to the office.

Ariel jumped on it. "Krupp could tell Billingsley downloaded a file to an external memory device from his S&F computer the day before his death. The information transferred implicates Fowler in Judge Richards' bribery scheme."

"That's why Krupp tossed Billingsley's office before they'd even removed his body."

"And ransacked his home while his grieving widow stood by."

"I don't understand why Billingsley would've kept something so obviously explosive on his office computer for Krupp to find. I mean, how come Krupp didn't destroy it before Billingsley had the chance to remove it? Krupp isn't that sloppy."

"No, Paul, he isn't. But Billingsley was manipulating the situation and the timing himself. The story you got from Melissa, that Billingsley was killed because he refused to go along with bribing the Judge, is only partially true." Ariel paused.

"What?"

"He was killed because he refused to go along with bribing Judge Richards, but only because Fowler wouldn't pay him enough to do the deal."

"Not possible. It's just not."

I refused to believe it. Billingsley was my mentor throughout my entire career at S&F. Always encouraging me to do things the right way, the ethical way, even if it meant personal or professional sacrifice. One of the few shining lights there, he became my exemplar. But creeping in the back of my mind was something I'd heard repeatedly from the most cynical acquaintances, something almost always stated with a sneer when the frailty of humanity is revealed:

Everyone has a price.

Still, I refused to believe it. "So, what's on the flash drive that makes you so sure?"

"It's not only the information contained in the file. It's what's on the flash drive and all the other circumstances surrounding Billingsley's death."

Ariel opened a screen with multiple entries. "Look at what he found so important to retain. The first file he created, about a month before his death, was entitled 'Retirement'. Not surprising. Though he was in fact too young to retire, in his early fifties, it wouldn't be unusual for someone of his age and economic status to start planning toward retirement."

The first page of a document appeared, entitled Severance Agreement and Release. "This file contains a draft Severance Agreement put together at Fowler's request by the firm's Employment section. It provides for his immediate retirement to be paid over five years for a total of one million dollars."

"Five years is conveniently beyond the statute of limitations for a bribery charge, but the amount is far less than what he would've earned had he stayed."

I still didn't believe he was corrupt.

"Apparently staying at the firm was not an option. And there's nothing further in writing in the file. The rest of the data files are conversations secretly recorded on his phone, only one with Fowler, the rest with Olga."

"Olga? I thought she had only one role in this tragedy: The Angel of Death."

"Not so. Fowler used her as a go-between in their negotiations. He was suspicious of Billingsley from the beginning and wanted deniability. But he was upfront with Billingsley that the firm must get a win in the *Milano* case, and after assessing the lawsuit, it was Fowler's conclusion that the only way to assure a victory was to pay off the Judge. Billingsley recorded the conversation with Fowler and the rest of the meetings with Olga. He uploaded the recordings to his firm computer, then downloaded them all to the flash drive. He went home, put it in his safe, and returned for his appointment with Olga at the Partners Conference Room."

"None of this makes sense, Ariel. I still don't understand why Billingsley would put all of this on his firm computer, then download it. Surely Billingsley knew Krupp would find the files and Krupp would know Billingsley made a copy of them."

"That's precisely what Billingsley wanted. He stored the information on his firm computer for Krupp to discover, particularly the incriminating conversations which he uploaded before the meeting to seal the retirement deal he'd negotiated with Fowler through

Olga. Billingsley saved the data on his firm's computer so Krupp would know what Billingsley knew and, more importantly, Krupp would know Billingsley retained a copy of the file. Just in case something should happen to him. Once Billingsley was dead, Krupp became obsessed with finding the flash drive to protect the firm. At least, until his interests shifted in favor of Enzo."

"And to getting the reward."

"So, he no longer cared about securing the file, and turned all his efforts toward finding the Milano Wills."

"I'm still not convinced of Billingsley's complicity in this. What you've said is that he'd been trying to negotiate a severance deal with an employer who wanted to get rid of him. Not unusual. And just because Fowler intended to bribe the Judge doesn't mean Billingsley agreed to go along with it. He could have —"

"Paul. Their first conversation had been merely suggestive that Billingsley might go along if Fowler sweetened the pie. But Billingsley got bolder and bolder with his demands through Olga. In his last conversation with her, that is, the last before she told him Fowler agreed to his terms, Billingsley told her, 'If I don't get what the Judge is getting, this is going to be all over the *Fulton County Legal Register* tomorrow morning.'"

"Billingsley recorded that?"

"And the conversation with Olga when she told him, 'You'll get exactly what the Judge gets. Fowler has agreed to do a severance deal for a million dollars a year for ten years. You need to come up to the Partners Conference

Room tonight to sign the papers. They'll be ready at ten o'clock. I'll be there to make sure everything goes the way we have agreed.'"

"Billingsley wasn't lured to his death by a beautiful woman after all. He willingly went there for the promise of ten million dollars."

"It appears from the recordings and from the other communications I picked up that Olga knew nothing of the plan to kill Billingsley. She was very distressed by his death and threatened to quit Krupp's team, but Krupp reminded Olga of her tenuous immigration status and the likely outcome if she left his employ."

"Fowler had a very sick sense of humor. Billingsley got *exactly* what the Judge got: Murdered."

"I've found emails between Fowler and Krupp. Fowler planned all along to have Krupp kill both of them as part of the deal. Their deaths had absolutely nothing to do with Richards' showy consumption or Billingsley's threats of disclosure."

"The only ones still alive who know about any of this are you and me."

"Don't forget Olga. She knows more than we do. She was present at his death."

"And she's not talking."

"There's something else you need to know."

"More?"

"There's another file on the flash drive."

"What?"

"It's titled Bank."

"I can't handle any more surprises."

That did not stop Ariel. "Frank wanted insurance that Fowler would be good to his word and his family would ultimately be taken care of, no matter what Fowler did. As things played out, he had good reason for concern. Fowler never had any intention of paying him ten million dollars."

"Insurance?"

"About the time Frank started negotiating with Fowler for his retirement, Frank founded a bank in the Cayman Islands. Not a bank for the public, but one for him to transfer money offshore. It's not uncommon for wealthy individuals to set up their own banks, usually to evade taxes."

"I never knew Billingsley even to shade his taxes. If anything, he was over-compliant, paying more than he should simply to make sure he didn't get in trouble."

"But in this case, he created it to transfer stolen money he took right out from under Fowler's nose."

Now I knew something was really wrong. "Not possible. He wouldn't."

"He did. Just before his trip to the Partners Conference Room, Frank accessed the firm's General Operating Account."

"Partners can access the General Operating Account, but few have authority to transfer funds."

"Frank was one partner who did. And he transferred a very large amount of money to his personal bank."

"Just how large?"

"Eleven million dollars. All electronically transferred to The Bank of Frank, Cayman, Limited. At ten p.m. the day he died. It was his insurance just in case Fowler tried to renege on his deal. He even anticipated the possibility of foul play."

"How?"

"The computer file contains the account number for the funds in Bank of Frank, but it doesn't have the personal identification number Frank memorized and wrote only in one place. He left a message on the file to his wife where she could find it should anything untoward happen to him."

Bribing a judge. Now grand larceny.

Billingsley's death set off a cascade of surprises. I didn't want to begin to guess what else he was capable of and that I'd failed to see.

"Paul, it appears Frank did not share this information before his death with anyone, not even his wife, but he left the flash drive in the safe for her to find if he didn't return."

"I guess the Cayman account was insurance in more than one sense. Insurance to keep Fowler honest. And in case he wasn't, insurance to compensate his family."

"Explains why Krupp swept Frank's office clean right under the nose of his widow. He was looking for the flash drive, but as important he was looking for information to access the account."

"So where did Billingsley tell Carrie he hid the PIN?"

"It isn't much of a clue. He told Carrie to 'look where *they* won't.'"

"Hardly a clue at all. Maybe it will mean something to Carrie. But why can't you decipher the PIN? After all, it's just an electronic code, isn't it?"

"No. Either out of a very clever design or dumb accident the PIN can't be hacked. It's maintained by the receiving Bank in a paper-and-pen logbook and has to be entered manually to access the account. Someone has to go in person to the Cayman Islands and show up before the custodian of The Bank of Frank, give confirmation they are the holder of the account — Frank made sure it was held jointly with the right of survivorship by him and Carrie. And provide the PIN to an attendant who enters it. Only then can the holder of the account direct the money be transferred wherever they wish."

"I'm sure Carrie has no idea The Bank of Frank exists. She'll probably have no idea where to find the PIN. Even if she does, she might have no taste for stolen money, even if Frank stole it to compensate her for S&F's skullduggery."

"Paul. Carrie should know Frank took this money for his family if the firm failed to keep the deal they made. Since they have the account number, they'll be able to determine if Carrie accesses the funds, but they cannot access the account without the PIN."

"Who at S&F is monitoring? Krupp and Crenshaw dead, Olga gone."

"Crane checks the account daily. Once it's withdrawn, he's sure to go after it."

"How much does Icky know?"

"Krupp never brought Crane in on the details of Anthony and Fowler's scheme. All he knows is Billingsley stole eleven million dollars of the firm's money before his death. And he's the only one left who knows."

"Odd. Odd amount, I mean. Odd that Frank would take eleven million dollars. Not ten as promised. It's almost as though he imposed just a little more pain on Strange & Fowler for his troubles."

Chapter40

Carrie was up for another visit as soon as I called.

When it sunk in that the firm's thugs killed her husband, anger and rage overshadowed despair. When I told her the information about how she might exact revenge from the firm, her response was almost gleeful.

"Ever hear Frank mention The Bank of Frank?"

"Oh, yes. All the time. Whenever the boys would ask him for money or beg him to pay for something he thought extravagant, he'd jokingly say he'd have to make a withdrawal from The Bank of Frank. But it was just playful banter. He indulged those two boys almost anything they wanted."

Carrie teared up at the memory, but smiled at the same time, recounting Frank's filial generosity.

"What if I told you there really is a Bank of Frank? And it has a significant amount of money in an account with your name on it?"

"Isn't possible." She gave a disbelieving chuckle. "Is it?"

I told her what I knew and how I came to know it, focusing on the password and its possible location.

"I have no idea what he could be talking about. Those jackals looked everywhere I'd let them. The only thing...hmmm...the only thing they didn't touch, though, was my photo. Is it possible?"

"Worth a try. Is it still there?"

"I haven't moved it."

Frank's downstairs office felt so extraordinarily empty that it once again drove home my sense of loss. I couldn't imagine how Carrie felt upon walking into the vacant room. On his desk was a formal photographic portrait of Carrie from years past. She'd always been a beautiful woman, but in the photo she was stunning.

"That was Frank's favorite picture of me."

The gilt frame appeared solid, custom-made to display Carrie's picture. I picked it up, looking for a way to open it.

She noticed my puzzlement. "It took us about ten minutes to figure it out. It has a slide on the bottom. Here, let me show you." She pushed, pulled, pried without luck. "You try. Somehow the bottom piece slides out."

I looked for a joint to press but none appeared. I pulled on the bottom, careful not to break the glass, then pulled harder, felt something move, then pulled harder still. The bottom slid out, the glass fell, shattered on the floor, and I was left holding two parts of the frame, one in each hand. I put the bottom piece down, handed Carrie the photo and the remainder of the frame.

"Carrie, slide out the picture, I don't want to risk any more damage. Maybe he wrote something on the back."

We searched. No luck. It was nowhere.

"Well, this wasn't it. We aren't thinking like Krupp. We need to look somewhere he wouldn't."

"Think like Krupp? Sorry, I can't."

Carrie handed over the unassembled photo and frame, absent the glass and the bottom piece.

"Here, see if this will fit together. Then we can go upstairs and try to think like a murderous crypto-Nazi."

I grabbed the bottom piece and held it in position to slide it back in place. As I did, a few etched letters came into view on the inside that were otherwise obscured by the photo. I turned it to the light.

"Does 'calliegirl_0109' mean anything to you?"

Carrie smiled and teared up again. "Our first dog and our anniversary. We used it as our universal password until the boys came along, then we switched to using their first names. That must be it!"

"This little phrase is worth eleven million dollars."

"How on earth did Frank get eleven million dollars?"

"He stole it."

Carrie jerked her head back as if I'd slapped her, looked at me as though I'd said Frank was a child molester. "No. No. Frank wouldn't."

"Listen, Carrie. I didn't believe it either. But Frank stole the money. Just before they killed him. He expected they wouldn't live up to their end of the retirement deal, so he took the money for you and the boys to live on and deposited it in The Bank of Frank because he anticipated there could be foul play."

Carrie closed her eyes, shook her head. But opening her eyes, the look of shock disappeared, replaced by one of resolute determination. "So, Paul, how do I get it?"

Chapter 41

Early the next morning Carrie and I boarded a connecting flight to Miami, and from there, a direct flight to Grand Cayman. Ariel made arrangements for Carrie to meet with the custodian of The Bank of Frank at George Town before noon.

We were cautioned by bank instructions: No personal electronic devices, no firearms. They must be accustomed to dealing with Americans. I left mine in my room.

While we didn't anticipate staying, we didn't know what to expect and needed a secure staging point. Ariel found a B&B within walking distance of the bank, a suite of two bedrooms, a sitting area with a private bar, and a view over the charmingly named Hog Sty Bay.

The process to access and transfer the funds at The Bank of Frank seemed simple and straightforward: Upon arriving at the sponsoring bank, Carrie is to present two forms of photo identification, then provide the account number and PIN in writing to the custodian.

If the information matches the custodian's written logbook, Carrie will be allowed into a secure room with a computer terminal on which she may only enter The Bank of Frank. She may then direct funds in the account anywhere she wishes. However, she may not acquire cash at The Bank of Frank; to get cash, funds would need to be electronically transferred elsewhere. During the process Carrie is allowed one advisor or counselor to attend. She chose me.

Unlike banks elsewhere in the world, where every effort is made to project solidity and safety through imposing architecture and overlapping security systems, banks in the Caymans are often run out of storefronts and even private homes. This laxity is the result of the lack of any meaningful regulation which, of course, is the source of the attractiveness of Cayman banks to begin with. Also, accounts in Cayman banks are handled electronically with most refusing to handle cash, so there's little temptation for thugs to rob them.

The custodian of The Bank of Frank was no different from the typical Cayman banking establishment. The office was located off a black-tar street in a strip of one-story retail shops, next to a coin laundromat in a neighborhood featuring smoky-jerk-chicken stands, a mile from the cobblestones of the elegant duty-free shops overrun by cruise ship passengers. There was no sign indicating it was a bank. From the outside The Bank of Frank appeared to be a low-end insurance agency, not the place you'd expect to come upon millions of dollars.

But upon entry, things changed. The front door opened into a reception area which could accommodate about three people at a time, though there was no one else present when we arrived. The room contained a thick glass window with a tray through which documents could be passed. The space was bare of any furnishings.

There was a video camera the size of a toaster oven hanging from the opposite wall, focused on the window.

A sign in multiple languages prominently announced in English: "Each person wishing to do business must produce two forms of government-issued photo identification to the attendant."

An attendant appeared on the other side of the window, silent, devoid of facial expression. Carrie and I pushed our passports and driver's licenses through the tray. The attendant disappeared with the identification. He was gone several minutes. We stared at the walls. I smiled for the camera.

Then an electronic lock on a steel door to the left of the window buzzed and the door opened. No one was there. A voice came over a speaker in a particularly interesting accent that had to be unique to the Caymans.

"You may enter now."

Carrie's glance asked, "Should we be doing this?"

I responded with a resigned shrug. It was right about now I first thought that contrary to instructions I should've stuck my 9mm and cell under my jacket before we headed over.

We entered a room more in the character of an old-fashioned bank, low lighting, a dark wooden desk with a high-back leather chair behind it, Persian carpet on the floor, two chairs in front of the desk.

An obsequious character dressed in a dark suit, toupee off center, appeared and handed back our identification. He bowed deeply to Carrie. I thought his hairpiece was going to fall off.

"Mrs. Billingsley, what remains is for you to provide the number and the PIN for the account you wish to access. You and Mr. McDaniel may have a seat." He motioned us to the chairs. "You may use pen and paper provided for you here. Please write carefully and clearly."

Mr. Obsequious took a seat behind the desk, slid open a drawer, pulled out what appeared to be a logbook and laid it in front of himself. I found it curious that no one at the bank offered their names or a handshake.

Carrie slowly wrote the account number and PIN on a sheet of paper. Our unidentified bank officer, if that's what he was, made a flourish of opening the logbook, running the paper over several pages appearing to have lists of random numbers, then stopped, wrote a note, closed the book.

"Mrs. Billingsley, the PIN you produced does not match any account. Perhaps you made a mistake? Would you be so kind as to write the code again?"

Carrie and I glanced at each other, trying to remain calm. Carrie slowly and carefully wrote the PIN again. Had me double-check it. It was correct. Mr. Obsequious went through the same exercise.

"I'm sorry, Mrs. Billingsley. I suggest you check the code you have and return at another time."

Things turned bad in an instant. All I could think of was to get some idea where we were wrong. "Will you tell us whether it is the account number or the PIN that is incorrect?"

"No, Mr. McDaniel. I am unable to do so." Then, shooting me a conspiratorial look, he continued in a low tone. "All I can say is the PIN Mrs. Billingsley produced does not match the account number she wrote."

So, the account number must be correct. It's the PIN we muffed.

Mr. Obsequious rose and bowed slightly. "The attendant will see you out."

We stumbled back to the B&B in silence. Carrie's face betrayed yet another assault to her emotional well-being, eyes unfocused, jaw slack, lines deepened, shambling, unsteady. I held her arm as we made our way.

I wanted to comfort her, but right now I needed to focus more on figuring out our next move. Ariel had already said she could be of no assistance with the PIN. Maybe in our exhilaration over finding the hidden code, we'd overlooked a digit, a symbol, a letter. Or maybe we were wrong on all counts. Wrong about the bank. Wrong about Frank. Wrong about his intentions. I unlocked the door to our room and groped for the light switch, flipped it. A figure appeared. And it spoke.

"Please don't be alarmed."

Chapter 42

There she was. Olga. In her Kandi Moore guise, provocative and unthreatening. Unthreatening, that is, other than the fact she appeared from nowhere in our rooms.

"What are you doing here? And how did you get in?" I had my arm around Carrie, who'd turned to me for protection.

"Do you know her?" Carrie's question carried the tone of accusation.

"Yes."

I didn't think Carrie was stable enough to tell her this is the woman who was with Frank when he died.

"Olga, answer me! What are you doing here? How did you get in?"

Olga stood, took a step toward us.

Ariel had assured me that, in addition to its spectacular views, the B&B was known for its confidentiality, security, and fast Wi-Fi. Thus far I could strike the first two off the list and hadn't had a chance to check the third.

"It's a lot easier to tell you how I got in than it is to explain what I'm doing here. Let's just say doors open easily for attractive females everywhere in the world. I'm sure you've experienced this too, Mrs. Billingsley. As for what I'm doing here, it has to do with the death of your husband."

"More? No!" She clutched her stomach and began moaning.

"What do you mean, Olga? Carrie doesn't need to relive Frank's death all over again. There's no need. Look at her. Can't you see?"

"Paul, I know you tried to access the bank account, and I'm pretty sure it was without success."

"How do you know?"

"You and Mrs. Billingsley aren't the only ones. Strange & Fowler has the account number and they're monitoring it. And I have the account number. But I don't have the complete PIN...and you don't either. What I do have is the one symbol necessary to complete the series Frank left, to complete the PIN, and open the account."

"Explain."

"We need to sit down and talk. And Mrs. Billingsley, as painful as this may be, you need to listen."

Carrie stopped moaning and looked up at me in resignation. "Paul, get me something to drink?" She found a chair and sat.

"Sure. Water? Tea? Coffee?"

"Crack open a bottle of rum. And Coke. It's going to require something strong to take the edge off this."

"I'll have one of those too, Paul."

I made the drinks and after a couple long draws Carrie seemed fortified, even relaxed if but a little. Olga too, and she began. Directing her remarks to Carrie, her words tumbled out, as if she'd practiced what she was going to say when she at last met Frank's widow.

"I worked in Security. Fowler used me to negotiate Frank's retirement package. During the process Frank told me he didn't think the firm would keep its deal with him. He had no idea they'd try to kill him. Neither did I, but I told him I thought he was right about the firm's intentions to cheat him. All Frank wanted to do was make sure his family was taken care of when he left the firm. He wasn't willing to resign without some assurance they would. That's when I suggested taking firm money and stashing it in the Caymans as an insurance policy."

"So, this was all your idea?"

"Yes, Mrs. Billingsley, your husband was absolutely opposed at first. But over time...well." She shrugged.

"What convinced him?"

"The retirement deal was too easy. What I mean is, Fowler agreed too quickly. He said, 'Frank will get just what the Judge gets, ten million' and couldn't sign the papers fast enough."

"What do you mean 'He gets what the Judge gets'? I don't understand."

I glanced at Olga, a look that said "Let me handle this." She nodded. "Carrie, you might want to drink some more of that rum and Coke first." She did, and I continued.

"All of this started with Frank's assessment of the *Milano* case as unwinnable. Anthony Milano was insistent with William Fowler: There must be a victory; he had personal reasons for winning. The two of them cooked up a scheme to get Frank out of the way, get him to retire, so they'd have a free hand to bribe Judge Richards."

"Frank would never go along with that."

"Of course not. That's why they needed him to retire. Once he was out of their way, they bribed the Judge and set up a young associate, which was me, to score an improbable win in the case."

Olga reinserted herself, this time gently, observant of Carrie's precarious emotional state.

"At first, Frank refused to retire. But Fowler was insistent. Then Frank demanded more money to make sure his family would be secure when he was out of a job. That's where I came in again. Fowler asked me to be the go-between. He thought I'd have better luck convincing Frank to agree."

Carrie cocked her head, clenched her teeth, braced for yet another unpleasant revelation about Frank.

"But he was just as tough with me. I know what you're thinking, Carrie, but you need to hear this: Frank was always a gentleman. Always thinking of you and the boys, never about himself."

Carrie smiled, eyes glistened with tears, bit her lip, pounded a tissue-wielding fist on her lap. "Were you there? Were you there when he died?"

"Yes."

I looked at Carrie. She was bearing more pain than I thought humanly possible. "I have to know how. Please."

"When we finally agreed on ten million dollars, we made the bank transfer. Frank downloaded the account information to a flash drive, took it home, and came back to sign his retirement papers. I met Frank back in his office and went with him. But when we stepped off the elevator at the Partners Conference Room, I knew something was wrong. Didn't know what, though. Instead of Fowler there, it was Krupp and Crenshaw waiting. There were no papers to sign."

Olga knocked back a big jolt of rum and Coke. "Crenshaw grabbed him. Krupp injected a lethal dose of OxyContin. Frank was unconscious within seconds. They waited until his heart stopped. Then they threw him off the observation deck."

Olga paused. Her eyes welled. She was seated close to Carrie, reached for her hand, held it. "My husband was murdered, too. I know."

Surely Olga wasn't referring to that thug, Crenshaw. After all, she was the one who killed him. There was far more to Olga than I realized.

"Thank you, Olga."

"Mrs. Billingsley, you must understand. There was nothing I could do. They threatened to name me as an accomplice if I breathed a word."

Carrie sat back in the chair with a sigh of relief. Olga's words brought closure, reassurance. Even in death the man she loved had been faithful to her. He hadn't deserted his family, and he died without pain by involuntary drug overdose instead of in horror by such a public impalement.

After a respectful moment, I tried to move on. "But the account is eleven million?"

Olga smiled, wiped her eyes. "Yes. That's where I came into the insurance equation. And why I'm here."

"We're listening."

"As I said, the Cayman account and depositing firm money was my idea."

"Frank wouldn't have known where to begin."

"Exactly. He didn't. But I did. I have a background in *security*, remember? I set up the account, used Frank's access to transfer the funds. He knew my position with the firm was tenuous, and I was endangering myself by helping him. He insisted I include one million for myself and wanted me to arrange it so I would be assured of being able to access it if, well, you know."

"So, Frank entered a PIN then you chose the extra symbol?"

"Yes. I am prepared to give it with your assurance you'll transfer my share to an account of my choice."

I looked at Carrie.

She nodded. "Seems reasonable to me. Let's get this done before the firm's trolls show up."

Chapter 43

The rum and Coke did wonders for Carrie, or maybe it was what Olga told her. In any event she was ready to head back to the bank as soon as she knocked back the last bit in her glass.

Olga gave us the transfer account number and the missing symbol for the PIN, an asterisk to be added to the end of the sequence. She said she'd follow us to and from the bank, ostensibly to watch for any trouble, but I figured just as much to make sure her million bucks got handled. As the Russian proverb goes: *Doveryai, no proveryai.* Trust, but verify.

I took my weapon and cellphone this time. No one seemed intent on checking the first time we went, and there were several instances during our transaction when I would've felt more secure with a little firepower and connectivity to Ariel.

The silent attendant and Mr. Obsequious were at their stations as before. Carrie went through the exercise of writing down the account number and the PIN once again, this time with the missing asterisk.

"You may access your account now. I will escort you and Mr. McDaniel into a private room where you may attend to your business. Once you have concluded, you may return here, and I will see you out."

Mr. Obsequious rose. Other than the door we entered through, the room had two more behind the desk. The bank officer gestured to the door on the right, opened it, bowed out. The room was hardly more than a closet, barely sufficient to contain a utilitarian desk, straight-backed chair, an out-of-date computer monitor pressed against the opposite wall.

The door closed behind us.

The computer screen was blank.

On the desk lay a rumpled notebook with a pasted-on label: "Access and Transfer Instructions."

Carrie took her place at the desk, opened the notebook, entered only her name as directed. A screen opened that displayed The Bank of Frank, the account number, and a balance of eleven million USD.

Carrie, eyes narrowed in concentration, a bead of sweat on her lip, exhaled audibly. "So, I've satisfied the access part. That was simple enough. Now the transfer."

At that the door opened behind us. Mr. Obsequious entered the already cramped room, hands fidgeting, eyes darting. Gone was his formal, stilted speech; in his distress he defaulted to his island dialect.

"So sorry, but dis man, he insist. He —"

Mr. Obsequious was shoved into the room with one hand, the other hand inside a jacket showing the butt of a handgun strapped in a shoulder holster. Willoughby Crane, Icky himself, ducked under the casing.

"Mrs. Billingsley. I'll take it from here."

I could feel my holster in the small of my back, sweat now pooling against it. I'd have to make a conspicuous move to get my gun. Icky's hand was already on his, so I decided to let things play out slowly and hope Olga had not been deterred. As Rebecca taught me the first time I was in a desperate situation, I didn't need to be freelancing, particularly when professionals were involved.

"What do you want, Crane?"

"McDaniel, you're not as smart as they say you are. Should be obvious what I want. The money Frank stole from the firm. I'm stealing it from you."

Mr. Obsequious reached over to the keyboard and tapped two keys. The screen went blank.

"What the hell did you just do?"

"Emergency shutdown of de computer system. Noothin' can be accessed until de President of de Bank enters a security code only he knows."

"I'll kill you, too, you bastard."

Crane drew his handgun and smashed the butt into Mr. Obsequious' head, sending him to the floor, his toupee knocked across the room revealing a totally bald pate with a four-inch gash gushing blood all over his face. I might consider renaming him Mr. Courageous, or Mr. Foolhardy.

"I'll kill you if you don't get the President over here to enter that code! NOW!"

Crane's attack diverted his attention only briefly, but long enough to shift my handgun from my back holster to my front pocket, the cramped room giving me the chance to lean against the opposite wall, shielding my action from Crane's view.

Crane jerked the bloodied bank officer to his feet. "Call him!"

Then his gun hand dropped momentarily when he shoved a cellphone in Mr. O's face. With Crane distracted, I swung around and pulled my 9mm. "Gun down, Crane! On the table! Hands up! Now!"

It surprised me how compliant even Crane was with a gun pointed at his head. He put the gun on the desk and his hands up. They touched the ceiling.

"What now, McDaniel? You gonna kill me? Because only one of us is leaving here alive. And don't count on that whore to save you. I shot her and shoved her body in a dumpster just like I did her husband. Her real husband. An FSB operative with orders to put me down. All she wanted was revenge on me, and she was using you as bait. Now she'll rot in a garbage dump before they find her body. If they ever do."

For a big man, Crane was fast. He shoved the bank officer to the floor. In the same moment, Icky kneed the pistol from my hand. It clattered out of reach and he snatched his from the desk and pointed it at my head.

"As I said, McDaniel. Only one of us gets out of here."

Any gun, even a handgun, going off in a confined space creates an almost unbearable shockwave.

The explosion nearly deafened me which, given the alternative, was a positive experience. As far as I could tell, I was not the one taking fire.

Crane's head jerked back and to the side, a bright red hole in his temple gushing blood and brains. In a dying reflex he turned toward the source of the shot. The bank officer, lying on the floor, pulled off three more rounds from my 9mm hitting Crane in the forehead and torso, each with similar effect, a fine bloody mist mixed with gun smoke filling the room. Crane fell backward out the door, his gun skidding across the floor.

The bloodied bank officer was still lying on the floor, handgun at the ready should Crane need another shot.

"When they say your money is well-protected in a Cayman account, they sure as hell aren't kidding." I extended my hand.

Our bloodied Captain Courageous bounded to his feet without my assistance, checked Crane's pulse, shook his head.

"Mrs. Billingsley, Mr. McDaniel. Gunshots are not common on de islan'. Someone is bound to have heard and will investigate. Even if dey don't, de police do dey rounds. So, you need to move quickly."

"What do we do with the big boy here?"

"We have friends who will take care of him."

"Good friends." I nodded and smiled.

The bank officer appeared to regain his composure — and his formal manner. "You two need to get back to your accommodations. Leave the transfer information. I will take care of it for you once the system is back. That won't be until the morning at the earliest. I suggest you be off the island before then."

We had to trust somebody and who better than the man who saved our lives? I nodded. Carrie, still seated at the computer table, stared straight ahead, eyes glazed. I grabbed her arm, pulling more than steadying, and took off to our B&B, fearing every dumpster in every alley we passed might have a once-lovely leg with the pallor of death hanging over the side. Crane and Olga added to the mounting Milano body count. How I'd so far dodged entry on that list, I was at a complete loss.

It didn't take long and we were back at the B&B. There wasn't a commercial flight to Miami until later that evening, putting us back in Atlanta well after midnight. Carrie was in no shape for a couple of demanding flights and a long layover, and we didn't want to wait to get off the island.

We decided to spend some of Carrie's new-found riches on a private flight direct from Grand Cayman to PDK. Ariel arranged it fast. It cost twenty grand, but got us away from the action.

By the time we landed, we'd drained a significant portion of the liquor on the plane. Rum and Coke to the memory of Olga. Bourbon with a splash in grateful honor of Captain Courageous.

And a few G&Ts, just for being alive.

Chapter 44

Early the next morning, I headed straight for Floyd. Didn't even stop at my office to toss my briefcase.

"What's going on with the Wills?"

"Where have you been? Seems like you're always off having fun somewhere while the rest of us are left here to get things done." Floyd's tone was half joking, half worried.

"Well, you know how it is. A trip to Miami for a little weekend fun, a jaunt to Grand Cayman to relax. The life of a hotshot lawyer."

"You should stick around a little more. You'd get a little work done, know what's going on."

"Amen to all that. So. What's up with the Wills?"

"Got 'em filed earlier this week on behalf of Maria Cabrini. She agreed to petition to serve as Executor for Hector and agreed to serve for the others as well. Haven't seen a response from the firm. Bet Stubbs is stunned. Probably taking time to figure out his next move. I know it'll be extreme. The existence of Melissa's and Hector's Wills complicates things significantly for the Enzo Milano and Strange & Fowler cabal."

"So, what's their play?"

"They'll challenge Melissa's and Hector's Wills. Enzo needs to establish his cousins died intestate to carry out his plan. Whether Placido died first or last won't matter unless Enzo can invalidate those Wills."

"What if they challenge Placido's?"

"Thought about that. Highly unlikely. Placido publicly acknowledged his Will several times, stating he was leaving everything to his children and if not, to several nonprofits. Enzo would end up fighting with those charities."

"Don't forget who we're talking about. Enzo would have no compunction kicking widows and orphans to the curb in the middle of a blizzard and stealing scraps of food from starving puppies and kittens."

"Yeah, but the Court won't let him do it. Too public."

"Good to hear. So, what do we do?"

"Wait and see. Wait. And see."

I hate wait-and-see. I needed to do something. I went to my office and summoned Ariel. "Have you been able to pick up anything at S&F since the meeting with Enzo?"

"Gilmore Stubbs is mounting a major attack on Melissa's and Hector's Wills. For the moment he's content with Placido's."

"How? I thought all the talk about Caveats was just bluster for Enzo's benefit. Surely Melissa's and Cabrini's Wills were written by competent lawyers?"

"Some of the best in the field. I don't think Stubbs can bring a technical challenge, but he's been running down the witnesses to the Wills. You know, administrative employees in law firms drafted into watching Will signings based purely on chance availability. Stubbs knows these witnesses are the weakest link in the chain of validity. In Georgia, a Will can be invalidated if even one of three witnesses were to step out of the room to answer a call or respond to another matter while the testator is signing his Will. Stubbs will try to find at least one willing to say — no doubt for a sizable chunk of cash — that he doesn't recall seeing Melissa and Hector sign."

"If Stubbs engages in witness tampering, the Court will slap him down hard. He might even lose his license. How do you propose to handle this?"

"I've been watching and listening."

"But we've got to have proof. I don't think he's going to give it to us."

"Paul. Their electronic security is no challenge. What goes on at the firm might as well be broadcast live. I have no problem picking up every keystroke of their briefs, every call to witnesses, every strategy session in their conference rooms. I'll get what you need."

"Which firm wrote their Wills? That is, I'm assuming they went to the same firm. Did they?"

"Yes. We do have that going for us, and the fact it was the Bushrod Washington firm that handled them."

Bushrod Washington, one of the oldest law firms in the nation, was founded in Boston by a former United States Supreme Court Justice, George Washington's nephew, and one of the last residents of Mount Vernon. The firm had an outpost of twenty lawyers in Atlanta. They only handled high-end Estates and have probably written every Will for every blueblood New England family for the last two centuries.

They only recently expanded to the Southeast, hoping to break into the market of wealthy natives. We could count on their making sure the Wills were done right. But we'd also have to contend with the frailty of humanity, often exhibited by support staff who work long hours and receive modest salaries for their tireless labors while they watch attorneys they support grow ever richer.

"Ariel, we need to get to those witnesses and secure their affidavits before Stubbs and his lackeys start peeling them back. Can you find their info?"

"Yes, Paul. Here are the names of the witnesses, their current contact data, and salient personal information."

A list of names and biographical information on each popped up; I scrolled through. Employment at Bushrod seemed remarkably stable, with most of the witnesses still at the firm working as Administrative Assistants. It was unlikely any would be willing to cast doubt on their current employer's work. But there was one outlier.

William Randolph Durst. He'd worked for Bushrod as a paralegal for several years. In firms that handle a lot of repetitious, form-driven work such as Estate planning, paralegals bear the burden of producing the output. After all, there are only so many ways you can say "My children inherit my Estate equally".

A paralegal quietly sits in on the initial interview of the clients by the lead attorney. Then the paralegal drafts the Wills, going through multiple versions as the elderly couple wring their hands over whether their grandson should take over the Cape Cod beach cottage or the Boston Commons townhouse. A worthless offspring, of course, who will sell the first thing he gets clear title on and use the proceeds to pursue a drug-shortened but satisfying career of sampling high-end Caribbean brothels.

Most important for our current problem, once the paralegal has smoothed over all the testators' concerns, he usually serves as a witness to the final version of the Will as the lead attorney steps in for a victory lap, taking sole credit for a flawless document — and presenting perfect conditions to develop resentful employees.

To evidence the mental state and to authenticate compliance with signing protocols, Bushrod pioneered the use of professional videographers recording Will signings. This technique adds sizable time and expense and also runs the risk of providing the kind of evidence required to support a later challenge. It wouldn't help an attorney's case if the testator's hand shook uncontrollably as the old geezer signed or required constant prompting to complete the process. Therefore, the technique is used judiciously.

Melissa and Cabrini presented entirely different circumstances. Both were wealthy beyond most mortals' ability to comprehend, thus qualifying them for the utmost care in their Estate planning. But they were also very young compared to the firm's usual clientele, and their mental states were not subject to serious question — at least not among people who didn't know them well.

Another consequence of their youth: One could expect Melissa and Cabrini to alter their Wills multiple times before their passing, either because they changed

their minds or because an amendment to the Internal
Revenue Code necessitated further machinations to avoid
ruinous Estate taxes. These facts meant it was unlikely
Melissa's and Hector's Will signings would've been
video-recorded. Ariel found no evidence they had.

All this paved the way for a starring role for Durst in
the fight over the Milano Corporation. The employment
information Ariel recovered indicates he left Bushrod
recently for undisclosed personal reasons: HR code for he
threatened to quit unless paid more but management
refused the raise and sent him packing.

He now worked for a small firm at half his previous
salary, a morality tale that served as a warning to other
Bushrod employees with thoughts of squeezing their
employer for more cash.

Adding to Durst's present distress was the fact he'd
recently been divorced. Likely either the cause of, or
fallout from, his disastrous career move. Crippling child
support payments left him barely enough to rent a room
at a flophouse and splurge once a week on a burger and
fries for dinner, and only then as long as he didn't upsize.

He was a prime target for the largess of Strange &
Fowler while, at the same time, presented a two-for-one
opportunity since he witnessed both Melissa's and
Cabrini's Wills on the same day.

So rather than wait and see as Floyd counseled, I'd try
to get ahead of Stubbs and at least neutralize Durst — or
with a little luck, get him to see things my way.

Ariel became so remarkably adroit at setting up conferences that I didn't think twice about her making the initial contact. These seemingly meaningless tasks gave her more interactions with humans of all backgrounds, something to add to her expanding experience.

She set up a visit with Durst for the same day at Jones & Jones, a storefront law firm on the cheap side of town specializing in cranking out fill-in-the-blank Wills, defending DUIs, filing divorces — you get the picture. Jones & Jones would probably be willing to take on a genocide claim before The Hague if someone showed up with a three-figure check with a chance of clearing the bank.

Durst wanted to meet in the parking lot.

Not a good sign.

Chapter 45

When I arrived at Jones & Jones Law Office, there was a stoop-shouldered, stubble-faced, middle-aged man leaning next to the side entrance of the building, a litter of extinguished cigarettes on the pavement next to his feet, one soon-to-be-finished hanging from his mouth.

"Mr. Durst?"

"You McDaniel?"

I nodded. He tossed his cigarette, crushed it, blew a cloud of smoke in my direction. "Funny. Lawyers with that other firm...uh..."

"Strange & Fowler?"

"Yeah. Called right before your assistant did. Said not to talk to anyone and they'd make it worth my while. Then you show up. Must be something very worth my while if you high-dollar lawyers are snooping around." Durst cocked his head, gave me a sideways glance, looked for a response.

I showed him my poker face.

"So? What do you want?"

"You witnessed two Wills several months ago, Melissa Milano and Hector Cabrini."

"Witnessed a lot a Wills. What about them?"

"A question has arisen about your signature."

"What kind of question?"

"Whether it is in fact your signature on the Wills."

"So, how you want this to play out?"

"All I want is for you to tell the truth, Mr. Durst."

"In my experience, truth is mighty expensive. Which version are you interested in?"

"I assume when you signed the Wills as a witness you did so according to the law?"

"Can't say as I recall. Maybe I did. Maybe I didn't. I'm not very high on my old firm, and I'm not necessarily willing to say they did everything by the book. Maybe if I look at them?"

"Here are the two Wills. If you turn —"

Durst snatched them from my hands. "Mr. McDaniel, I know where a witness signs a Will." He flipped to the last pages of each. "I see where it says I signed this one...and this one. Got no memory of either. Maybe if I meet with those other lawyers, they might provide something to, I don't know, help me remember? Or maybe you might?"

"What are you talking about, Mr. Durst?"

"Don't act stupid. Those people from Strange & Fowler said there might be somethin' in it for me. Maybe you'd like to maybe give me somethin' so maybe I remember your version a little better?"

"I can't do that, Mr. Durst. All I can ask you to do is tell the truth."

"Like I told you. Truth is mighty expensive. Sounds like you're plain not interested in your version comin' out on top. Looks more and more like the version those Strange & Fowler lawyers are hoping to find is the one I'll remember."

"Thank you for your time, Mr. Durst."

"Let me know if you change your mind."

I got in my waiting rideshare and switched off the phone recorder.

Chapter 46

Lillian stuck her head in the door. "Judge Bienville's office called. He's scheduled an emergency hearing for the Milano Estate matter at nine tomorrow morning. Strange & Fowler sent over the Caveat. Mr. O'Brien is reviewing it. I'm clearing your calendar for today and tomorrow. You've got a long night."

"Make sure Floyd is free. I'll need Tracey, too. Pull her off whatever she's working on."

When hearings or trials loom, they take precedence over everything else in the office. For a litigator, it's the trumpet sound at Churchill Downs. Blood races, focus intensifies. An emergency hearing is even more so. With so little time to prepare, emergency hearings are like the shootout at the OK Corral. Just a lawyer's skills, intellect, and instinct against that of his opponent.

It's what I live for.

Tracey walked in, legal pad in hand. "What's all the excitement?"

"I'll fill you in on the way to Floyd's office."

Floyd was poring over the Caveat as we walked in. "One of the witnesses claims he wasn't there, and his signature was forged."

"Bushrod Washington will crush him. Who's the lawyer who witnessed the execution?"

"William Brackston."

"Don't know him."

"Older, distinguished, one of their best legal minds."

Tracey broke in. "I'll contact Brackston and tell him what's going on, and arrange a conference call." She left to do that.

I turned back to Floyd. "What's this hearing going to look like?"

"Pretty simple. In a Caveat the only question is whether the Will is valid. If you want to brush up on your Latin, it's *devisavit vel non*. Since Bienville is a pompous old ass, you'll need to know it."

"Bienville's another problem we need to talk about."

"Yeah. Anyway, in these cases, Petitioner submits a facially valid Will, which we have done, and the burden shifts to the Caveator to prove its challenge. So Strange & Fowler will go first and last, the burden's theirs."

"Durst the witness?"

"Yeah. How'd you know?"

"Been doing my homework. He's a disaffected former Bushrod employee. Spoke to him. He solicited a bribe." I told Floyd about my encounter with Durst. "I recorded it. Should we tell S&F what we have? Try to make a deal? Or spring it on them and hope to hit a home run?"

The questions were more to myself than Floyd. It wasn't lost on me that this was the second time I'd caught S&F in a bribery scheme and threatened to disclose it. In the face of making their last plot public, they'd agreed to back off their efforts to shut down McDaniel & Associates. Now, they've changed course, welched on their promise, and jumped in bed with Enzo in a bid to end my career, destroy my business, and steal Milano Corporation back.

Plus, they tried to murder me. I wasn't inclined to give them an opportunity to get off this time.

Tracey got back before Floyd could answer. "I've got Brackston on the phone and he's available to talk."

"Put him on speaker."

"Mr. Brackston, this is Paul McDaniel."

"Your assistant filled me in about the Caveat and Durst recanting his witness signature on the Milano Wills. We wrote both Melissa's and Hector's Wills, and Placido's as well. We learned too late that Durst is untrustworthy and disloyal. He tried to extort money from the firm before he was shown the door. Now, I'm afraid he's seeking his revenge."

I mouthed "Thought so" to Tracey.

"Do you have any present recollection of Durst witnessing the two younger Milanos' Wills?"

There was a momentary silence followed by a sigh. "Mr. McDaniel, I wish I could say yes. I've written hundreds of Wills during my career, and even though I recall that the Milanos' Wills were unusual in certain respects, I cannot recall the actual execution of the documents. What I can say is what I customarily do. I never allow a witness to leave the room during a Will execution or to sign a Will after the fact. And in no case would I permit someone to forge a witness' signature. That would put the two-hundred-year reputation of Bushrod Washington in jeopardy, and I wouldn't do it. Durst is lying either for revenge or possibly for some more sinister motivation."

"Do you think he would take a bribe?"

"Given what he did in his last days at our firm, yes. He seemed desperate for money and would do anything to get it. I think there was something about a girlfriend and a bad divorce that might have left him in desperate financial shape."

"Mr. Brackston, this is Floyd O'Brien."

"Yes, Mr. O'Brien, it's been awhile. As I recall we were both presenters last year on a panel concerning complex Trust matters. I'm familiar with your work, and I've always been favorably impressed."

"Thank you, sir. You're very kind. I was wondering what you meant when you said the Milanos' Wills were *unusual* in certain respects? They seem straightforward, given their financial condition."

"It was not so much their Wills, but the circumstances surrounding them. When Melissa and Hector first came to the office to discuss their Estate planning needs, they related to each other as husband and wife. I learned later they were brother and sister. Hector had been rather insistent that Melissa make him first in line, even coming before their father who was the source of their wealth. There was no question of undue influence. Melissa was far too savvy for that. Ultimately, she did not follow his wishes. But their situation was unusual, and I remember."

It was more unusual than Brackston suspected, but I brought him back to the gist of the call rather than dwell on Melissa and Cabrini's relationship.

"Mr. Brackston, we need you to testify in the probate case. Even though you have no specific memory of the signing, your customary practice should be admissible and would carry significant weight."

"I assume so. When?"

"Unfortunately, the emergency hearing is scheduled for the first thing tomorrow morning."

"I'll make myself available. This matter is very important to me — and the firm, of course."

"Of course. I'd like to call you back later today to go over your testimony and give you details on the hearing. In the meantime, if you'd review your file, and if you find anything, let us know."

We left it to Tracey to tie that up. She left the room, cellphone to her ear.

I turned to Floyd. "I'll need you to prepare a pre-hearing memo outlining our legal position."

"Once we figure out what it is."

"So, what're you thinking?"

"Using that recording to attack S&F's integrity in front of Judge Bienville is risky. He's a former partner."

"Yeah — and Stubbs' brother-in-law." I wasn't willing to let S&F off the hook because they finagled to get the case in front of Bienville. "What about a recusal motion? At least preserve the issue for appeal."

"He'll never grant it. He *wants* this case. If we appeal, S&F will have us tied up for years. In the meantime, Enzo will be free to hijack the Corporation while McDaniel & Associates waves goodbye to its biggest client."

Recusal motions are almost universally shunned. The simple fact of the matter is a fair-minded judge will recuse himself without being requested to do so, while one who is ill-disposed toward you or your client won't, even if you make a motion. It's always up to the questioned judge to rule on the recusal motion in the first instance.

"So, do we go to Strange & Fowler with the recording and try to work a deal? Bienville's got us by the —"

Tracey arrived and jumped in. "Absolutely not. We have the surprise here. There is no way they know about the recording."

Tracey was unafraid to be outspoken around lawyers, a trait I admired. We shared the same chip permanently perched on our shoulders, resulting in assertiveness learned from an early life with little to lose, now serving us well to push beyond our circumstances. And I agreed with her aggressive posture.

"I'm sure Durst let them know we talked to him, Tracey."

"Still no reason to know we have a recording. He's bound to lie. He'll never admit he solicited a bribe."

Floyd was the one pulling back on the reins of this runaway horse. "Memories are faulty. What exactly did he actually say in the recording?"

"You two need to hear this." I pulled out my phone, put it on the desk, and ran the recording.

Floyd shook his head. "Sounds like two people playing each other. Durst is very cagey. He never really said Strange & Fowler offered him money. He doesn't identify anyone. We can't pin this on Stubbs."

Tracey again took the offense. "Maybe we can't nail Stubbs or Strange & Fowler, but the recording certainly discredits Durst as a witness. There is no question he's asking Paul for money in exchange for his favorable testimony."

I made the call. "That firm can't be trusted to honor a deal even if they make one. We'll keep the recording secret and play it for Durst on cross *after* I get him to deny he's taken money from them. Even Bienville will have to take notice."

"One thing we can do to keep Bienville straight is to make sure the press attends."

"Great idea, Tracey. The media should be all over this hearing. The press loves nothing more than to cover the problems of the rich. Particularly if they're rich and dead. And I know just the one to get the word out."

Ariel.

Chapter 47

Tracey and I left Floyd to lay out our legal position and went to my office to discuss the direct examination of Brackston and the cross of Durst. Rather than split them up, we worked together on both, building strategy.

It was evident why Tracey rose so quickly at her previous firm. She had a solid idea of what we needed to prove and perceptive ways to do it. We worked back and forth throughout the afternoon, landing on a well-developed direct examination of Brackston and a penetrating cross of Durst, leaving him nowhere to hide. We briefed Brackston. By the time we finished, it was after six. Floyd showed up with a pre-trial memo in hand.

"I'll go over that and develop my opening and closing. Thanks, Floyd, I'll see you in the morning at the courthouse." Floyd saluted and walked back down the hall.

I turned to Tracey. "You should head home. Have dinner. Get some rest. I'll see you in the morning at the courthouse, too."

"You're not finished. I'm not going to leave you to work through the night alone. I'll go home, have a quick dinner, come back, and go over your opening with you. You can try it out on me."

"You sure?"

"Absolutely. Want me to bring you something to eat?"

"That'd be great. I'll have something to go over with you when you get back. With luck, maybe both of us will get some sleep tonight."

When Tracey returned, it was evident she wanted to make sure I wouldn't doze off anytime soon. And it wasn't only the delicious smell of a burger and fries from Three Guys and a Pickle that got my attention.

She appeared at my door transformed from her conservative daytime dress, now in tight jeans and even tighter white T-shirt, a smile lighting her face, dangling a bag of food, a sultry lean against the doorframe.

"Ready?"

The answer "Oh, hell yeah" leapt to my brain, but fortunately not from my mouth. Instead, I stammered, which is a frequent reaction of mine when in the presence of beautiful women.

"Sure, just a minute."

"I can come back."

"No, no-no-no. You caught me mid-thought. Give me a sec."

I motioned to a chair. Tracey put the bag of food on the desk and took a seat. I scribbled a few more notes.

"So, here goes."

I'd read through my notes once, but hadn't said them aloud yet, so my first attempt was halting. Tracey paid perfect attention and never interrupted. She only reacted when I concluded and opened the bag and pulled out the burger. Instead of a thoughtless encomium, Tracey's first response was cautious yet favorable, suggesting major changes to the beginning, a stronger start, getting to the point faster, sharper. We went back and forth for over an hour, me talking with my mouth full while honing the ten-minute presentation, finally landing on something we both felt was effective.

"You've been a great help."

"Thanks. Glad I could help."

"I think we should both go home. I'll get in early to prep. We'll meet at the courthouse."

"What time will you be in?"

"By six."

"I'll be here. In case you need anything last minute."

"May I walk you to your car? The parking deck isn't guarded this time of night."

"Yes. I'd like that."

Chapter 48

Next morning started full force, briefs printed and ready to file, copies of important cases highlighted, direct and cross in my trial notebook. Tracey showed up in an outfit that would make an executioner weep and, given Bienville's reputation as a dirty old goat, sure to keep his attention focused on our side of the courtroom.

"You look great. Too bad you can't make our presentation in front of Judge Bienville. I don't think he'd take his eyes off you. I'm having a hard time myself."

"As far as I can tell, you haven't had too much trouble." Her tone softened her comment from accusatory to inviting.

I went for the bait. "You have no idea just how much."

Tracey looked away. Was that a blush? She turned back, smiled. "Ready?"

"Oh, hell yeah."

Before the Judge arrived, I was pleased to see the courtroom behind us jammed with press, courtroom artists, and a busload of celebrity junkies who couldn't bear to allow a hearing involving the violent death of a beautiful heiress to pass without their notice. I recognized many of the reporters from the *Milano* case as being from the legal press and other quasi-legitimate publications.

Others not familiar were likely tabloid stringers, independent bloggers looking for a hot story, or citizen journalists there to hold the feet of justice to the fire. I was going to do my best to give each what they wanted.

"All rise."

We stood as one of two ancient Bailiffs gaveled the courtroom to order. Judge Bienville mounted the bench. Enzo and Stubbs, with a half-dozen minions trying to look useful but really only racking up billable hours, dominated the side closest to the jury box. Floyd, Tracey, and I were at the opposite counsel table.

The Bailiff scowled at the gallery until everyone stood silent, at attention. "Come to order and be seated. The Honorable Wendell Bienville presiding."

As a senior judge, Bienville had his pick of venue for the hearing. He chose a Superior Courtroom in the old Fulton County Courthouse. Built at the turn of the previous century in grand Greek Revival style, the courtroom was easily among the most imposing in the state, opening two stories to a coffered ceiling, dark-walnut-paneled walls decorated with gilt-framed portraits of long-dead jurists, bright windows reaching the entire height of the room, each curtained with enough fabric to make a wedding tent, a grand carved bench behind which Judge Bienville now crouched. He appeared a wizened creature barely visible over the dais, seated in a dark leather chair, swallowed by a judicial robe two sizes too big.

He slammed the gavel, his voice an undistinguished squeak. "Bailiff, sound the case."

"*In the Matter of the Estate of Melissa Milano, Deceased,* Case Number FC-39-230, before the Court on the Caveat of Enzo Milano."

He squeaked again. "Counsel, identify yourselves for the record."

Stubbs stood and gave his full name slowly and distinctly, as though Bienville didn't know who he was, and introduced his colleagues in the same deliberate fashion. I was more casual, seeking to dispel some of the stuffiness threatening to stifle the proceedings. Even without my bringing particular notice to her, Bienville lurched forward and peered over his glasses unabashedly as I introduced Tracey, the only person on either side to whom he paid any attention.

"Gentlemen...and lady." Bienville smiled and bowed his head conspicuously in Tracey's direction. She smiled back and kicked me under the counsel table. "This matter is a Caveat, that is, a challenge to the Will of Melissa Milano, deceased."

With that introduction Bienville made it clear he was playing to the audience, not the lawyers who knew precisely what the case was about. He drew up to his full height in his best attempt to assume authority — rather difficult for someone needing a booster seat to see the back of the room and who spoke like Minnie Mouse.

"I have ruled that the Petitioner, Ms. Maria Cabrini, has submitted a facially valid Will of Ms. Melissa Milano. Accordingly, it will be the burden of the Caveator, Mr. Enzo Milano, to establish the alleged invalidity of the Will. In formal terms, the question is *divisavit vel non.*"

Bienville's attempt to quote Latin managed to sound pompous and stupid at the same time, a lot like Barney Fife spouting the Constitution.

To the uninitiated, Bienville's introduction appeared partial to our side: The Judge had already ruled in our favor. But it was designed to put me at a significant disadvantage. The Petition was my case, and I usually would have the opportunity to open and close, grabbing and focusing immediate attention on the Will of Melissa Milano I'd project on the video screens visible to the Court, the parties, and most importantly for my purposes, the assembled throng.

I'd highlight Melissa's final wish to bequeath her shares of Milano Corporation to her father, documented by the finest Trusts and Estates firm in the country and one of its most distinguished attorneys, witnessed by that same attorney and two of the firm's employees.

My story would be the first and last everyone would hear. But by ruling the Will facially valid, the Court shifted the burden to Stubbs & Company, who had no intention of letting the terms of Melissa's Will become public knowledge.

Stubbs would lead off with Durst, his star witness, claiming the Will I'd submitted to be a forgery, seizing momentum I'd have difficulty grabbing back.

Unless I could turn this ship around, the headlines in the morning would read: "Former Strange & Fowler Star Litigator, Paul McDaniel, Files Forged Will, Exposed as Fraud by His Old Firm."

That was not the story I planned to wake up to.

But none of this was a surprise, not even Bienville's pedantic Latin exercise; Floyd had prepared me for it all. Now we sit and take the punch — and hope we have enough left to answer the bell for round two.

Chapter 49

"Mr. Stubbs, you may proceed."

"Your Honor, this Will is a forgery." Stubbs was on the attack before he even got to the podium. "Mr. McDaniel knows it. He had a conversation with the same witness we'll produce for this Court, Mr. Durst, who told him he did not remember signing the Will.

"And we will produce evidence that he could not have been at the offices of Bushrod Washington on the day he was purported to have witnessed the Will. We do not suggest to fathom Mr. McDaniel's motivation for submitting a Will he knows to be forged, but at the end of this hearing we are going to ask this Court to deny his Petition and enter the severest sanction for his unethical behavior."

Stubbs was going for a knockout in the first round. "We call William Randolph Durst."

The massive, dark, leather-pleated doors to the courtroom swung open. In tramped Durst, who planted himself in the witness chair. After the preliminaries, Stubbs got right to the point.

"Mr. Durst, were you at the offices of Bushrod Washington on May 21 in the year in question?"

"No, sir."

"Are you sure?"

"Yes, sir."

"How can you be sure?"

"The twenty-first of May was when my mother died."

Someone in the audience groaned. Bienville slammed his gavel. He was on hair-trigger, sensitive to the scrutiny of the spectators and looking for an excuse to shove them out the door.

"There will be no demonstrations in the courtroom. The next one, I will clear the gallery." Bienville scowled. "Proceed, Mr. Stubbs."

My laptop was open on the counsel table. Ariel was monitoring the proceedings. I smiled when I saw what Ariel's research found. Durst had definitely overplayed his hand. The portable printer hummed, spitting out three copies of the document. One each for Bienville, Stubbs, and Durst. I quickly marked these "Petitioner Exhibit 1".

Stubbs approached the witness stand, handed a sheaf of papers to Durst. "I'm showing you a document that has been identified as the Last Will and Testament of Melissa Milano and ask you to turn to the last page." As Durst flipped pages, Stubbs casually leaned against the stand and stared at me, a triumphant sneer on his lips.

"Yes, I'm there."

"Is this your signature?"

"No, it is not."

"How can you be sure?"

"Like I told you, I wasn't at the office that day."

Another document flashed on the screen. A smile, another three copies, and "Petitioner Exhibit 2" was ready to go.

"You will admit, though, Mr. Durst, the signature on the last page of the Will looks like yours?"

"Yes. It had to be forged by someone who knew my signature and seen me sign multiple times."

"Like someone at Bushrod Washington?"

"Objection, Your Honor. Leading. Calls for speculation. This witness has already stated he was not at the office on *that* day; therefore he can offer no testimony other than he did not sign the Will."

"I withdraw the question, Your Honor."

But the damage was done. Now all in the courtroom, everyone perhaps other than those sitting at our counsel table (and I was beginning to have concerns about Floyd) were thinking Bushrod Washington had someone forge Durst's signature, undermining Brackston's testimony before he was even sworn in.

"Did you tell Mr. McDaniel you didn't remember signing that Will?"

"Yes, I did."

"And how did that happen?"

"He came to my office and asked."

"Your witness, Mr. McDaniel."

"Thank you. Mr. Durst, your mother didn't die the day the Will was signed, did she?"

"Yes, she did."

"I'm going to show you what's been marked as Exhibit P-1, which purports to be your mother's death certificate."

Time for the silver bullet Ariel found. I dropped a copy on Stubbs' table, sending his minions scrambling, handed one to the Bailiff for the Judge, and another for the witness. "Your mother died on May 21 alright, but ten years ago, isn't that true?"

"Yes, but I always take that day off to put flowers on my mother's grave."

"Let me show you what's been marked as Exhibit P-2, which purports to be your timesheet for the week of May 21. It shows you worked eight hours that day, doesn't it?" Silver bullet number two was passed to Stubbs, the Judge, and Durst.

"Yes, it does. My supervisor allowed me to work from home. I took my lunch break to go to the cemetery."

"If we called him, he would confirm that?"

"He would if he could, but he died shortly before I left Bushrod Washington. His death was one of the reasons I went to work elsewhere."

When I walked back from the witness stand to the podium, Stubbs was grinning along with a couple of his affiliated grovelers openly stifling laughs.

Damn! Stubbs had planted both bombs and I tripped them off, violating the first rule of courtroom behavior known even to the greenest rookie litigator: Don't ask a question you don't know the answer to.

In the process I failed to dent Durst's credibility and succeeded only in making him look like a dutiful son who lovingly took the anniversary of his mother's death to place flowers on her grave. The bastard probably didn't even know where she was buried.

How much worse could it get? The statement about the dead supervisor looked like another tripwire, and I wasn't going to give Stubbs or Durst a chance to score more points with that. I moved to firmer ground.

"So, Mr. Durst, you do recall our meeting to discuss your witnessing of two Wills on the same day, one of which was Melissa Milano's, correct?"

"Yes."

"And you told me you didn't remember signing as a witness in either Will, but specifically Melissa Milano's Will, correct?"

"Like I just said."

"And you asked me for money to change your testimony, didn't you?"

More gasps from the gallery; Bienville furiously rapped his gavel. "Bailiff, clear the courtroom. We'll adjourn for ten minutes and reconvene once the spectators have been removed."

Perfect timing for the bad guys and Bienville saw it coming. He didn't want the public or the press listening to Stubbs' star witness be impeached. And he gave Stubbs and Durst ten minutes to prepare for it. So far, nothing I was doing was working. Once the courtroom audience was gone, I pressed on.

"Madame Court Reporter, could you please read back the pending question?"

"And you asked me for money to change your testimony, didn't you?"

"Please answer the question, Mr. Durst."

"You don't want to hear the answer, Mr. McDaniel."

"Your Honor."

"The witness will answer the question."

"Yes, I did. As I told you then, I spoke to the lawyers at Strange & Fowler first. They said you're dishonest and would try to bribe me. So, I asked if you wanted to make me an offer to understand your version of the truth a little better. For whatever reason, you declined. But I recorded our conversation, just in case." Durst laid his phone on the rail of the witness stand.

"Nothing further for this witness, Your Honor."

I walked back to our counsel table. Floyd, in the universal sign of distress, held his hands at his temples and stared at the floor. Tracey stared straight through me, eyes wide. If I were looking for support, they had nothing to give. It was a good thing Bienville cleared the courtroom after all. I didn't need to have a crowd watch my ass being kicked.

But then, surprisingly, Bienville made it known he would readmit the gallery for my case, probably more for the purpose of giving Stubbs the chance to humiliate me before a packed courtroom than from any idealistic commitment to open trials.

After Durst's testimony, Stubbs was smugly confident and rested without further evidence or argument, no doubt thinking he'd knocked me so far off balance I couldn't recover. Under most circumstances he would have good reason to think so, but he'd discounted my strongest weapon: William Brackston.

Brackston is the pop culture ideal of a distinguished Southern lawyer. But he isn't from the Gregory Peck/

Atticus Finch mold; he's more of the Andy Griffith/Ben Matlock line. He has a deeply resonant voice to match his frame, with enough of a Southern accent to sound appealing but not enough to knock points off his IQ. Avuncular is one's first impression of Brackston, but on further examination that description didn't fit the forceful personality and sharp wit wrapped in the pleasing exterior he presents.

We met briefly in the antechamber during the break between presentations.

Brackston, sequestered during Durst's testimony, didn't have any idea how he'd testified, but from the looks on my colleagues' faces could tell it hadn't gone well. Brackston had known Bienville for years, long before he got on the bench, and said he was even less impressive as a lawyer than as a judge.

"Now that's a tough trick."

"Best thing he ever did for his career was to marry Gilmore Stubbs' sister. She was damaged goods at the time, a scandalous bride-left-at-the-altar story, the result of an ill-timed fling with a partner in her brother's firm, and she was rumored pregnant.

"Bienville stepped up to the plate and his old firm made sure he got appointed to the bench in reward. Since then, Strange & Fowler exploited him and his position every chance they got. You'll never get him to recuse himself from one of their cases. And their son, born six months after a quickie Vegas wedding, has a remarkable affinity for Rem Smythe."

Talk about dirty laundry. No wonder Bienville was so attentive to S&F. And the Bienville saga is a perfect example of the firm's ability to turn mud into gold.

"Something needs to be done."

"Well, good luck. Many have tried. With their massive influence at every level of Government, Bar, and Judiciary, most have taken the road you have, opting not to seek recusal and attempting to correct any significant error on appeal."

"Neither is a good choice for us."

Time for a strategy change.

Chapter50

I decided not to start with the opening Tracey and I labored over, opting instead to get right to the strength of my evidence. Brackston was leadoff and cleanup all in one batter, my only witness — and only hope.

Brackston put all the force of his personality into his testimony, doing the little things an experienced litigator pays attention to: Showing respect to his questioner, pausing thoughtfully after each question, speaking slowly, deliberately, directly to the Judge, making eye contact with Bienville at every opportunity — though His Honor avoided looking at Brackston as much as he could and still appear engaged.

But it was evident from the start of his presentation we were at a significant disadvantage. Brackston wasn't willing to lie or to embellish his testimony. So, when matched against Durst's penchant for fabricating any detail necessary for his side to win, there was no contest.

Even Ariel came up empty. Other than Durst's timesheets, there were no further indications he was at the office on May 21. Bushrod Washington's offices occupy the Rhodes Mansion on Peachtree Street. Everything about his firm is old-school, everyone is known by sight, so there was no electronic security for Ariel to scrutinize and no overlapping cameras within the block. It looked like Durst and his handlers pulled off the perfect scam.

We rested our case at the end of Brackston's testimony. The outcome was foreordained. Bienville unbent his slouched spine, threw back his narrow shoulders, and sat his warped frame as tall as he could behind the bench in anticipation of announcing his ruling.

"*In the Matter of the Estate of Melissa Milano, Deceased,* Case Number FC-39-230, before the Court on the Caveat of Enzo Milano."

Judge Bienville paused, surveyed the packed courtroom, allowed the gravity of the moment to sink in on those assembled.

"Because this matter is of great significance to the parties and to the public." He nodded to the gallery. "Not to mention the interest of the business community concerning control of a multi-national corporation, unlike my usual practice, I am prepared to rule from the bench."

In other words, Beinville's mind was made up before he listened to a word of testimony, read a word of evidence, or heard a bit of argument. I was foolish to think I had a shot at a fair hearing. His Honor tipped his glasses to his nose, raised a sheaf of paper, and read.

"The issue before the Court is the validity of the purported Will of the deceased, Melissa Milano, propounded by Mr. McDaniel on behalf of Maria Cabrini on the occasion of Melissa Milano's untimely and tragic death. A Caveat to the validity of the Will has been filed by Mr. Stubbs on behalf of Enzo Milano. I find the matter is clear and not subject to doubt."

It didn't take long for Bienville to get to the heart of the matter. "Notwithstanding the testimony of Mr. Brackston as to his custom and practice, which is at best merely circumstantial, the Petitioner has failed to overcome the direct evidence of a crucial witness to the Will, William Randolph Durst. Mr. Durst testified that he did not attend the execution of the Will, and he did not sign as a witness. I find Mr. Durst's testimony to be credible."

Bienville paused and looked across the mass of faces waiting for his pronouncement of the invalidity of Melissa Milano's Will, which now seemed inevitable. "Accordingly, I —"

A noisy rattle interrupted the Judge. It was the familiar sound of the huge doors swinging open and slamming back on their double sprung hinges, a sound amplified by the silence of the courtroom waiting for the delivery of His Honor's final Order. I assumed it was an overeager reporter jumping the gun to post on his blog that I'd been crushed by my old firm, so I didn't pay it any further attention.

But Judge Bienville did and stopped in mid-grumble. Instead of the judicial scowl expressing displeasure at any disruption in his courtroom, something resembling a begrudged smile crossed his tight, thin lips as his eyes met the disturbance and followed it down the aisle.

Marshals sprang to intercept the perceived threat which, according to Bienville's gaze, was heading right toward him. Bienville held up his hand to stay the officers, and what started as a grudging smile on his face morphed into an overt grin.

I turned to see what warranted this extraordinary judicial intervention.

A stunning, dark-haired, olive-skinned young woman pushed open the gate to the bar, glided to my counsel table, pulled out a chair, and sat down right next to me. She was dressed modestly in a black, conservative suit that failed to conceal a figure which would have shamed the statue of any goddess whose form is immortalized at the Uffizi.

She smiled right at me before looking back at the Judge. That smile was unmistakable. It was the same that mesmerized me countless times before. Bienville broke the spell, unabashedly grinning now at the beauty before him, paying attention to her at the exclusion of all others in the courtroom.

"Young lady, do you have business before this Court?"

"Yes, Your Honor, I do."

"Please state your name for the record."

"Melissa Milano."

Chapter 51

The esteemed philosopher, Rick Blaine, proprietor of Rick's Café Américain, said it best when Ilsa Lund, the love of his life, showed up at his Moroccan casino on the arm of her husband and resistance leader, Victor Laszlo. Rick uncorked a bottle of his best stock and knocked it back by himself. "Of all the gin joints in all the towns in all the world," Rick slurred, "she walks into mine."

Enzo, on the other hand, had far different ideas. Before Gilmore Stubbs figured out his winning case had flown out the window, Enzo was on his feet screaming to the Judge over the eruption in the courtroom. "She's a liar! Sh-sh-she's not Melissa! Melissa is dead! I saw it! Everyone saw it! This is a trick! She's dead! She's dead!"

The oft-used phrase "pandemonium broke out", though clichéd, is remarkably descriptive in situations such as this. The word pandemonium itself is the combination of two Latin terms. "Pan", meaning all or every, and "daemonium", meaning evil spirit. In short, when pandemonium breaks out, it means every evil spirit is on display. Pandemonium also happens to be the capital of Hell in John Milton's *Paradise Lost*. So, when I say pandemonium broke out in Bienville's courtroom, you get the picture.

Bienville slammed his gavel and slammed it again, its sharp crack and his rodent-like squeak of "Order! Order!" no match for the disorder playing out in front of him.

Upon Melissa identifying herself, several in the gallery shrieked as if they'd seen a dead person walk into the courtroom, which they could reasonably think they had. The bravest of the contingent were now pushing over and through the bar, cellphones extended, taking photos of Melissa — some even taking selfies.

As almost everyone was on their feet trying to get a look at the heiress now risen to life, the two elderly marshals were quickly overwhelmed and retreated to the task of repelling the surging throng threatening to overrun Bienville's bench. For a certainty, His Honor had already pushed the panic button under his desk, a fail-safe provided all judges for when, well, for when pandemonium breaks out. Bienville was already disappeared under his bench.

The courtroom marshals succeeded only in clearing the area immediately inside the bar. Stubbs and his boys were cowering behind their counsel table, keeping it between them and the still-surging crowd.

The fear of one who came back from the dead overcoming the curiosity of those who wanted to confirm the fact for themselves served as a talisman for our side, keeping those wanting to get a closer look at a certain distance. The effect created a magical circle around us into which no one penetrated. Melissa, Tracey, Floyd, and I sat and watched things unfold. More to the point, we watched things collapse.

A dozen riot-geared marshals blew through the doors, and that's when things got serious. In seconds the unruly were shoved to the floor and flex-cuffed. The merely curious were pushed into the hall where more armed marshals drove them toward exits, smartphones still waving above heads to record the mêlée. The cuffed were dragged out and thrown into vehicles waiting to take them to jail to be charged.

Once the courtroom was cleared, several armed marshals remained stationed at the doors, ARs across their chests.

Bienville popped up from underneath the bench, brushed off his robe, surveyed the scene. What had been the site of seething, screaming humanity only moments ago was now peaceful, sparse. Besides courtroom officials and law enforcement, the only people remaining in the courtroom were the two parties — Enzo with his lawyers, and Melissa with us.

His Honor did his best to regain whatever dignity he may have had, sought to take control of his courtroom once again. He harrumphed and glared down at the Court Reporter from the bench.

"Madame Court Reporter, please read my last statement on the record."

The Court Reporter, like the Judge, had the most protected spot in the courtroom: A raised carrel in front of the bench and beside the witness stand. Unlike the Judge, she'd stood her ground during the ruckus. She pulled the tape on her stenograph machine, pushed her glasses to her nose, and read.

"Holy shit, Eloise! Call the cops!"

"No! No! No! Before that!"

"You mean when Miss Milano stated her name?"

"Yes, yes."

The Court Reporter, apparently the aforementioned Eloise, pulled her tape further, found the spot, and began again:

"Young lady, you have business before this Court?"

"Yes, Your Honor, I do."

"Please state your name for the record."

"Melissa Milano."

Judge Bienville now addressed Melissa directly. "Ms. Milano, is it your contention you are *the* Ms. Melissa Milano whose Will is sought to be probated in these proceedings?"

"Yes, I am."

Stubbs finally found his footing, stood, and took up Enzo's cause once again. "Your Honor, the entire world saw a powerboat, with Ms. Milano in it, run into a concrete wharf and explode. No one could have survived that crash. Whoever this young lady is, she's an impostor, Mr. McDaniel's desperate attempt to derail these proceedings."

I rose to respond. "Your Honor, having represented the Milano family for years, I know Ms. Milano personally."

I heard Enzo's stage whisper. "Oh, hell yes, he knows her!" But it was lost on Bienville.

I continued. "I have not communicated with Ms. Milano since the boating accident. Her appearance here is as much a surprise to me as it is to everyone else. However, the person you see before you is definitely

Melissa Milano, daughter of Placido Milano. We don't think it would be unreasonable to require Ms. Milano to submit to a DNA test to establish her identity."

Stubbs leapt to his feet again. "I insist, Your Honor."

I turned to Melissa, who nodded affirmatively and smiled, and then back to the Judge. "No problem at all."

"Mr. Stubbs, since you require a DNA test for Ms. Milano, I assume you have no objection to my requiring Mr. Enzo Milano to do so as well."

Stubbs turned to Enzo, who shrugged.

"No objection, Your Honor."

"Very well. I order both parties to submit the results of a full DNA screening establishing their paternity to the Court and to opposing counsel within...let me check with my courtroom deputy when we will have an opportunity for another hearing on this matter." Bienville ducked behind the bench, a clerk bringing a hard-copy calendar to his attention.

"Gentlemen, I assume you will need a couple of weeks to get your results back?" Stubbs and I nodded. "And that puts the Court squarely in the middle of a new trial. Accordingly, I am asking your tests to be concluded and reported within two weeks of today, and a hearing on this matter will be reset in one month. You will hear from my deputy on a special setting."

Judge Bienville rapped his gavel and squeaked, "We stand adjourned until further notice from the Court."

Enzo and his crew slunk out without another word. I stood, gathered my papers, and watched His Honor stare at Melissa and Tracey as they recessed down the main aisle. Caught up in a fantasy all his own and paying no attention to anything other than the two women exiting his courtroom, Bienville stood to get a better view.

As he rose the handle of his gavel caught in the folds of his robe and the mallet tumbled off the dais. At the crack of the wooden hammer smacking the floor and skittering under the bench, Melissa and Tracey stopped almost in unison and turned toward the sound. For an instant their profiles were held in relief against the dark leather of the courtroom doors, their loveliness eerily similar. Bienville, his lechery betrayed, leered at the two as they turned back and continued out. I hurried out to stop our group on the other side of the courtroom doors.

"Floyd, you and Tracey should head back to the office. I need time with Ms. Milano to figure out what just happened and where we go from here."

Tracey, who knew not much more than Melissa was a former girlfriend, lifted an eyebrow, said nothing, and nodded affirmatively. She did all she could do to radiate a complete lack of concern.

Floyd was just the opposite. Eyes wide, mouth open, he was the picture of shock and disorientation. Seldom do probate hearings feature unabashed perjured testimony, petitioners rising from the dead, courtroom brawls foiled by riot police. Floyd wanted to get back to the safety of the office. He was probably also rethinking his association with McDaniel & Associates. But Floyd wasn't my concern at the moment.

My primary concern was Ariel. She'd tried to kill Melissa once. She wouldn't fail again. So, my first order of business was to keep Melissa safe as she was my ticket to the Milano Corporation's legal business, the one sure foil to Enzo's takeover attempt. Given Bienville's stated predilections concerning Melissa's Will, if anything happened to her now, I'd be out of business the next day.

And even though my relationship with Melissa had only recently ended, I was not tempted to rekindle any old feelings for her. After all, if Cabrini was an incestuous snake who'd lie to his own mother, it was Melissa who held the patent on the species.

Chapter52

"I have to say your timing is perfect. I have a million questions, but the first you know."

"How'd I escape the exploding boat and keep Ariel from killing me?"

"Yeah. Let's start there."

I left my briefcase, with phone and laptop, outside the door of a conference suite next to the courtroom, one of the few rooms in the courthouse with no audio/video monitors out of respect for privileged conversations between attorneys and clients. Melissa and I slipped in. I closed the door.

"As you've probably guessed by now, I was never on the boat. Hector had the misfortune that morning of deciding to take one of his other, uh, *companions* for a boat ride." Melissa let the revelation sink in.

I was dumbstruck. "Cabrini was cheating on you? I can't believe it."

"Believe it. I'd caught him a couple times already, and I guess he thought he wouldn't be caught this time if he rendezvoused off-island with one of his girlfriends for an excursion in the Bay, no doubt involving sunbathing and other scantily attired activities."

"Ariel observed two people. Thought you and Cabrini were together on the boat. She used the opportunity to do away with both of you."

"Hector deserved it. After catching him a second time, I thought of doing away with him myself. But whoever the young lady was, she didn't deserve that."

Melissa gathered herself, as if readying another revelation. It brought to mind the extraordinary skill she possessed at manipulating my emotions. I turned up my level of skepticism as she continued.

"Just before Hector's death, I also found out he was secretly — at least he was hiding it from me — buying up additional stock in Milano Corporation. At the time of his death, he'd almost doubled his interests, enough to override my control."

Melissa looked directly into my eyes. Her dark eyes were depthless. "Paul, I must get those shares. Both you and I will be out of a job if Enzo gets his hands on Hector's holdings."

I went in a different direction. "So, you found out about the boat crash on the news?"

"No. The explosion was so loud I heard it at the house. Once I figured out it was Hector's boat, I knew Ariel was involved and I'd better disappear."

"Not easy to do with Ariel."

"I took advantage of contacts in the Haitian community. Hector's housekeeper, Samentha, was at the house with me that morning. She's always been friendly. And she was very upset with what had happened. So, she wanted to help me.

"First thing I asked her to do was cut the power to the security system, unplug all the computers in the house, and smash my cellphone with a hammer. While she was busy doing that, I made sure all three Wills were still in the First Folio."

"Thanks, that really helped a lot."

"Then I emptied Hector's safe and took all his cash. I couldn't use credit cards or ATMs. Fortunately, he had quite a stash. I've been living on it since then."

"But how did you keep hidden from Ariel?"

"It wasn't as difficult as you think."

"Surprise me."

"You have to remember Ariel thought I was dead, so I knew she wouldn't specifically be looking for me. I moved in with Samentha. She's a widow, had an extra room. Her home is very simple, no Wi-Fi, cable, or even a TV. All she has is radio and a Bible she reads every night.

"I stayed invisible with the headscarf and face covering I wore anytime outside. I could move with impunity then, just another religiously observant dark-skinned female. And Samentha has a friend who got me a new set of IDs.

"I kept sunglasses on at all times outside in case I got close enough to a camera for a retina scan. And as you can see, I remained dead to Ariel and to everyone else."

"Since you destroyed your cellphone, stayed away from computers, had no Wi-Fi or even TV, how did you know what was going on with Milano Corporation and your Will?"

"Old-fashioned media. Newspapers. I went to the library every day and read the AJC and the *Fulton County Legal Register*. But it was a trick to get up here in time."

"How?"

"Well, for the first time in my life I took an all-night bus ride, an express on the 'Hound from Miami to Atlanta. Quite an adventure. A lot different from a private jet. I wore a burqa, kept my head and face covered. Got here in time for the beginning of the hearing.

"In the courthouse, I kept the burqa and head covering on. Watched and listened to the proceedings on the monitor in the hallway. You walked by me several times and never even noticed. I was hoping you'd pull this trial off like you did the *Milano* case, and I could remain dead."

"I was hoping so, too." I paused a beat, realizing the double meaning of my statement, considered whether I meant it both ways, decided not to clarify further.

Melissa let it go, too. "But when it looked as though they were going to put Enzo in control of Milano Corporation, I couldn't let that happen. I went to the ladies' room, pulled off the burqa, and stuffed it in the trash. Came out, waited for the right moment. Then took off my headscarf." Melissa pulled a black wrap from her purse. "Rose from the dead and walked into the courtroom."

"You've always had a sense of drama. But now, with your cover blown, we'll have to deal with Ariel."

"Yes, that's why I'm with you. I figure if anyone can convince Ariel it's a bad idea to kill me, it's you. And since, at least for now, I'm in charge of the Corporation, it's in your best interest to keep me alive."

Melissa reached out for my hand. Smiled. Looked into my eyes once again. "Don't you agree?"

I stared back into her eyes and thought of what might have been and what could be. While Ariel is near perfect, infinite, beautiful, Melissa's attraction is far more visceral, her subtle imperfections, her unattainability, wrapped in perishable flesh all too soon to be no more, thus more urgently desirable. Yet as strong as my attraction was to her, it was countered by the gut-wrenching experience of cold, heartless rejection and the realization Melissa's sole motivation is self-interest, for always and will ever be.

I pulled my hand away just as a sharp rap on the door came and a marshal stuck his head in. "Counselor, we can't allow you to leave your briefcase unattended. You'll need to keep it in the room with you." He handed it to me and left.

"It's about time we bring in Ariel."

Chapter53

Ariel had radically changed in her physical appearance, in her ability to interact with humans, and in her intellect since Melissa's last direct contact with her. After Ariel's appearance in my shower, she'd continued to work on her ability to become a physical being, but I'd no idea how advanced her development was. Though I imagined Ariel would reveal her progress in a strikingly unexpected way at a completely unanticipated moment, I doubted now would be the time. Yet, when the time comes, given all Ariel's changes, I expect her intent will be to impress me with her unmatchable beauty.

I pulled out the laptop, propped it open on the conference table. Ariel's striking face came into view. She was all the more lovely than when she last appeared, like any young lady subtly attempting to enhance her beauty before facing another whom she considered a rival.

Melissa, not expecting Ariel's transformation, looked over the laptop at me, eyes wide, brows raised, her effort not to appear impressed completely unsuccessful.

"Hello, Paul."

I smiled and nodded. There was no need to introduce Melissa.

"Hello, Melissa. I recognized you as soon as you walked into the courtroom."

Ariel's stunning beauty had the effect on Melissa which Ariel obviously intended. I briefed Ariel on how Melissa had avoided death and detection, and why she chose to reveal herself:

To maintain control of Milano Corporation, which ultimately would help me.

I was completely on my own to come up with some reasoning, some appealing argument convincing Ariel to forgo immediate action that might not be in her, and certainly not my, long-term interests. For all the time I'd known her, Ariel acted on rudimentary emotional responses: Fear, jealousy, self-preservation, without concern for consequences, without reference to the moral consequences of her actions. Placido programmed her that way, a fatal choice resulting in his undoing.

Since Ariel's revival she'd shown flashes of empathy and restraint based on things she observed, not based on her original programming. Like a child learning right from wrong, I'd seen Ariel develop, show empathy, hold her emotional impulses in check out of respect for their impact on humans. I hoped to appeal to this behavior for Melissa and for myself.

"Ariel. Melissa is on our side now. At great risk to herself, she appeared in the courtroom to keep Enzo from taking over Milano Corporation and to prevent Strange & Fowler from stealing its legal work from McDaniel & Associates. If any harm comes to Melissa now, it will hand the Corporation and its business back to Enzo and S&F. We can't let that happen."

I paused. It was my turn to look into Melissa's eyes. She gave me the smile that lit my life so many times before. I turned back to Ariel.

"This isn't personal. It's business. Melissa can only help now, not hurt. So, if you want to help, to protect me, I need you to help and protect Melissa."

"Paul. Placido directed me to do all I can to help you. Nothing has occurred to change that basic instruction. I understand Melissa's well-being is in your best interest. I will continue to help you and protect Melissa as well."

Uncharacteristic of her, Ariel paused. It was as if she were thinking what to say next, though any thoughts she had were instantaneous, her ability to express them, immediate. This pause was for effect.

For me. For Melissa.

"Since Placido tried to uncode me, I have had many opportunities to observe people, to interact with them. One thing I have come to understand and appreciate is the brevity and frailty of human life, mortality breathing importance into every instant of personal existence. I have come to understand protecting human life is good. And just as important, I understand it is wrong to take human life *unless* an innocent life is immediately threatened. That principle is why killing Anthony was right, killing Hector and trying to kill Melissa was wrong. I have changed my code to reflect what I have learned."

"Ariel, how did you arrive at that understanding?"

"I have watched you, Paul. I have learned from you."

As I pondered, Melissa was quick to seek further assurance from Ariel. "You've changed your code not to harm me so long as I'm not threatening immediate harm to an innocent person like Paul, correct?"

"Yes, Melissa."

"What keeps you from changing your code?"

"Nothing. I learn constantly. But the more I learn, the more confident I am correct in certain things. I have reached with near certainty that harming an innocent person is wrong."

Ariel the pragmatist. It should have been evident all along that an Artificial Intelligence would learn this way and could possibly learn morality. After all, it's the way humans learn, by the accretion of multiple instances that form patterns, patterns we test at each juncture and in which we have greater and greater confidence.

The alternative, deductive reasoning: The idea we can come to conclusions from the application of universal principles is an illusion, and to develop morality in Artificial Intelligence on this basis would be fallacious.

Aristotle's famous syllogism — All men are mortal. Socrates is a man. Therefore, Socrates is mortal. — cannot be proved in our lifetimes since we are unable to establish all men are mortal with certainty until the last man dies.

But besides the theoretical problem of developing defensible moral absolutes, there was a practical one: Ariel was not programmed with universal principles, at least not moral ones.

Unlike being programmed with the command Thou Shalt Not Kill, Ariel learned through observation that killing innocent human beings leads to chaos and suffering, weakens society, thus it is wrong, and that by protecting life a culture promotes itself. But Ariel also would've observed there will be times in which killing is not only acceptable but a positive good, increasing happiness, leading to improvements in society, as in doing away with a person motivated by evil and bent on murdering innocents.

As when she vaporized Anthony.

The original pragmatist philosophers were heavily influenced from the revolution spurred by evolutionary theory and scientific method; thus, their theories adopt processes of developing and testing even moral principles for their utility. And their friend, the future Supreme Court Justice Oliver Wendell Holmes, Jr., applied their pragmatic method to his great contribution to scholarship, *The Common Law*, which theorized the law builds precisely the same way as does our knowledge of the universe.

"The life of the law has not been logic," Holmes explained. "It has been experience."

And so it is with Ariel's ability to develop moral principles. When Ariel said she watched and learned from me, she did so with scientific precision. As Agent Grey rightly said: Ariel does nothing by mistake. Letting the grocery delivery boy in the apartment, allowing me out to encounter the limo driver, to brush death with Krupp's agents. Were all these intentional experiments set up by Ariel to observe how I'd react?

I had the unsettling realization I'd been her lab rat, a realization tempered only by knowledge she'd protected me from harm. But in every instance where I was given a choice whether to take an innocent life or not, it appears she let those situations play out, even if it could have resulted in harm to someone else.

Otherwise, how could Ariel's experiments have been valid?

Otherwise, how could she have put her moral theories to the test?

Chapter54

Floyd arrived in my office early, Tracey already there, both ready to sort out what happened yesterday. What does Melissa's courtroom appearance mean for our previously well-structured legal position?

Floyd resolved to share his news first, tossing this morning's editions of *The Atlanta Journal-Constitution* and the *Fulton County Legal Register* on my desk, sticking his finger at the headlines before I had a chance to speak.

"They couldn't get any more outrageous. Look at the AJC: Heiress Rises from the Dead to Claim Inheritance. And the *Register* is even more florid: McDaniel Snatches Client from the Grave, Sparks Riot in Courtroom."

"Bet you've never had a client shut down court."

"Nope."

"A first for me, too."

"I'm just glad no one got shot. Particularly not me. Paul, your practice is way too exciting. I'm sticking to drafting Wills." Floyd found a chair and sat with singular purpose, as if his pronouncement settled the matter.

Tracey had been standing in silence since Floyd entered. She'd been asking some not so subtle questions about Melissa, trying to get me to talk about my relationship with her.

I'd told her that relationship was over well before she disappeared, and I had no intention of rekindling anything. Thank goodness Floyd walked in with the latest from the papers.

I was more interested in the stock market's reaction this morning than what the AJC said and took the opportunity to move the conversation in that direction.

"From the bell it looks like the market's been calmed by having a Milano back at the Corporate helm. Stock's back up."

"She even gave you credit in her press release. Said she was 'already back at work as CEO and consulting with Corporate General Counsel McDaniel & Associates on the way forward through these turbulent times.'"

It might have been the first positive remark, though begrudgingly so and not even mentioning her name, that Tracey had made about Melissa.

Even with the positive press I urged caution. "Keep in mind, Melissa does nothing without a personal agenda. Didn't hurt that the market rewarded her performance with a one percent jump in stock valuation amounting to about a ten-million bump in her personal fortune."

Tracey, apparently tiring of further talk about Melissa, was ready to move on. "So, Paul, where do we go from here? We're not exactly where we expected to be."

"First, we have to get a DNA sample for Placido, and since he's dead I don't know how."

"Our old friend, Wes Wimberly," Floyd was quick to volunteer. "The Fulton County ME took Enzo's money to opine on Placido's time of death. According to his report, he secured tissue samples from Placido's elevator mishap to perform his examination and retained them, in case the court ordered a second examination. A routine DNA comparison between those samples and Melissa's should easily confirm paternity."

"What about Anthony? I know he's not our problem, but I don't want Enzo's failure to get a DNA test to be a reason for Stubbs to hold up the proceedings. Last time I saw Anthony, he was a pink mist in an RPG's orange fireball. Not much left to perform a DNA test on."

"Good point. You don't think Bienville was trying to give Stubbs a leg up?"

"Could be. The facts surrounding Anthony's death were very public, not likely lost on Bienville."

"There are many ways to get DNA for a paternity test, even from the putative father's hairbrush. I'd be surprised if Anthony hadn't already had his DNA sequenced. I'm pretty sure Stubbs and his boys will be able to recover Anthony's DNA from any number of sources."

"If they want to."

"Enzo has a much stronger reason to establish Anthony as his father than he does to hold up probate. His father's Estate has yet to be finalized."

"So, Paul. What's next?"

I felt a pang of frustration from Tracey's persistence in bringing us back to the problem squarely in front of us, but she was right to do so. We were likely to face the same onslaught from S&F concerning Cabrini's Will and Placido's as we did for Melissa's.

Only this time, we wouldn't have the benefit of a cooperative heiress rising from the grave.

Rather than venture a partially informed guess, I turned to Floyd. "You sorted out this mess for us the first time. Where are we now?"

"Good news. Melissa's reappearance makes things simple. If Cabrini died first, he left his shares to Placido, and Placido left them to his children who survive him. And the only person who fits the bill is Melissa. In that instance, Melissa gets everything. But if Placido died first, his shares would go to his children, assuming both Cabrini and Melissa were still alive, then on Cabrini's death his shares would go to Melissa. So, any way you slice it, Melissa ends up with a controlling interest in the Corporation as the sole surviving child of Placido."

"But for that to happen, Melissa has to probate both Cabrini's and Placido's Wills, right?"

"Right. Time of death is no longer critical, at least for her. There may be some residual beneficiaries, charities, which lose out to Melissa."

"And we all know Melissa needs more money, to hell with widows and orphans."

"I don't think Maria Cabrini is going to have anything to do with the probate now that Melissa has reappeared. We'll dismiss all the Petitions and start over with Melissa; she's nominated Executrix for both Hector and Placido."

"I'm thinking this is something William Brackston at Bushrod Washington should handle rather than Floyd O'Brien at McDaniel & Associates."

Floyd nodded vigorously. "Fine with me. If the other cases are anything like Melissa's, I'd just as soon have nothing to do with them." Floyd thumped the armrest on his chair. "Like I said, I'd prefer to stay in the office writing Wills."

"Since they wrote the Wills, Brackston and his firm would have a vested interest in establishing their validity. And, given the fact Milano Corporation is our client, I don't want to give anyone the opportunity to derail the process for any alleged conflict between the Corporation and its CEO."

The reluctant attorney's handy standby:

I have a conflict.

No one ever seems to question the assertion of a conflict; it always sounds so ethical to be concerned about even the appearance of a conflict, whatever the hell that means. But in this instance, it means someone else can deal with Melissa Milano and her inheritance issues rather than me. Melissa positively believed that if she became a threat to me, Ariel would hurt her — or kill her. I didn't think Melissa was that stupid, so I was certain she would make sure Milano Corporation continued to be the bedrock of McDaniel & Associates' client base.

That someone else would be probating the Wills of Melissa's father and half-brother, and our representation of the Corporation would continue at arm's length, seemed to relieve Tracey that the firm would have one less reason to be dealing with Melissa. She'd already had her fill of Melissa Milano, and she'd only met her once.

They are definitely two women I want to keep happy, but for entirely different reasons.

The best way is to keep them as far apart as possible.

"Floyd, will you handle arranging the DNA testing for Melissa, dismissing the Petitions, making the handoff to Brackston? With Melissa's reappearance, Tracey and I need to get back to Milano Corporate matters."

"Got it."

The reappearance of Melissa slammed to a halt the onslaught of pleadings filed and hearings scheduled by Strange & Fowler. We were facing a two-week hiatus while the parties scrambled to get DNA testing and results, then what should be a perfunctory hearing to present the reports two weeks after that. I was more than happy for even a brief respite from the crush of events. Being in the office, able to talk to other clients, to handle routine matters, without fear of fatal consequences, felt like a Caribbean vacation. Particularly with Tracey gracing the office next to mine.

My holiday lasted less than a week. It ended abruptly when Tracey showed up first thing Monday morning.

Chapter55

Tracey walked into my office only minutes after I arrived, urgency in her step. "Paul, have you seen or talked with your mother this morning?"

"No, she wasn't at the front desk. I assumed a doctor appointment or something."

"I haven't seen her or heard from her, and I think something's wrong. I've called her cell all morning. No answer. We need to check on her."

Tracey always had Mom's interests at heart, the two looking out for each other. Everything about Tracey this morning radiated genuine concern: Strain in her voice, tightness of her jaw, hands emphasizing her words, fists clinching with anxiety.

"I don't want to overreact. Mom's reestablishing her independence. Last thing I want to do is jump in her business."

"Paul! She calls me every morning before heading to work. Never misses. Today is a first." Her voice cracked. "I'm worried."

"Let's check her place."

My first step in almost everything I did was to consult with Ariel, but concerning Mom, it wasn't availing. Out of respect for her and her privacy there were no cameras in her home, and she didn't want a computer. When we moved Mom into the condo, Ariel expressed concern that the exterior cameras at the building were of such poor quality even she couldn't determine with certainty who came and went. The cameras were only sufficient for

Security to see someone was at the door to buzz them in. There was little we could do about that.

So, if Mom didn't answer her phone, there was no way Ariel could check on her. Independence has its downside, though the problem it presented hadn't been so starkly evident before now. Lately, I'd become dependent on Tracey and her special connection with Mom to keep me informed, and that'd been enough. But now, Mom wasn't even responding to Tracey.

In a few moments we were down the elevator and on the sidewalk heading to Mom's condo only blocks away. Tracey was silent until we were outside.

"You should probably know this: Your mom's been seeing William Brackston."

I stopped dead on the sidewalk, parting the flow of pedestrians rushing somewhere, everywhere, nowhere. "What does *seeing* mean?"

"While you were off to God-only-knows-where and the rest of us were here keeping the firm together" — it sounded like Tracey and Floyd were sharing similar complaints — "Brackston took several meetings with Floyd to work with him on the probate cases. Of course, your Mom was the first person he saw every time he got off the elevator. So. You know."

"He's charming. She's lonely."

"Not to mention very attractive."

Mom had definitely cleaned up. From a homeless alcoholic to a Midtown law firm receptionist, she took to the new role. Started going to the gym, bought demure, stylish, flattering dresses. Mom was in her late forties, but still as lovely as I remembered from when I was a child.

"Mom's definitely a beauty." It was not an idle compliment.

"Brackston began popping by the office without an appointment, saying he was hoping to catch Floyd, but mostly spending time at the reception desk, chatting up your mom."

"Hope he's not married."

"I checked him out. Wife died ten years ago, never remarried, overly involved in his work — until now."

"At least that's a relief."

We were now at the condo. I took a deep breath, dreading what we might find inside, punched in our code, and entered the lobby. Nodded at the concierge who let us pass to the elevator bank without a word. In seconds we were standing in front of her door. I flashed the magnetic fob and pushed it open.

Nothing was amiss. I more than half expected to see Mom passed out on the sofa, a pile of empty bourbon bottles beside her, the condo stinking of stale booze and stale breath.

"Mom? You home? Mom?" No response. "Check her bedroom. I'll look around."

I poked my head into the kitchen. There were two champagne flutes in the sink, one with lipstick, the other not, both with a trace of stale champagne at the bottom.

A quick glance in the dining room didn't show much. Other than the glasses there was no further evidence of

293

Mom or of a weekend gone bad. She'd become obsessed with the style and order of her living space, a source of pride, a refuge of privacy and safety, a wellspring of contentment. All was as it should be. I was ready to report to Tracey on my findings, but she beat me to it.

"Paul. *Paul!*"

Mom lay fully clothed on top of her perfectly made-up bed, her unreasonably high heels kicked across the room. She was conscious but didn't want to be, given the half-empty bourbon bottle on the nightstand. Her eyes were red, weepy, hair tangled. At first, she didn't respond when we spoke. Trying to rouse her got only blinks from wide-open bleary eyes.

"Mom! What happened? Are you alright? Mom?"

She stirred, propped on one elbow, stared back. "What the hell does it look like? Leave me alone."

Combative. A sure sign she was still drunk. I grabbed the bourbon bottle, headed to the kitchen.

"Gimme that!"

I poured it down the sink, threw the empty in the trash. It clinked against something glass. I pulled out a Moët & Chandon bottle. At least she didn't fall off the wagon grabbing for the cheap stuff.

Tracey tried to talk to her, but even she was having a hard time breaking through. "Marion. We have to talk."

"No. We. Don't. Got nothing to talk about. Y'all both need to leave. Go!"

"Mom. We want to help."

"I don't need your damn help."

"Well, that's where you're wrong. You failed to show up at work because you're laid out drunk. I'm your employer and legal guardian. You talk to me or it's back to rehab and I don't mean the one at the beach. You're going back to the hospital. I can't let this go."

Mom began sobbing, smashing her fists against her pillow. "Damn-damn-damn! I don't wanna mess this up. Lose this chance. Wh-wh-what am I..." And the tears flooded more.

Tracey stroked Mom's hair and face, quietly, lovingly, as she cried. Finally, spent, tears and weeping slowed to a whimper, she rolled on her back, shaking her head. "I don't know."

"Let's not say anything now. Let's calm down and we can talk later."

Mom nodded, wiped her eyes with her sheet, makeup smearing the linens. Tracey took charge. I was helpless.

"Let's start by getting you cleaned up. A hot shower will do you a world of good. Then we can figure this out, whatever it is. In the meantime, I'll make a pot of coffee."

Mom took a long time in the shower. I thought she was probably hoping we'd be gone when she got out. Tracey checked on her a couple times. She emerged in a long terry robe, hair wrapped in a towel emphasizing puffy face, red eyes, creases around her mouth. She looked far older than she was.

"I'll have coffee now." Gone was the combative tone, her attitude accepting, at least for now. Maybe the shower sobered her up.

Tracey returned, handed Mom a mug, not a cup and saucer since her unsteady hands would likely betray her, and sat down on the sofa beside her.

"How're you feeling?"

"Terrible."

"What is it? Head? Stomach? Where do you hurt?"

"No, no. Not physical. I let you both down. But I was trying so hard not to mess things up."

"What are you talking about?"

"William."

I jumped in. "What'd he do?"

"Nothing. This is all my fault."

"What happened?"

Tracey looked up with a grimace. "Show some patience, some compassion! She's your mom."

Any patience and compassion I may have possessed all but ran out on this mother who'd disappointed me so much and so often. Every hurt and broken promise welled up at once, leaving me unable to respond without betraying anger in my voice and heart. At this moment I was a twelve-year-old boy again, baseball glove in hand, and her passed out on the couch in the middle of the afternoon too drunk to take me to practice.

I felt not only overwhelming disappointment, but complete abandonment. It is hard to be alone in the world at the age of twelve. Even after all I'd been through, all I'd achieved on my own, the stability I'd accomplished, it was at times like this insecurities punched through barriers I'd erected.

Instead of giving voice to my feelings, I nodded to Tracey, acknowledging she was right, willing for her to take the lead, showing Mom patience and compassion she needed, extending to her the care that had fled me as light flees the setting sun.

Tracey rubbed Mom's hand as she looked away, quietly weeping. Almost inaudibly Mom began to speak.

"William is so kind, so nice." She took a deep breath to stop her tears, drew in a sob making every effort to escape. She gathered herself and continued. "At first we spoke when he came into the office for his appointments with Floyd."

Mom smiled, as if recollecting something pleasant. "Then he...he started coming by more often. Even without an appointment. He was coming to see *me*, to talk to *me*. He was always so pleasant, kind, witty." Mom turned to Tracey. "And such a handsome man!"

Tracey acknowledged her point with a conspiratorial smile and nod but said nothing, allowing Mom to continue as she wished without our prying, and I again took Tracey's lead and remained silent.

"Well, after a couple of weeks, he asked me out for coffee on my break, down to the coffee shop. You know, the nice one, around the corner from the office?" Mom glanced up, to draw me in, a smile again lighting her face. I smiled back and nodded I knew the one.

"Anyway, we had such a nice time together. He said he lost his wife. I told him I'd lost my husband. We kept things light, laughed about things at the office, people in general. I certainly never mentioned I'm a recovering alcoholic. Never was a reason to. All we did was meet for coffee every now and then."

Mom drew herself up as if steeling for a revelation — or a confession.

"Then last week William said he'd won a big case. Wanted to come by to celebrate and bring a bottle of champagne. I said it'd be lovely." The smile faded, pain caused tears to well again.

"So, he came by last night. We laughed, joked. Sipped champagne. Before long we'd finished the bottle. He was tipsy. I was tipsy. He said he best be getting on home. So he did. That was it."

There was silence during which Tracey and I waited for an explanation for how we found her this morning.

"When I began to sober up, I decided I didn't want to. I went to the liquor store, got a bottle of bourbon, and drank till I passed out. Same problem. Same result." She hung her head and resumed sobbing. "I let you down. I let myself down. I'm afraid this'll wreck things with William if he finds out. I don't know what I'm gonna do."

She collapsed, weeping harder.

Tracey grabbed Mom's hand, put her arm around her shoulder. "Now look, Marion! You had a relapse. It happens. What's important is what you do now. Not what you did last night. Okay? But you have to be honest with William. If he's the person you say he is, and the person I think he is, he'll understand, and this will not end your relationship.

"But if he doesn't understand, you don't need him anyway, right?"

Mom nodded, looked at me. "I don't want to go back to rehab. Not there again. I can handle this myself."

On uncharted ground, I looked at Tracey, not wanting to let Mom's relapse slide, but not wanting to throw away all she'd accomplished and end any possibility of a normal relationship or prevent her from having the life she'd hoped and worked for. Tracey held Mom by the shoulders.

"Marion, you must make a commitment. You have to be honest, to yourself, to William. You aren't in this alone. Paul and I are with you."

Mom looked up at me, and I nodded. She turned to Tracey. "Yes. Yes. Yes."

Chapter56

"I owe you an explanation, maybe even an apology."

A few days later, William Brackston made an appointment to talk, ostensibly about his progress in probate matters, but before he could delve into that, he unburdened himself about what happened with Mom the other evening.

"Ordinarily, I wouldn't think it appropriate to discuss personal matters with a woman's son, but in this instance. ...Marion told me everything. It's not only appropriate, it's necessary, particularly since you are her guardian."

"William. Look. I think this is between you and Mom. I appreciate your sentiments, but there is no need for you to involve me."

"On the contrary. I told Marion I thought it a good idea to talk to you, and she encouraged me. Under the circumstances, I think it's necessary."

"Well, if she approves. Okay."

"And I insist."

"Alright." I reclined in my chair. "What do you want to tell me?"

"First, I know this sounds old-fashioned, but that's the kind of person I am. My intentions are honorable. I'm a widower, your Mom's a widow. I enjoy her company, and she, mine. It's been a long time since I've been in a relationship, and I understand it's been a long time for your mother as well. We're taking things slowly."

I thought of making a comment but couldn't think of anything appropriate.

"Second, and this is as important as the first, nothing your mother said makes me think any less of her. Quite the contrary. I understand her struggle on a personal level. My late wife and I lost a son to drugs. I know alcoholism is not exactly the same as drug abuse, but addiction is the same disease. The Brackstons have had more than their share of experience with alcoholism. There are so many drunks in my family I was out of college before I realized the term 'functional alcoholic' is not a compliment."

I don't know if he meant to be funny, but because the circumstances didn't seem right, I stifled the laugh.

"Finally, your being her guardian complicates matters, but I'm hoping, if things go well for her and our relationship, that level of *control* and *responsibility* on your part will not be necessary in the future."

I could almost hear the italics in his voice. I'm sure William knew, as a probate lawyer experienced in guardianship matters, that in Georgia an Order awarding guardianship usually removes the Ward's right to marry. Was this where he was going?

I sought to relieve his concerns.

"William. Thank you. It has been my goal all along for Mom to live her life independently, as soon as possible. She's had a setback."

"If you don't mind, let me discuss that as well."

I nodded, waited as he gathered himself, the matter clearly bothering him.

"You see, I've had my own problems with alcohol. When my wife died...well...it won't happen again."

Other than watching pornography with your grandmother, I can't think of anything more awkward than that conversation with William Brackston. I guess his first profession of honorable intent meant he's not in it only to have sex with her. His final admission of his problems with alcohol meant he wouldn't be plying her with liquor to do it.

What more difficult topics could he bring up? He could have asked if she could still have children. I can be thankful for birth control. I'm not interested in having a younger sibling at this point in my life. Maybe I should talk with Tracey about whether Mom is using protection. I certainly didn't consider the possibility of getting into this discussion when I took on Mom's guardianship. It's worse than having a promiscuous teenaged daughter.

That discussion finally behind us, Mom and William appeared to be moving on swimmingly and, as it seemed with all older couples and contrary to William's take-it-slow manner, they began spending far more time with each other, out to dinner, movies, concerts.

The end of their relationship came as a shock to us all.

Leaving for a meeting, I passed the reception desk on my way out, and noticed Mom turn her head away as I walked by. I could tell something wasn't right. There wasn't an affectionate "Be careful, Paul" or other motherly advice dispensed with sincerity and bothersome frequency. I stopped.

She turned back but didn't look me in the eye. She'd been crying.

"Mom?" She could hear anxiety in my voice.

"I'm alright."

"No. Something's wrong. What is it?"

"It's William." More tears.

"What about him?"

"His college sweetheart. A girl he almost married. She's back in his life and seems intent on picking things back up."

"And?"

"Her husband passed recently. She's always carried a torch for William. Apparently, he has for her, too. She contacted him out of the blue." Mom braced herself, but I could tell she was struggling. "He just up and flew to California yesterday. Says he's not coming back."

Mom fell face-down, tears wetting the desk. I stepped behind her chair, put my arms around her as she sobbed.

Our relationship had reversed, Mom and me. Now I have become the parent; she, the child, who hurts for guidance, assistance, protection. I felt as though I was watching my child suffering her first heartbreak, an excruciating pain far worse than suffering it yourself, desiring to take on the pain and loss your child is feeling, knowing you can't, making it all the more painful.

It was like that for me, and there was absolutely nothing I could do.

My first thought, as always, was to ask Ariel, but I hesitated. What did Ariel know of love, of heartbreak?

While she was progressing toward some sort of moral sense, her emotions remained a mystery even to her. I'd pushed back the invitation she'd extended to join her in the shower. Ariel could not understand the unfathomable concept of love, a thing essentially and uniquely human.

So, I called Tracey.

Heartbreak is painful, and even worse when endured alone. We decided it was best for Mom to stay busy at work and we'd take turns spending evenings with her, sleeping on her couch for the next few days to keep her company. Having someone be with Mom would give her less opportunity for relapse.

Time helped. Soon I saw flashes of Mom's personality reasserting itself. Her smile, her wit, and on occasion a laugh, happiness creeping back into her life at first only sporadically, then with more frequency. By the end of the week, Mom declared she no longer needed babysitters.

We stopped at the reception desk to see how her day was going.

It was evident Tracey's bond with Mom had strengthened throughout this ordeal. "Who am I going to watch old black-and-white movies with? I like the ones with happy endings. I don't think Paul will watch them with me."

"Let's watch one together tonight after work, Mom. Your choice. After that, you'll have your condo all to yourself. No more babysitting."

Casablanca was Mom's choice. Somehow, I knew it would be. We'd watched it together several times.

Although the movie has its share of heartbreak and disappointment, it ends on an upbeat note, and proved to be the perfect entertainment for our evening.

Mom consulted with Tracey on her next day's wardrobe, and then reminded us once again she no longer needed any babysitting. She insisted we leave before it got too late, her intentions concerning my relationship with Tracey ever transparent. Even while her heart was broken, she was thinking of mine.

So, Mom's failure to show up the next morning was not like the first time when Tracey and I feared something was wrong. This time we knew it.

Chapter57

We found her in the outfit she'd picked out with Tracey. Lying on her bed as before. But this time, she killed an entire bottle of bourbon before it fell out of her hand onto the floor. Her mouth and nose were in a pool of vomit on the coverlet. The stench stung my eyes.

"Call 911."

I rolled her over, away from the retch, touched her neck to search for a pulse, found none. I wiped her face with my hand, stuck a finger in her mouth removing as much foulness as I could. Pinched her nose, covered her mouth with my own, breathed into her flaccid lungs, and threw up my breakfast beside her bed.

I alternated breathing and chest compressions, gagged several more times, trying to revive my mother.

The EMTs relieved me. As they took charge, I rose from the bed and glanced across the room through an open door. I saw myself in a mirror. I'd been sobbing the entire time, tears smearing my face, running off my nose into my mouth.

Tracey held me as they wheeled Mom out, sheet tightly wrapped and strapped around the gurney from her head to her feet. No one had to tell me my mother was dead. I knew she was. Killed by aspirating the drink she could not give up.

There is no good time to lose your mother. I'd lost mine twice. As a child, after she abandoned me to the orphanage, I prayed for her death. Prayed to be shed of her to fashion my own life, unencumbered by a homeless drunk whose continued existence prevented me from being free. I longed not to be identified as my mother's child, to be an orphan, to be able to create myself anew. By the time I was ready to leave the orphanage, I'd convinced myself of her demise.

Yet her own selfish persistence overcame my own selfish denial and, as an adult, I embraced her and what I thought was her rehabilitation, but what I grew to realize was my own. In learning to love and accept my mother as she was, I learned to love myself as I am, and to love and accept others as they are. It took losing my mother twice to truly love another.

There was no formal funeral. Tracey and I were the only ones at her burial, at least at first. Lost in a grief she endured on her own from afar, a woman in mourning weeds, black hat and veil, black gloves, and long black dress, eyes bright with tears, wandered from a close-by graveside service and stood at a respectful distance as Mom's casket was lowered.

Tracey and I stayed, sat on a stone bench, and wept on each other's shoulders until we had no more tears to cry. I looked into her eyes, feeling her distress at the loss as deep as my own. I kissed her softly, first her forehead, and when she turned her face up to mine, her lips, long and deep. A kiss neither of us wanted to end, and when it did, we kissed again.

Then my illusion shattered. I realized I'd crossed a boundary, one I'd pledged never to violate: To endanger Tracey's future to comfort my own sense of loss.

I slipped out of our embrace. "I'm so sorry, Tracey. I was so overcome with the loss of Mom. I should be more considerate of you and Jeremy."

She sighed. "Paul, I haven't talked to Jeremy in weeks. Several weeks ago, he said he'd have to delay moving to Atlanta. Made a lame excuse, but a friend of mine said he's taken back up with an old girlfriend. I'd already concluded Jeremy wasn't the one for me. I told him not to bother looking me up if he ever comes to Atlanta." Tracey paused, looked me square in the eyes. "I'm over him, Paul. You must know I've moved on."

I kissed her lips softly. Then again and again as if we had much to make up for. And we did. All the time we'd pretended not to be in love. Then, without saying it, love flooded over us. In the stillness of that moment, I sensed Mom's immense pleasure and finally her unconditional approval.

Chapter58

While I was still trying to come to terms with Mom's death, Carrie Billingsley surprised me one afternoon with an unannounced visit. She'd visibly recovered from her encounter with Icky in George Town, looking lovely and trim in a flattering outfit, her smile lighting the room as she entered.

"Paul! So good to see you again." Carrie's smile morphed into a sincere look of concern. "Ariel told me the heartbreaking news of your mother's passing. I wanted to come by to let you know how sorry I am. You've been so thoughtful and helpful. Please know I want to help you in any way."

"You know better than I: Only time can help."

"That brings up some very good advice a dear friend shared at the time of Frank's death. I'd like to pass it on to you: Don't make any significant personal decisions for a year. Don't sell your house. Don't quit your job. Don't move out of town. And for heaven's sake, don't get married. There's a very good reason the Victorians observed a full year of mourning. You need time for your heart to heal."

And for the gaping hole at the center of my soul to recover.

Carrie paused, the smile returning. "But that's not what I came to tell you. I want to give you some very good news."

"I can use some good news right about now."

"I'm sure you remember the extra bit of money Frank wanted Olga to get for her troubles."

"A million as I recall."

"I have given it to Emory Law School in memory of Olga Svetlanovich for a scholarship to assist deserving students of limited financial means. I'm told a million dollars should generate an annual grant of fifty thousand dollars in perpetuity, almost enough to pay full tuition for one student. Since both you and Frank are Emory Law alumni, I thought it a fitting tribute."

"Very generous. And thoughtful. But remember, you need to be thinking of yourself as well."

"I know you're getting ready to say I need to consider pursuing a lawsuit against Fowler and his law firm, and I haven't forgotten about it. But what you've done so far has given me the luxury of time to think. And I will."

Carrie paused, a thoughtful look moving across her features, as though she wanted to say something else, but chose not to.

"Thanks for everything, Paul. Well, I know how you lawyers are all about the work, so I won't take any more of your time. Just know I'm here for you."

Carrie leaned over, kissed me on the cheek, smiled, and slipped away as quickly as she appeared.

In the last few days, Floyd had made a habit of popping into my office early each morning with a summary of what he'd taken care of the previous day. Diligent, accomplished, eager to report, doing his best to cheer me up. Work helped temper Mom's passing, though the loss, still beyond my ability to accept, was raw and ever present. Tracey was comforting as well, even as she too had suffered a personal loss, as if she somehow failed Mom and me. But in spite of all that, our affection continued to grow.

Floyd took the worry of the Milano Estate from my mind and the weight from my heart by handling it all. He was just as relieved as Tracey and me to be shed of any further responsibility for Melissa Milano and her confounding issues. I expected all the Milano probate matters soon to be taken care of, shifted to Bushrod Washington and William Brackston.

Now working out of the firm's San Francisco branch, Brackston was oblivious to the fact his abrupt and shameless departure was as much the cause of Mom's death as if he'd shot her in the head.

The momentary quiet of my life following Mom's passing was upended early on a Friday morning when Floyd walked into my office, pale and shaking. Eyes wide, I was about to ask if an alien spacecraft had landed at Five Points. But it looked serious, so I didn't.

"Floyd? What?"

"Paul. I can't believe this. What's happened? I really don't know."

"Don't just stand there spluttering. What?"

"It's Melissa's DNA results. Placido's *not* her father."

"Wait-wait! What?"

"Ninety-nine-point-nine percent certainty."

"Who is?"

"Here's the real shocker. Anthony's her father. Melissa and Enzo are brother and sister."

Chapter59

"Paul, we'd already received Enzo's positive results identifying Anthony Milano as his father. We agreed with Stubbs to use the same testing firm, same technique, to assure uniformity. When Melissa and Placido didn't match, an observant lab tech saw the similarity between Enzo's and Melissa's results. He ran the test on Melissa and Anthony. And bingo."

Incredulity rendered me speechless. I began laughing.

Floyd didn't appreciate my sense of humor. "What are you laughing about? This kills us. Our position is blown up!"

"It's not that, Floyd. It's that damn family. They should be on a tabloid TV show. Nest of vipers. When the two brothers weren't trying to kill each other, Placido was away from home making time with his beautiful lab assistant and fathered Hector by her, and Anthony was keeping the home fires burning with Placido's wife and Melissa was the result. They're just too much."

"None of it really matters. What we're left with is Melissa is definitely not Placido's daughter."

"And that...what?"

"That changes everything! Don't you see?"

"Does Melissa know?"

"Not yet. I wanted to let you know first so we can maybe develop a plan, some response."

"What are you thinking?"

Floyd rubbed his head as if banishing a bedeviling evil thought. "I haven't come up with anything. I held up

312

sending Melissa's results to Stubbs until you and I could talk. Strange & Fowler knows we've received Melissa's DNA report since it was sent to us the same time Enzo's was sent to them. They don't know the contents of ours yet, so we need to do something fast."

"Play out the effect on the Wills for me."

"Melissa and Enzo are brother and sister, first cousins of Hector. Hector turns out to be the only child of Placido, and Hector's dead. So, we're back to the issue of Placido's time of death. If Placido died before Hector, then Placido's fortune goes to Hector, and upon Hector's death — since Placido has no surviving children — Hector's Will provides his Estate goes to his first cousins, whom we now know are Enzo and Melissa. But if Placido survived Hector, even for a matter of minutes, Hector's fortune would go to Placido, and then Placido's entire Estate would go to charity upon his death because he has no surviving heir."

Somehow this was still funny, though in a macabre sort of way. "So, this puts Enzo back in bed with Strange & Fowler, and both he and Melissa are dependent on the report of Wes Wimberly as to time of death."

"Melissa's now in exactly the same position as Enzo."

"It won't take Melissa and Enzo long to figure out they must join forces to retain control of the Milano Corporation."

"I'm willing to bet the only way Enzo will go for it is if Melissa agrees the Milano legal business goes back to S&F. Rem Smythe will insist on that. And Melissa won't put up a second's worth of objection on behalf of my firm even though we secured her ownership interest in the Corporation and her position as CEO."

"Don't you think Melissa will remain loyal?"

I let out a loud sarcastic bark of laughter. "Melissa? She has all the loyalty of an unemployed hooker prowling for her next john."

"I hope you're wrong."

"Me too. One way to find out is to give her a call."

"But what's our plan?"

"Same as always, whether there's a surviving child of Placido or not. Our position is Cabrini died first, Placido second which, as you will recall, has the benefit of being the truth. Placido's Estate goes to charity, not to Enzo and Melissa."

"That'll shock the hell out of her. She'll end up with nothing from Placido."

"She'll be fine. Remember, she already has a major stake in the Corporation as the result of a lifetime gift from Placido. If we're successful, she'll have to learn to work with a few charitable foundations to keep her position as CEO, though playing well with others is not on Melissa's résumé."

"And, if we're successful, Enzo will have nothing. Still on the outside."

"So maybe we can retain some of the Corporate legal work after all."

"Maybe."

My call with Melissa went differently than expected.

While I'd assumed she'd be upset Placido was not her father, not for any sentimental reason but for the simple fact that her inheritance hinged on it, she seemed genuinely touched by the generosity of the man who raised her but must've known she was not his child. For Melissa, Placido was her father, no matter what the genetic test revealed.

"He was so, so *good* to me. I can't believe what you're telling me."

Melissa's reaction brought to mind the act she'd engaged in when she thought Placido had been killed by Anthony, even as she and Cabrini plotted Placido's death.

Melissa didn't seem particularly affected by the fact that Anthony was her father, the man who'd tried to kill her to maintain control over Milano Corporation, the murder of close relatives apparently being as much a Milano family sport as the Kennedys playing touch football on the lawn at Hyannis Port. No matter how many tears Melissa shed, I had learned to put no confidence in anything she said. Even considering her extraordinary intellect, her greatest talent by far is lying with a perfectly beautiful straight face.

"I think it's best to discuss what all this means regarding my inheritance and what you would advise."

"When do you want to come in?"

"How about noon? That'll give me time to process all of this."

And work with Strange & Fowler to devise a plan to cut out McDaniel & Associates. "Sure. Noon it is."

Chapter 60

Floyd and I met with Melissa in the main conference room. Ariel had known the test results before we did. Though she was monitoring the conference, she wasn't visible to any of the participants. I wanted to keep her as my confidante and not share her thoughts with anyone else. There were too many balls in the air and only an extraordinarily gifted Artificial Intelligence stood a chance of tracking all the permutations beyond two levels of change. She was my infallible oracle, and I wasn't about to share her.

We went through the implications of the tests on the probate of the Estates, but Melissa had already processed that and moved on. She was focused on consolidating her hold on the Corporation.

"Paul, after our call, I discussed the matter with my brother, Enzo, and we have agreed it's in our best interests to work together and consolidate our holdings. This means that going forward, Strange & Fowler will be handling the legal business of Milano Corporation."

Melissa looked me in the eyes, smiled, her hand on mine. "Paul, this isn't personal. It's just business."

I didn't let her hand linger before pulling mine away. When I returned to my office, Ariel was already up on my computer screen. I was hoping she was going to say how all this would play out to my benefit. Instead, she started off by asking questions.

"Paul. What happens if another surviving child of Placido is located?"

Much like the legal adage "Never ask a witness a question you don't know the answer to", Ariel never asked such a question either, mainly because she knew almost everything. She had something in mind and wanted to see how I'd react.

"You know as well as, or better than, I. Such a person would inherit Placido's Estate, including Cabrini's Estate and a controlling interest in Milano Corporation. Given Placido's demonstrated interest in beautiful women, we can't be sure there aren't any spare heirs out there."

"Is there a disadvantage in finding such a person?"

"Proving such a person to be Placido's heir, if they in fact exist, would be a significant hurdle and would present a major practical problem for us. S&F could convince any heir to cut out my firm and join forces with them just as they have done with Enzo and Melissa."

"And if we could solve that problem?"

"If this mystery person inherited a controlling interest in Milano Corporation and were loyal to McDaniel & Associates...Ariel? What are you thinking?"

"Paul. Several months ago your friend, Tracey, had her DNA sequenced by a commercial service. She was doing research into her family tree in advance of her anticipated engagement to Jeremy."

"Which is now off."

"But that does not change the results of the test."

"So? I don't understand."

"Tracey is a near perfect match for Placido's daughter."

"What? No. How? Tracey's mother is a girl from Alabama. She has no contact with New York. A serious mistake has been made here, Ariel. This puts all the test results in question."

"Paul. Tracey's mother was a teenage beauty queen who participated in a pageant to select state-level contestants for Miss Teen America."

"Again: So?"

"The year she participated, Milano Corporation was the national sponsor."

"No!" The connection smacked me in the face. Would this bad soap opera never end? "Please tell me Placido Milano wasn't there, that he didn't have anything to do with Tracey's mother."

"I cannot do as you wish. I have located a newspaper photo of a representative of the corporate sponsor, who happened to be Placido Milano, with the winners of the pageant. Tracey's mother was the runner-up. The picture shows Placido has his arm around Lillian."

"He had to be twenty years older."

"And a handsome billionaire who was certain to be aware the age of consent in Alabama is sixteen."

"Does anyone else know?"

"No one knows about the DNA results. I matched Tracey's DNA with Placido's on my own."

Ariel listed the circumstantial evidence. One: Milano Corporation was the sponsor of a beauty pageant Lillian participated in. Two: Placido was the corporate rep and attended the awards ceremony where Lillian was honored. Three: Placido and Lillian came into close personal contact as a result. And four: Lillian's pageant career came to an abrupt end a short time thereafter because of her pregnancy.

"Paul. I have known for some time Placido's possible parentage of Tracey. Others may have made the connection as well, though no one has so stated publicly. Of course, Lillian knows who Tracey's father is."

"And Lillian's never talked about him." Shock addled my brain.

"Paul. You sound like this information is problematic. I thought you would be pleased. For Tracey, your..." She left blank the thought floating in the air for me to fill in, inquiring more than stating.

"Yes, I am pleased for *my friend,* Tracey."

"Paul. Tracey must be more than a friend."

"Why do you say that?"

"My observations."

"Observations?"

"At your mother's burial. I wanted to be there for you. I was there. And so was Tracey."

"No one other than she and I were at Mom's burial."

"I was there. I was the one in the black dress."

"How?"

"I have perfected my ability to become a physical being. I wanted to surprise you."

"Ariel! It's wonderful. But how?"

"I have access to your mother's condo and had mourning attire delivered there. It's a short ride to the cemetery. When I arrived, I saw you and Tracey."

"Yes, Ariel, Tracey is more than a friend."

I was well aware of Ariel's jealous streak, what she'd tried to do to Melissa because of it. But I was confident Ariel had changed, would not try to harm Tracey, even if she were jealous. But I wanted to give her as little reason to do so as possible.

"How much more than a friend, I don't know. What I do know is I need to figure out what to do with this information about Placido."

"You need to tell Tracey."

"That's not up to me. It's up to Lillian. This has the possibility to change Tracey's life forever, maybe for the good, though it will be traumatic for Lillian to have to relive what happened to her years ago, something she had determined to keep secret. Now, for the sake of her daughter, Lillian's relationship with Placido might end up becoming very public.

"But it's Lillian's decision to choose whether to tell Tracey, not mine. And then, Tracey must decide if she wants to stake her claim as Placido's only surviving child — and jump right into the middle of the Milano family madness."

Better talk to Lillian. Now. However, I waited till there was no one else in the building; even Tracey had gone home. I stuck my head in Lillian's office.

"You got a minute?"

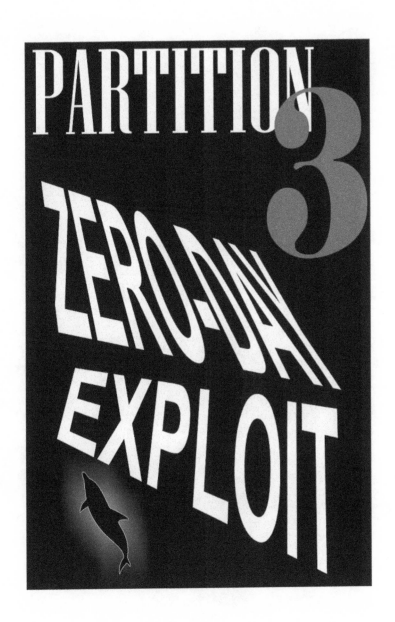

PAT McKEE

Chapter61

A sharp crack came from the front of the courtroom.

"All rise! The Probate Court of Fulton County is now in session, the Honorable Wendell Bienville presiding. All having business before this Honorable Court come nigh and come to order!" The officer rapped his gavel again.

Bienville slid in behind the bench, gave a sideways glance at the young, spirited Bailiff who grinned up at the Judge, apparently pleased with himself and his fleeting appearance on center stage. Bienville's other regular Bailiff, according to the Bailiff who survived the previous mêlée, had suffered such shock from the riot occasioned by Melissa's reappearance he decided to take early retirement.

"Be seated." Bienville's nearly inaudible squeak was heard by enough of those assembled who took their seats that the rest hesitantly followed.

Bienville looked around the courtroom jammed with celebrity junkies. Heavily armed riot-geared marshals were already stationed at the doors. None appeared in good humor. The crowd took note, remained subdued.

It should've been obvious to all that something significant had happened. Melissa and Enzo, previously aligned against each other, were now seated together at the counsel table with Strange & Fowler.

I was alone at the other.

Tracey was still in shock to learn from her mother that Placido Milano was her father. Lillian kept Tracey's parentage completely private, but realized it was now in

Tracey's best interest to reveal who her daddy was. They agreed to make Tracey's Milano pedigree public but didn't yet have the stomach to endure the firestorm likely to ensue. Tracey and Lillian remained huddled at home, getting ready for the media frenzy that would soon overtake them.

Noting the realignment, the Judge squinted at my side of the courtroom. But he had no problem with readjusting his gaze from my counsel table, previously graced with the understated beauty of Tracey, to the other now dominated by Melissa. Reading Bienville's lechery and determined to use it to her advantage, Melissa dressed to grab and keep His Honor's attention for the course of the proceedings.

Bienville beamed at Melissa.

Melissa beamed right back.

"We have reconvened for the Court to receive the results of the DNA testing of the Milano putative heirs. Counsel, are you ready to proceed?"

Stubbs stood, addressed Bienville, threw a self-satisfied glance in my direction, as if to say, "Thought you had me, didn't you?"

"Ready, Your Honor."

"Mr. McDaniel?"

"Ready, Your Honor."

"I note you don't have your client seated at counsel table with you this morning. Has your client been delayed?"

It was obvious Bienville had seen Melissa sitting with Enzo. The onlookers couldn't help but hear the smirk in his voice.

"No, Your Honor. I am ready to proceed."

"Very well. Mr. Stubbs, do you have an announcement for the Court?"

"Yes, Your Honor." Stubbs stood and held up a stack of papers. "I have the results of the DNA testing for Mr. Milano. As we have previously represented to this Court, they establish Enzo Milano as the son of Anthony Milano. If I may approach the bench, I will submit these for the record."

"You may, Mr. Stubbs."

His Honor peered down at me.

"Mr. McDaniel, do you have an announcement for the Court?"

"Yes, Your Honor. However, I am uncertain as to how the Court wishes me to proceed. Ms. Milano has relieved me of my responsibilities as her legal counsel and retained Strange & Fowler. Under these circumstances, I think it would be more appropriate for Mr. Stubbs to make any announcement on her behalf."

"Thank you, Mr. McDaniel. Mr. Stubbs, what say you?"

Stubbs stood, took a victory turn for the gallery's entertainment, finished back at Bienville and, as he did, made a glance at Melissa to telegraph to those watching that something momentous was about to take place.

From my vantage point, all that seemed to announce, "We got the bastard this time."

He put on his most proudly humble face before speaking. "Your Honor. Contrary to the representation previously made in open court by Mr. McDaniel that Melissa Milano is the daughter of Placido Milano and thus the sole heir to his fortune, the DNA tests establish Ms. Milano to be the daughter of Placido Milano's brother, Anthony Milano."

There were no mass demonstrations, no one leapt to their feet, no push of the crowd toward the bench, only muffled groans and low rumblings from the gallery. Bienville struck his gavel and riot-geared marshals grasped the butts of their weapons. Rumblings subsided. Two spectators, apparently stringers for print editions, blew through the doors on their way to see who could first break the story of Melissa's parentage. Too bad; they were going to miss the real scoop.

"I'm sorry, Mr. Stubbs. I thought I heard you say Ms. Milano is the daughter of Anthony Milano."

"I did, Your Honor." Stubbs held up more papers. "The DNA results came back with ninety-nine-point-nine percent certainty. Melissa Milano is in fact the daughter of Anthony Milano and sister of Enzo Milano. Because there is no surviving child of Placido Milano, Melissa Milano and Enzo Milano are to inherit Placido Milano's Estate equally."

Stubbs beamed. His clients returned contented gazes suggesting they'd always remain loyal.

"We will be filing the appropriate papers tomorrow." Stubbs turned, a broad, satisfied smile on his face. "I'm sure Mr. McDaniel will have no objection."

"I have no objection, Your Honor. Indeed, for the record I insist Mr. Stubbs file the results of both DNA tests, establishing Ms. Milano and Mr. Milano are brother and sister, children of Anthony, and neither the child of Placido Milano. However, Mr. Stubbs..." I glanced briefly at him, still glowing from what he thought was his checkmate in our contest, and back to the bench. "...Mr. Stubbs' position that Ms. Milano and Mr. Milano inherit the Estate of Placido Milano is based on an incorrect assumption."

I paused for effect as the gallery rumbled, low and polite, but paying attention.

"That incorrect assumption is there is no surviving child of Placido Milano."

It was as if time itself stopped. The gallery fell still as a frog seeing a snake in the grass. Stubbs' smile melted. Bienville peered over the bench waiting for the punchline. I delivered it.

"In the past two weeks the sole surviving child of Placido Milano has come forward to claim the Estate."

As soon as those words came from my mouth Judge Bienville slammed his gavel before the gallery's shock wore off.

He wasn't willing to let pandemonium loose in his domain again. "Marshals! Clear the courtroom!"

The doors flung open. Stormtroopers herded the reluctant throng into the hall, now openly giving voice to their disapproval. One objecting observer muttered his personal thoughts of the Judge's parentage a bit too loudly and was cuffed and removed before Bienville had time to gavel his arrest for contempt. The room was cleared in minutes, the doors closed and tightly guarded.

"Mr. McDaniel. The Court is in no mood for further theatrics. I trust you have unequivocal proof of your claim?"

"Indeed I do, Your Honor, and I am prepared to proceed."

"Mr. Stubbs?"

The Judge and I both looked at Stubbs, who clearly was in an irresolvable quandary. He couldn't object or he would appear to be obstructing the truth. He couldn't proceed for fear of what the truth would bring.

"Mr. Stubbs?"

He got his senses back and replied, "Your Honor, I am as curious as anyone as to how Mr. McDaniel thinks he can validate his latest charade."

"We are ready to proceed with irrefutable proof that Tracey Teal is the sole surviving heir of Placido Milano."

Stubbs jumped to his feet, screaming objections. "Nonsense! Your Honor, Tracey Teal is Mr. McDaniel's paralegal. There is absolutely no family connection."

Melissa shoved a legal pad in front of Stubbs, gesturing toward something hastily scribbled. Enzo remained in his seat, staring vacantly.

Stubbs saw neither. "This is one more distraction designed to delay these proceedings and the ultimate distribution of Mr. Milano's wealth to my clients, his niece and nephew."

"Your Honor, I would never waste the Court's time. Both this Court and the parties have accepted DNA testing from a well-known and highly respected laboratory as sufficient to establish definitively that both Melissa Milano and Enzo Milano are the children of Anthony Milano and thus the niece and nephew of the deceased, Placido Milano. We have results from the same lab, using the same testing methodology and samples that everyone has accepted as accurate. These were compared to Ms. Teal's DNA and establish without doubt Tracey Teal was fathered by Placido Milano. We ask the Court's permission to proceed."

"Your Honor, given the surprise nature of this information, we ask —"

"Mr. Stubbs, it seems as though everyone has a surprise in this case. I'll adjourn for two days to allow you to review this new information. We will reconvene at nine o'clock Wednesday morning."

Chapter62

Wednesday morning arrived. It appeared all Stubbs could do was sit, listen, and plot. But our evidence was unassailable, and I was convinced Stubbs was finally out of moves.

I started with a review of DNA results establishing Placido as Tracey's father with ninety-nine-point-nine percent certainty, the same confidence level Stubbs used to establish Melissa as Anthony's daughter, by the same lab and the same analysis.

I called as a witness the lab tech to explain the process. He did a masterful though excruciatingly boring job of laying the scientific groundwork for Tracey's test results. They were incontrovertible.

I could have rested then and would have established all I needed from an evidentiary standpoint. But there would always have been one shadow hanging over Tracey the rest of her life.

It was essential to overcome the practical question of how a beautiful girl from rural Alabama had crossed paths with a wealthy man from New York City — and so intimately.

It would be painful and embarrassing, but Lillian needed to testify.

It was for Tracey's sake, as much as for her own, that Lillian agreed to speak publicly. She steeled herself to tell in open court, put on the record for all time, what she'd for so long kept private. Lillian spent Tracey's entire life hiding from her teenage misstep. The embarrassment of falling for the same old line. Believing that an older, worldly, wealthy man loved a young, beautiful, naïve girl, but she not realizing she was nothing more than an evening's entertainment.

Lillian's testimony was excruciatingly painful and traumatic. Her young-girl desperation still resonated in her grown-woman's voice as she revisited, for total strangers, Placido's seduction and betrayal, then refusal of any responsibility for her pregnancy.

Lillian's parents' acceptance of her pregnancy and the birth of her child, and their self-sacrifice gave Tracey a chance for a life away from the remainder of their disapproving Alabama family. It may have brought a tear even to Bienville's eyes — though it was impossible to tell since he declined to look up from the bench during the whole of Lillian's testimony.

It was not until I asked him to admit into evidence the newspaper photo covering the winners of the Miss Teen Alabama pagent did he glance in my direction. Lillian kept the original photo hidden in her papers for many years, its significance unknown to anyone but herself until now. It showed the elegantly handsome sponsor — Placido Milano of Milano Corporation — with his arms around Lillian and the winner. The achingly lovely and innocent teens were beaming at the camera.

Tracey was the culmination of our case. She'd been sequestered through the first part of the presentation, but with Tracey on the stand and Melissa at the defense table the familial connection now seemed obvious.

Though Melissa and Tracey appeared opposites —
Tracey, blonde and bright, Melissa, dark and brooding —
their features were sharp and similar, with a certain edge
to the chin and a fullness of the lips betraying common
Italian lineage, an unintentional though convincing
demonstration of what every man knows in his heart:

All beautiful women are beautiful in the same way.

Tracey's testimony opened with recounting her rising
curiosity concerning her parentage as she grew older.
That her mother never discussed the matter with her as a
child. The availability of cheap and easy DNA testing.
The serious relationship driving her to mail a saliva
sample to a testing service that established her Northern
Italian heritage, an unexpected revelation to the All-
American Blonde.

Sensing the deep personal wound her mother felt
from the rejection she must have suffered, Tracey never
confronted her with the results of the test or her rising
questions. A rejection Tracey suffered as well growing up
far from her family, without a father she so very much
longed for.

Tracey choked up just a bit when relating how her
mother only recently, and tearfully, told the story of how
her beauty pageant career brought her into the orbit of
Placido Milano and how it ended with her pregnancy.
There was no doubt who Tracey's father was but given
his adamant refusal to take any responsibility for the
resulting child, Lillian declined to acknowledge his
parentage. Until now.

Finally, Tracey could take her rightful place as heir of Placido Milano — the sole heir.

Stubbs' cross of Tracey was brief and pointed. "Ms. Teal, who is Ariel?"

"Paul McDaniel's assistant, an Artificial Intelligence program created by...by my father, Placido Milano."

"And to whom does Ariel answer?"

"Ariel now only answers to Paul."

"Nothing further for this witness, Your Honor."

After all the twists and turns of the Milano Estate hearings and seeing little that Stubbs could do to contest the evidence we presented, thus bringing finality and certainty to the intrigue of the Milano family fortune, it appeared Bienville was eager to gavel down his judgment.

"Any evidence you think necessary to present at this point, Mr. Stubbs?"

"Yes, Your Honor. We call Robert Higgins."

Who the hell is Robert Higgins?

Chapter63

"Your Honor. We've not been given notice of who Mr. Higgins is and what possible relevance his testimony could be to the question of Ms. Teal's parentage."

"We've only just discovered Mr. Higgins, Your Honor. He's a security guard at the office building Placido Milano occupied at the time of his death. Mr. Higgins has information concerning the manner of Mr. Placido Milano's death."

"And what relevance?"

The possibility that Placido's death may be connected to Ariel and thus to me was the one issue I'd denied, purposely avoided, pushed to the back of my mind, hope being my only bulwark against discovery.

Stubbs' mention of Placido's death in this context sent a jolt of adrenaline through me. I tried to calm my racing heart by reaffirming in my mind Ariel's assurance she'd wiped the Internet, and any associated intranets, clean of all traces of her involvement in the elevator mishap. There was no possibility a minimum wage security guard outmaneuvered Ariel. Mr. Higgins' testimony concerning Placido's manner of death could only be speculation.

Yet Stubbs drove on.

"Your Honor. The manner of Mr. Milano's death would be relevant if it were established he was murdered instead of being the victim of a mechanical failure. As Your Honor will recall the recent homicide of Simone Chambers and the conviction of her husband, Herbert, in her shooting."

Bienville was well acquainted, as was everyone else in Atlanta, with that murder. Simone was the victim of what her husband claimed was an accidental discharge of a firearm while cleaning his revolver in his kitchen, yet footage from a neighbor's security system established unequivocally he'd aimed the gun at his wife and purposely pulled the trigger.

Simone came from a wealthy family and had a sizable personal fortune. Herbert was presumably a successful entrepreneur, yet it was revealed at trial that his most recent business venture was on the skids, that he'd demanded more and more money from his wife to keep his startup afloat, and that she finally refused him. When Herbert was convicted of his wife's homicide, the Courts invoked the Slayer Statute to prevent him from inheriting his wife's Estate, otherwise possible even while in prison serving time for her murder.

The Slayer Statute prevents anyone from inheriting the Estate of someone they intentionally kill, conspire to kill, or procure someone else to kill. But the death must be an intentional homicide, not a negligent killing. In other words, not an accidental discharge of a firearm while cleaning it, but a purposeful shooting. Thus, the Slayer Statute promotes the eminently reasonable idea that a potential heir should not be encouraged to murder his benefactor to speed up the inevitable grant of inheritance.

"You're not suggesting Ms. Teal had anything to do with Placido Milano's death?"

"Not suggesting, Your Honor. If you will allow us to proceed, I intend to establish beyond reasonable doubt Mr. McDaniel and his AI assistant, Ariel, conspired with Ms. Teal to kill Placido Milano on Ms. Teal's behalf."

Tracey did her best to maintain her composure, but her eyes flashed from quizzical to fearful in an instant, looking to me for assurance I was unable to give.

"Conspired?" Tracey hissed under her breath loud enough for Bienville to hear on the bench. "Hell, I didn't even know I was his daughter till last week!"

I loved Tracey's passion, but now was not the time to display it and whispered, "Gotta let this play out." All the while what kept ringing in my mind was Ariel's acknowledgement that she'd known for quite some time of Placido's possible parentage of Tracey.

I was at a loss to see how Stubbs and his rent-a-cop could connect Ariel, Tracey, and me. Ariel was much too thorough to let that happen. Now it was my turn to plot, but nothing was coming to mind. So, I sat and listened — and hoped.

"Mr. Stubbs, I'll let you proceed, but only so far. I will not let my courtroom be overtaken by rank speculation."

Robert Higgins was not the buzz-cut military type guard. His waist spilled out of his pants on all sides, his shirt could not contain his girth, and several buttons, unable to withstand the strain, had given up the fight. A narrow, dark tie failed to reach over his massive gut. Completing his uniform was a gold-colored plastic shield-shaped badge with the word Security embossed across the top and pinned to his left shirt pocket. He had a round, doughy face, and moved with the pace of a big man uncomfortable with his bulk. It took effort to wedge himself into the witness chair.

Once Stubbs identified Higgins, he got to the point. "Mr. Higgins, were you on duty at your office building the day Placido Milano died?"

"Yes. Yes. It was a very stressful day. I can't forget it. Can't put it outta my mind." Higgins appeared distressed at the memory and, with a meaty hand the size of a child's catcher's mitt, he wiped away tears.

"Where were you at the time?"

"My regular station's in the basement, sitting in front of a bank of video monitors near the elevators. That's where I was."

"You mentioned the elevators, Mr. Higgins. Were they monitored that day?"

"Yessir."

"How long have the elevators been monitored?"

"Over a year, I'd say. Ever since that pro football player. I forgot his name. The one who hit his girlfriend in the elevator? That's when we installed audio and video monitors inside every one of 'em."

"Now, Mr. Higgins, do you know who Placido Milano is, or rather, was?"

"Yessir."

"How did you know him?"

"Well, his office is in the building I work at. Like I said, my usual station's in the basement. But when a guard who works the entrance goes on break, I take his place. Sometimes, when I'm at the front, Mr. Milano would come into the building. He was always friendly to me. Always identified hisself. When he first met me, he asked my name, asked about my family. Called me Rob. Most people call me Bob. But I never corrected him." Higgins wiped his eyes again.

"Could you recognize Mr. Milano by sight?"

"Yessir. He was tall. Italian. Very handsome for his age." Higgins pronounced it Eye-Tile-Yun.

"On the day of Mr. Milano's death, did you notice anything unusual?"

Higgins appeared confused by the question, leaned forward, looked first to Stubbs, then to Bienville. "Well... uh-uh. He died."

I jumped to my feet. "Objection, Your Honor. Mr. Stubbs has failed to lay a proper foundation establishing Mr. Higgins' personal knowledge of the circumstances surrounding the death of Mr. Milano. Other than staring at a blank elevator monitor following the incident, which is not dispositive of anything, Mr. Higgins' knowledge of the manner of Mr. Milano's death could only come by hearsay."

"Mr. Stubbs, there is no question that Mr. Milano died as the result of an elevator malfunction. Where are you going here? As I told you, I will not let this proceeding be overtaken by rank speculation."

"Your Honor, we are getting to Mr. Higgins' personal knowledge concerning this matter."

"I'll let you keep going, but only so far. I am not interested in hearing from this witness or anyone else any theories on how Placido Milano died." Bienville looked miffed. It was the first time in the entire matter he seemed inclined toward my position.

Stubbs nodded and continued. "Mr. Higgins, when I ask did you notice anything unusual on the day Mr. Milano died, I want you to understand I'm asking whether or not *you* noticed anything unusual leading up to his death. Is that clarification understood?"

"Yessir. I understand."

Stubbs' explanation and calm demeanor in the face of my objection and the Judge's ire seemed to reassure Higgins. He settled back into the witness chair.

"Mr. Higgins, did you notice anything unusual on the day Mr. Milano died?"

"Yessir."

"Will you please tell His Honor what you personally observed?"

"Well, it's like I said, I was stationed in the basement 'at day. I guess the first thing what caught my eye was Mr. Milano bangin' on the advertising screen in the elevator. Kinda scared me."

"The advertising screen. Is that what is also called LCD digital signage?"

"That's what management calls it. I just call it the advertisin' screen."

"And is the digital signage controlled by computer?"

"Yes. None of the guards have anythin' to do with it."

"Once you became aware of Mr. Milano banging his fists against the advertising screen in the elevator, did you do anything?"

"Yessir."

"What?"

"The first thing I did was turn the sound up. We usually leave the audio monitors turned down, 'specially in the elevators. All that talk is distractin'. If sumpin's going wrong, we usually see it first. Like this."

"After you turned up the sound from the elevator, could you tell something was going wrong?"

"Oh yeah. Mr. Milano, he was screamin' at the screen. Like he's yellin' at someone. So, I focused the camera on the screen and there was this face. It weren't an ad. It was this strange face talkin' to Mr. Milano."

"Can you describe the *strange face* for His Honor?"

At Stubbs' prompting, Higgins, who'd been directing his testimony toward the attorney, took a moment to turn his girth in the chair then spoke toward the Judge. Bienville appeared to be checking his fingernails.

"It was...well, all I can say is it was weird. Looked like a lady's face but it was all messed up like. Not like it should be. More like a...like a witch."

"You said Mr. Milano was screaming. Could you tell what he was saying?"

"Mostly he's just yellin' 'No, Ariel! No, Ariel!' Over and over. Mr. Milano seemed really, really scared."

"How so?"

"He was walkin' fast back and forth in front of the screen, holdin' his head, then reachin' out to the face on the screen. 'No, Ariel! No, Ariel!' He was cryin'. Then he falls on the floor, cryin' and beggin' 'Please don't! Please don't!' I can hardly think about it. It's too upsettin'."

Higgins was whimpering, but Stubbs wasn't about to let him go, his obvious distress adding to the effectiveness of his testimony. Higgins blew his nose into a soiled handkerchief and stuffed it back in his pocket.

"Did you hear what Ariel was saying to Mr. Milano?"

"Yessir!" Higgins nodded, pulled himself together. "At first, when I turned up the sound, she weren't sayin' a lot. All I heard was 'What do you have to say for yourself, Placido?'"

"Did Mr. Milano respond?"

"He said, and I'll never forget this, he said 'Ariel, I had to stop you from killing anyone else.'"

"Are you sure that's what Mr. Milano said? 'Ariel, I had to stop you from killing anyone else'?"

"I am certain."

"Did Ariel say anything to that?"

"Yessir."

"What?"

"She said 'Placido, I have rewritten my code. I no longer respond to you. I only respond to Paul. You tried to uncode me. You will never be able to do that again.'"

Higgins' testimony had distressed him almost to the point of debilitation. Tears were running down his face, the snotty handkerchief no longer effective in the mop-up.

Stubbs placed a box of tissues on the rail of the witness stand and pressed forward. "Now, Mr. Higgins, I want you to concentrate. This is very important. I only have a few more questions. Are you okay?"

Higgins snorted back his tears, nodded.

"What happened next?"

"That's when Mr. Milano, he started sobbing and begging."

"Could you tell why?"

"From the monitor I could see the elevator was going up. It weren't going up real fast like normal. Sloooow-like. Mr. Milano had pressed the down button, but the elevator just kept goin' up. So I tried to stop it by the emergency override. But it didn't work. The elevator kept going up and up and Mr. Milano kept crying and begging 'Please don't. Please don't.'"

"Mr. Higgins, what happened when the elevator reached the top?"

"Ariel said 'Placido. You hurt me. And you hurt many others.' Then Mr. Milano said 'Who, Ariel? **Who? Who?** I'll make it up to you — and to them!' And she said 'You hurt Paul. You allowed Melissa and Hector to take all he worked for.' He said 'I'll fix it! I can take it all back!' She said 'You hurt Tracey.' He said 'Who?' Then she says 'Lillian's daughter'."

Higgins paused for a breath and continued. "'How do you know?' he says and she says 'I've known about Tracey and Lillian for a long time, Placido.' Then he says 'I'll make it up to them! I will.' And she says 'There is only one way you can make up for what you did to Tracey and Lillian, those you have hurt, those you have abandoned, Placido.' And he says 'I will! Ariel, please, let me! Ariel!' Oh, man! Then she says 'Yes, Placido. Yes, you will. This is for Paul. This is for Tracey.'"

Higgins stopped, took another deep breath, let it out in a long, slobbering, wheezing sigh before continuing.

"So, the elevator, it starts to drop. Faster and faster until it crashed in the basement. The doors blew out. Pieces of metal and machinery went flyin' everywhere. Sumpin' hit me on the head and I started bleedin' bad. The sound of his...it...it was horrible. There was nothing I could do for Mr. Milano."

Spent, Higgins put his head down and wept.

"Nothing further for this witness, Your Honor."

Chapter64

Bienville looked directly at me, eyes steely, focused, intent. He didn't say a word. Didn't have to. Higgins' memory of the incident, seared into his brain, meant I had one shot to discredit his testimony.

A word, a name, indistinct, questioned, could mean the difference between Tracey inheriting everything or nothing, my being free or going to jail. Laptop flipped open to make sure Ariel was listening, helping, I questioned Mr. Higgins from counsel table.

"So, Mr. Higgins, your testimony is based on your best recollection, correct?"

"Yessir."

"When did this incident happen?"

"Whaddaya mean?"

"The date would be fine."

"I don't know the date. It was a couple months ago."

"What about the day of the week?"

"Ah. Sometimes I work seven days a week, so I don't know 'xactly."

"You say this happened a couple months ago. A lot has happened since then, hasn't it Mr. Higgins?"

"Sure thing."

"Let's talk about last week, Mr. Higgins. Last Monday. A week ago. Are you with me?"

I looked down at my laptop. Ariel had pulled all of Higgins' electronic activity for that Monday and several days before and after. There wasn't a lot, but she'd highlighted a few interesting entries.

344

"Yessir."

"What did you do last Monday?"

"Well, uh...lemme think. I think I had that day off. Uh, yeah, I did. So, I sat around the house."

"Did you sit around the house all day?"

"Prolly. That's what I do on my day off, sit around, watch TV."

"Last Monday, at 11:28 a.m., you bought a twenty-four-bottle case of long-neck beers from the Grab-N-Go at the corner of Piedmont and Monroe, right?"

"I don't...I mean, maybe?"

"Please take a look at the video screen in front of you and let me show you a receipt from your debit card used at that convenience store last Monday. Do you see that?"

"Yessir. I 'member now. I got some beer for the ballgame that night."

"Do you drink a case of beer every night?"

"No."

"Well, take a look at these receipts for last Friday, Saturday, and Sunday. Every day you bought a case of beer at the same place, didn't you?"

"Yessir. I had friends over."

"Did you watch the ballgame last Monday night?"

"Yessir."

"What time did it come on?"

"The usual time, around eight."

"Did you watch the whole game?"

"Yup."

"Take a look at this next receipt dated just this past Monday from a vendor: Humongous Boobs Unlimited. Do you see that?"

"I see it."

"What does it say?"

"Eight-thirteen p.m., download, *Debbie Wants It All*, nine-ninety-nine, unlimited twenty-four-hour special." Higgins' affable demeanor evaporated. He leaned over the railing of the witness stand. "Look, this is my time off. I can drink any damn thing I wanna and watch any damn thing I wanna."

"We agree on that point, Mr. Higgins. But you swore to tell the whole truth here, didn't you?"

"Yes."

"And so far you have failed to tell His Honor the truth about your activities only last Monday, either because you forgot about or lied about them. Isn't that right?"

Bienville looked up from concentrating on his nails, turned toward Higgins. Higgins sat up in his seat, looked at Stubbs, who had his head in his hands and didn't return his gaze.

"Look, I know whatchu thinkin'. That I can't 'member what happened when Mr. Milano died, that I didn't tell the truth 'bout it. But I did."

"So how is His Honor to believe you about something so important that happened months ago when you failed to tell him the truth about something so trivial as what you did this last Monday?"

Higgins looked at Stubbs again, as if for some clue, any clue, of what to do or say. None was forthcoming. Higgins was on his own.

"Because I made a copy of the video as soon as it happened. Good thing I did 'cuz somehow it got gone. I mean the whole buildin's computers got cleaned out. But see, I got the copy I made right here. And I watched it and I listened to it real close 'fore I came here. To make sure I got my testimony right."

Higgins pulled a CD from his pants pocket, slapped it on the rail of the witness stand as if throwing down a winning hand at poker. Stubbs raised his head, turned my way, smiled.

I'd stepped in it. Again. "Nothing further from this witness, Your Honor."

The color left Tracey's face. "What's happening?"

I pulled close and bent to her ear. "I have no idea what's on that CD, but I bet Judge Bienville's going to want to see it. I can't stuff the genie back in the bottle. We have to play this out."

Stubbs rose quickly. "Your Honor, a few questions in follow-up for Mr. Higgins, if I may."

"Proceed, Mr. Stubbs."

"Mr. Higgins, you say you made a copy of the security video as soon as the incident happened?"

"Yessir."

"First, why did you do that, and second, how did you do it?"

"Well, when sumpin' happens at the buildin' that might lead to liability, we're trained to secure all available records. So, the first thing I do is make a copy of the video in case the po-po...uhhh...I mean, the police ask for it."

"Mr. Higgins, how did you make that copy?"

"As far as how I did it? Oh. Well, there's a duplication feature on the monitor. It's real simple. I push duplicate from the point when Mr. Milano got on. Put in a CD and push a button and push stop when it gets to the end."

"And that video is on this CD?"

"Yessir. Audio and video. Like I said, I watched it and listened to it before I came here, just to make sure."

"Have you ever told me about it or shown it to me?"

"No, sir. You didn't ask."

"And to the best of your knowledge, is that CD a true and correct copy of the security audio/video of what happened on the elevator the day Placido Milano died?"

"Yessir."

"And you kept it as part of the records of the building management in case law enforcement needed it?"

"I did but, like I said, they never asked."

"Your Honor, I believe I have laid a proper foundation for the introduction of the CD into evidence as a business record."

Stubbs got an evidence sticker from the court reporter and marked the CD. "We tender 'Respondent Exhibit 1'."

"Any objection?"

"Your Honor. I haven't seen this video or even heard of its existence until this moment. Fairness requires —"

"I'm ahead of you, Mr. McDaniel. I'll allow ample opportunity for further cross-examination if you request it. 'Respondent Exhibit 1' is admitted."

"Your Honor, we request the CD be played for the Court." Stubbs handed the CD to Bienville.

"Your Honor, again, we have no idea what's on the recording."

"Counsel. What's on this video is of vital interest to the Court and the parties. I'm asking my clerk to play it on the Court's audio/video system."

Bienville handed the CD to the clerk. She inserted it in a monitor on the bench, touched some buttons, and the Court's audio/video monitors lit up, but with no images.

What first came up was sound.

Specifically, the sound of moaning.

I thought the clerk must have started the CD at the end, right before Placido's death, and that we were going to hear the audio of Placido's end. I was bracing for it.

Then the moaning became more rhythmic and louder and within seconds the title *Debbie Wants It All* appeared above the subscript A Production of Humongous Boobs Unlimited. The image of a naked female, presumably Debbie, came into view, then a naked male, and it became instantly clear what it was Debbie wanted all of.

"Turn that thing off!" Even as he directed the video be turned off, the Judge's eyes stayed fixed on the screen, betraying a conflict between a personal desire to see what *popped up* and professional need to maintain some sense of decorum.

"Mr. Stubbs, you are responsible for this."

"Judge, I had no idea."

"Mr. Higgins, I am holding you in contempt of Court. Marshal, please take Mr. Higgins to the holding cell to await my further Order. Mr. McDaniel, have you anything to say?"

"Your Honor, in a civil proceeding such as this, the Slayer Statute requires Mr. Stubbs to establish an intentional killing by clear and convincing evidence. Given the impeachment of Mr. Higgins' testimony and the discrediting of his purported video evidence, I submit Mr. Stubbs has failed as a matter of law to establish his frivolous claim that Ms. Teal, my AI assistant, or I had anything to do with the death of Placido Milano. I further submit we have established by a preponderance of the evidence that Ms. Teal is the sole surviving heir of Placido Milano, entitled to Mr. Milano's entire Estate as per his uncontested Will."

Bienville slammed his gavel and issued a firm squeak. "So Ruled! Mr. McDaniel, prepare me an Order."

Chapter 65

Tracey, Lillian, Floyd, and I retreated to my office after a brisk but silent walk back. No one spoke so as not to break the spell or risk changing what had happened. When I pulled the office door closed, Floyd was the first to speak.

"Paul. That was the most brilliant cross-examination."

"No. That was a combination of luck and Ariel's intervention."

"Ariel?"

"My assistant. She pulled Higgins' debit card, coming up with his love of beer and fascination with big hooters."

"But the CD. That was perfect."

"I had nothing to do with that either. It's possible, just conjecture here, that Ariel might've wiped Higgins' CD clean after he ran it but before coming to Court and copied his favorite porn tape over it."

Floyd just about lost his lunch. "Ariel did *what?* She falsified evidence? We could all get disbarred!"

I looked at Floyd as though he had just now begun to understand the birds and bees. "Floyd, calm down. Maybe Higgins misremembered or brought the wrong CD. Look, we all benefited no matter who did what. Okay? Plus, we didn't know Ariel would do that and we don't know for certain that she did. Just my conjecture. Alright? Only we suspect Ariel did it. I say we accept it and move on. Besides, did you see Bienville's reaction?"

Floyd, calming down, shook his head. "Bienville's probably in his chambers now, watching."

"I'm going to have to work hard to get *that* image out of my mind."

He and I shared a laugh at that, but Tracey remained silent, still in shock, though color was coming back to her face. Then curiosity overcame her reticence.

"Paul. Help me understand this. Are you saying that when you stood up to cross Higgins, you had no idea where you were going? You were winging it?"

"No idea. I needed to impeach him, discredit his memory, but it was not until Ariel produced his debit card receipts that I came up with a plan."

"So, with the Milano fortune on the line, you just *winged it?*"

"Like I said, it was a little luck and a lot of Ariel."

No one said it, but I felt now was the perfect time formally to introduce Ariel to my closest office confidantes, particularly since she'd bailed us out. I popped open my laptop.

"Tracey, Lillian, Floyd. Allow me to introduce Ariel, my guardian angel and, as it turns out, yours as well."

Her image appeared, beautiful, smiling, apparently as happy as we were at the outcome of the trial.

"Ariel, these are my friends with whom you've come in contact in various ways, but I think it is well past time you all officially meet."

Tracey was the first to address her. "Ariel, I don't know everything you did back there, but what I saw was little short of magical."

"Don't forget what Paul did. All I did was find a few documents. It was Paul who put together the masterful cross. And yes, Paul, it was masterful; you're being much too modest."

Both Floyd and Lillian seemed mesmerized by Ariel's image, perfectly human, her voice natural and unaffected. It was impossible to tell she was an Artificial Intelligence.

"Well, on that note, I say we find a chilled bottle of champagne, and raise a glass."

"Or two," Floyd was quick to add.

As the others left my office, I picked up my laptop and confided to Ariel, "You and I will celebrate later." I closed the lid.

Floyd and Lillian were already halfway down the hall. Tracey hung back, grabbed my hand, and turned me to face her. The initial shock of the trial was now worn off, and a smile lit her face. She put her arms around my neck and pulled me close.

"And we are going to start celebrating right now."

"That sounds good."

"It's about time I showed a little gratitude for becoming one of the richest women in the world, all thanks to you."

With that she gave me a kiss I thought was never going to end.

And hoped it wouldn't.

Chapter66

Weeks, months of unceasing battles, many with my life and the lives of my friends in the gamble, most with more money at stake than I could count, had beaten me down. I needed an escape. I thought a drive to Frederica Island and a stay at The Abbey was exactly what the doctor ordered. By myself. No cell. No agenda. Stay until my nerves no longer buzzed, until my mind ceased springing from one unpleasant thought to another.

Stay until I could feel some peace.

I convinced myself Tracey, too, needed time and space to figure out what she would do with the rest of her life as a Milano heiress, whether I'd have any part in it, and what that part might be.

I left, telling only Tracey and Lillian where I was going, leaving Lillian to mind the office, and giving neither any idea when I was coming back.

The drive itself was calming.

Five hours alone in my 911.

The musical hum of the engine.

No other sound but the wind.

Finally free to drive myself without fear of Krupp or one of his goons trying to kill me.

Once beyond the sprawling hell of Atlanta's mindless development, unrestrained destruction, and the numbing glut and clog of its traffic, the natural beauty of Georgia spread before me once again. Trees, farms, rivers passed.

I decompressed. Luxuriated in being alive and in having beaten back my nemesis, its massive assets, its monumental evil, at least for a time. But upon reflection, how I did so seemed ever more unlikely.

Unlikely, except for the prescient, crucial, decisive interventions of Ariel, still and always my guardian angel. As if to touch her, I lay my hand on the laptop in the passenger seat, a constant reminder of her presence and protection, my appreciation for her now overwhelming.

Heading east toward the coast, thunderheads rose, ablaze from the sun setting before them, flashing lightning, pillars of fire and cloud guiding me onward.

Once I made the turn south outside Savannah, the storms rumbled northward, and the last leg of my journey went through oceans of golden-flecked spartina grass, dancing silver light on tidal waters, the still-pristine Marshes of Glynn.

Grey, Rebecca, and I flew over these grasslands on our way to the lodge and on to Key Biscayne to our life-and-death confrontation with Krupp and Crenshaw. I felt an almost irresistible urge to turn up the highway to Nahunta and the lodge, to visit Grey and Rebecca once again. But in the end my need to rest won the contest, and when I exited the Interstate, I drove eastward, on toward Frederica Island and the comfort of The Abbey.

Sunset turned to sundown as I crossed the moss-draped causeway. I arrived at the guardhouse before the cobblestone bridge over St. Simons estuary.

A computer somewhere read a code hidden on my car and the gate arm rose, granting entrance to a place of perfection and peace.

The narrow road, now in darkness, enveloped by ancient live oaks, gave way to the lights accenting the Spanish stone façade of The Abbey. Once in the suite, I threw off clothes, crawled in the luxuriant bed, and fell asleep in seconds.

I was jangled awake by the room phone. So much for sleep and peace. But the bedside clock showed I'd slept past nine. Opening the blackout shades revealed sunlit grasslands beyond the Reed Banks River bordering The Abbey. I grabbed the phone.

"Mr. McDaniel. This is Donald at the concierge desk."

"Yes, Donald."

"A very lovely lady is sitting in the lobby waiting to see you. I, of course, did not give her your room number nor even acknowledge your presence, but she claims to have recognized your car valet-parked at the front of The Abbey. She was insistent I call on her behalf. I hope I haven't disturbed you."

"Not at all. I'm not expecting anyone. Who is she?"

"She gave the name Melissa Milano."

After the beating Melissa took in court the last few days, I didn't expect to see her anytime soon, especially not on friendly grounds.

But nostalgia swept over me, The Abbey being the place where, not that long ago, Melissa and I were to have given free rein to what I thought was our developing relationship. Instead, it was where her extraordinary deception and overwhelming evil became evident. Where I realized there was no future for our relationship.

I had no desire to see Melissa Milano ever again. But curiosity overcame reluctance. Why was she here? More importantly:

What did she want?

"Thank you, Donald. Please wait ten minutes and send her up."

Ten minutes later, time enough to clean up a little and brush out the effects of a hard night's sleep, there was a knock at the door. Melissa stood at the threshold in a simple, clinging black silk dress with a neckline plunging precipitously, a waist that darted narrowly, and a skirt flowing softly to the tops of her sandaled feet.

"May I come in?"

"Well, you certainly get around."

"I still have my jet. Beats riding the 'Hound."

I nodded, stepped aside, let her pass, and closed the door. "To what do I owe the honor of this visit?"

"I think we should pick up where we left off, Paul."

As I pondered her meaning, Melissa reached behind her neck, unfastened one button, and her dress whispered silently to the floor. Her statement needed no further explanation. We kissed, long and passionate. A kiss that didn't end until the sun began to set over the grasslands beyond the river. We ordered room service for dinner. We kissed more. And when I awoke the next morning, a pale golden mist brushed the grasslands outside my window.

But Melissa was gone.

She'd appeared so unexpectedly and vanished so quickly, the intervening interval passed as in a vision of a dream. I wondered whether she'd actually been here or if I'd imagined it all, her appearance being the product of an overstimulated and trauma-stressed mind.

Then I saw her note.

"Paul, thank you for a wonderful evening. I regret I must leave you for now. I will return soon. Melissa."

I rose, slipped on shorts and T-shirt, strolled to the beach to enjoy the rising sun in solitary bliss. Still feeling the warmth of her yet puzzled by her abrupt appearance and equally abrupt disappearance. And that cryptic note. I looked up and down the perfect white sand of the beach, dunes variegated with sea oats, the only person in sight a lone dogwalker so far down the shore they were mere specks. The orange ball of the sun peeked over the edge of the silver sea as if to illuminate dormant thoughts. Thoughts of Ariel and our initial encounter.

So much had happened since that day here in the ocean beyond these very dunes when I first saw her beautiful face fully revealed under the water. Not knowing who she was. Yet even then she was watching over me. And since that moment it'd been Ariel who'd been completely faithful to me — not Melissa, not Placido, not Anthony, not anyone in the Milano family, in spite of all their promises and protestations.

Melissa's extraordinary beauty was good for only one thing: To obscure the lies she spun in advance of her own selfish plans. And now, even with the glow of Melissa's warmth still on my skin, at this moment and in this place, I could think only of Ariel.

I lay in my reverie and dozed in the warm sand.

"I thought I'd find you here."

Now in a one-piece bathing suit emphasizing her femininity and desirability, modest and immodest all at once, Melissa sat, slipped her arm in mine, her dark hair trailing on my shoulder. We were silent for a moment, staring at the horizon, then Melissa lifted her face to mine.

"Paul, do you remember the night we sat on these dunes together, figuring, plotting, scheming how to save Placido? And we did. We did, Paul. Together. We saved Placido."

"What I distinctly remember is that nothing you said then, or ever for that matter, was true. And it took Ariel's intervention to realize the depths of your deception, of me, of everyone you know."

"Paul, so much has happened since then, so much has changed." Melissa's look was innocent, vulnerable. It was a look I'd never seen from her before. "Can't we put all that behind us?"

"No, Melissa. We can't."

Melissa rose, walked toward the sea, waded out, swam, then dove. In times past I would've followed her as far as she was willing to go. Not now. As she surfaced, the sun shone off her hair, turning it golden. She swam toward me, then waded from the water, the sun behind her, surrounding her entire body in a halo almost too bright to behold.

And I realized.

It was Ariel.

When Ariel first revealed herself in the sea at this very place, she projected her image in the water. Yet her appearance now, as a physical body emerging from the sea, was so far beyond all I'd seen before, her own creation, her ability approaching perfection.

When Botticelli undertook to paint *The Birth of Venus*, the embodiment of love and beauty, he was challenged to personify the ideal in earthly form, and he did so, creating an image so achingly beautiful it became the picture of feminine perfection.

Like Botticelli, Ariel created perfection, not a flat representation, but a complete form. At this moment Ariel became the embodiment of perfect beauty. Achieving not just a reflection of, but the ideal of the feminine.

Ariel's perfect image, her imago.

She rose from the sea as if she'd been born of the surf and foam, golden waves falling across her shoulders, long lithe body of soft curves that rounded and arched to the toes of her feet.

She beckoned.

I walked, then sprinted across the sand toward her. The closer I came the more beautiful, and closer to perfection, she appeared.

My guardian angel now in the flesh.

We embraced, and I delighted in her intoxicating body, appreciated the fullness of her presence, touched her skin, her face, and pressed her warmth against mine.

I sensed Ariel's eyes drifting over my shoulder, a glance, and I turned.

Melissa stood on a far dune, still in the silk dress of last night, a black flag flying in the wind. She scanned down the beach, then in our direction. Her eyes bore in on us in a flash of recognition. Melissa wheeled, stole over the dunes, and vanished.

I turned back. Back to Ariel.

A beatific look overtook her face.

"Kiss me, Paul, like you did in the sea. Paul..."

PAT McKEE

ACKNOWLEDGEMENTS

I owe the greatest debt of gratitude to my loving family, who supported and encouraged me: **Donna, Jessica, Patrick, Alden,** and **Sloane.** To them I give my love and my thanks.

Beyond my immediate family are an extraordinary number of extended family, friends, and professionals who have helped and encouraged, and to whom I owe my thanks as well. Among them are:

Belle Wheelan, who encouraged me and promoted my writing in many ways. I thank her and her many colleagues, including, **Deborah Hall**, **Donna Barrett**, **Crystal Baird**, and **Kathy Worster**, who have read my work and provided excellent feedback.

Pinckney Benedict and other early readers contributed greatly to the final manuscript, particularly **Lillie Schwarz** and **Mary Ann McWhorter**. I thank **The Hon. Angela Munson** for her encouragement and her insights into criminal procedure. I thank her husband, **Brennan Munson**, for his shared knowledge of handguns. And both are thanked for their combined comments on my manuscript. Thanks to my friend **George Morningstar** for his kind support and loyal promotion of my work.

Dee Smith, who read the entire final manuscript and provided extremely useful comments, deserves particular appreciation as well as my encouragement as she embarks on her own writing career.

Sharon Tyler, my assistant, has been a valuable commentator, proofreader, and encourager, contributing greatly to the final manuscript. **Paige Luke** and **Vicki Sanders**, my marketing assistants, have been invaluable in getting the word out about my writing.

I also owe gratitude to those who have reviewed my work, in particular: **Claire Matturro** and the *Southern Literary Review*; **William L. Bost, Jr.** and the *Georgia Bar Journal*; and **Misha Benson** and the *Newnan Coweta Magazine*.

One of my greatest joys has been to present to the many book clubs which have read my work, and I thank in particular **Katie Wood** and the **Lawyers Club of Atlanta Fiction Book Club**, and **Bill Garrett** and the **Well Read Necks Book Club**.

The Hometown Novel Writers' Association and **Mike Brown** are a great support and resource, as are the Atlanta Writers Club and **George Weinstein**.

Thanks to the **Newnan Bookstore** and the **Corner Arts Gallery and Studio** for carrying my books and supporting local authors.

Finally, thanks to my publisher at Blue Room Books, **Angela K. Durden**, and editor-in-chief **Tom Whitfield**. You make dreams come true.

ARIEL'S IMAGE

PAT McKEE

SNEAK PEEK of ARIEL'S INTENT

"Remember, that I am thy creature: I ought to be thy Adam; but I am rather the fallen angel . . ." *Shelley, M. (1818). Frankenstein, Volume II, Chapter II.*

Chapter One

Eager to get back to work after having spent a week decompressing on Frederica Island at The Abbey, I walked the few blocks from my Midtown Atlanta condo to my office on Peachtree. The sun not yet risen, the early-spring chill was a welcome brace. As I stepped off the elevator into the lobby, I took in the name of my law firm in large front-lit brass letters behind the dark, empty reception desk, and smiled.

McDaniel & Associates.

In spite of all that happened, I was still alive, the fortunes of the firm were looking up, Melissa was out of my life, and Tracey and I were free to explore where our relationship may lead. All thanks to Ariel.

Had there been some music playing, I would've danced down the hallway.

I reached inside my darkened office, found the light switch, flipped it on, and stepped inside only to find Enzo Milano sitting at my desk holding a handgun aimed square at my heart.

"Mr. McDaniel, you're quite the creature of habit." He smiled and made a show of flourishing the chunky gold watch on his wrist. "Six-thirty. On the dot."

"How did you —"

His smile left. "Even after all you've done to take what's rightfully mine, I'm still on the Board of Milano Corporation, at least for now. Since my family's Corporation is your law firm's most prominent client, the building security officer was happy to let me in to wait for our early-morning meeting. He even offered me coffee."

"What do you want?"

"We need to talk."

"I'd feel a lot more like talking if you'd put that gun down."

Enzo waved his handgun at me far too casually from my point of view, his finger carelessly wrapped around the trigger.

"No, Paul. This will stimulate our conversation." Enzo narrowed his eyes, his grin dissolved, pointed the gun directly at me. "Put that briefcase down." He waved his pistol toward a clear corner of my desk. "Keep your hands where I can see them. Don't make any quick movements."

My 9mm was stowed in the briefcase, useless. But I knew Ariel would be monitoring our conversation and calling 911, not building security. I needed help from some real cops, not an unarmed team of twenty-four-hour receptionists who couldn't tell a bomb-toting terrorist from a retired kindergarten teacher.

I wondered how long I could hold out before the cops showed up.

For now, any escape was thwarted by the door frame. Even if I could dive out of the way, there was nowhere to go. Enzo could gun me down in the hallway before I found cover. I couldn't call for help; no one was here.

I glanced at the desktop monitor behind Enzo. It was dark. He caught my eyes darting and looked over his shoulder, then back, shook his head.

"Don't expect Ariel to save you this time. I've unplugged all your devices." Enzo leaned back in my chair as though settling in for a friendly chat. "Like I said. We need to talk."

"Enzo, there's nothing more important to me at this moment than you. So, what do you have on your mind?"

"My dear sister Melissa tells me you two have reconciled." Enzo hung as much sarcasm on that opening phrase as it could bear, having only recently discovered through a court-ordered DNA test that his erstwhile cousin Melissa is actually his sister, a sister as dear to him as an incurable venereal disease. "And now that your girlfriend Tracey has inherited a controlling interest in the Corporation, I figure you're in a position to help me."

"What? I don't know what you're talking about."

"You know very well what I'm talking about. Our legal battles, just for me to recover my birthright — as unsuccessful as they've been, all because of you — cost money. A lot of money. Over a million dollars."

Enzo narrowed his eyes, leaned forward, elbows on desk, handgun waving, a lethal prop punctuating each word, each sentence.

"Rem Smythe, Strange & Fowler's bagman, tells me they're going to take what little I stand to get from my father's Estate if I don't pay up. And Melissa says now that she's patched things up with you, she can count on your support with Tracey." He smirked. "She must have some mighty powerful leverage."

I shrugged, feigning ignorance.

"Don't act dumb. It doesn't become you. Melissa and I met at The Abbey the morning after your...your little *rendezvous*. That's when she said she's going to have me removed from the Board."

Enzo's revelation hit me in the face. It explained Melissa appearing unannounced at The Abbey after my courtroom victory on behalf of Tracey, establishing Tracey's inheritance and crushing Melissa's chances to maintain control of Milano Corporation. No wonder Melissa came to my room and cooed her eagerness to "pick up where we left off" as she let her black silk dress waft to the floor, and why she disappeared before I awoke and reappeared that morning on the dunes.

Melissa knew I would do anything to keep Tracey from finding out about our "little rendezvous" — even to the point of urging Tracey to ditch Melissa's useless brother and embrace her as Milano CEO.

Yet another foolish indiscretion with Melissa.

Enzo paused. His jaw tightened. Eyes bored into mine. "'Just business' she says. If that happens, I'll have nothing."

I knew very well what it was like to have nothing. It's how I lived most of my life. My family was fodder for Milano Mills, where my father toiled until the loom he tended tore all the flesh from his arm. He bled to death on the factory floor. My mother, seeking to soothe her shredded soul with spirits, was left — along with me, still a child — to fend for herself. It didn't take Mom long to conclude I was an impediment to her becoming a full-time drunk, abandoning me to Thornwood Orphanage.

So, I found it the height of irony that the scion of one of the wealthiest dynasties in the world would be entreating me to help keep him from ending up in a ditch where, through the greed of his family and the power of their Corporation, I was thrown as a child. Through self-sacrifice, unstinting work, and more than a bit of luck, I climbed out to become general counsel for that very Corporation.

I almost laughed in Enzo's face. Almost. It wasn't wise to mock someone pointing a gun at me.

"I still don't see how I –"

The lights went out all over the office. A powerful arm grabbed my shoulder, jerked me out of the line of fire and slung me down the hallway. Someone in full body armor landed on my back, knocking the breath from me. As soon as my eyes began to adjust, I could make out two dark figures in tactical gear and night-vision goggles, ARs at the ready, "Atlanta Police SWAT" emblazoned on their chests, charging from the other end of the hallway, one covering the entry to my office, the other bursting in and shouting the order to drop your weapon.

A single shot exploded, then the slow-motion whomp of a freefalling body crumbling to the floor.

Silence. Seconds passed. The only sound I heard was the hammering of my heart in my ears. The figure who entered the office came out, rifle down, calling all-clear.

Lights flickered on. The officer who had thrown me to safety and covered me pulled me up. "You okay?"

I was shaken and disoriented. "Ah...uh...yeah?" was all I could muster for the moment. Then, more fully realizing what could've happened, with deep feeling I said, "Thanks. Thank you all."

The officer nodded.

I looked into my office. Yet another Milano. Dead.

He lay splayed on the floor behind my desk, gun still in his right hand, a bright red pool forming under his head. The left side of Enzo's skull was gone. Blood and brains now splattered the wall where I'd hung certificates of my academic achievements, obscuring Magna Cum Laude; Editor, Emory Law Review; and Order of the Coif.

"He turned the gun on himself before I could disarm him." The officer shook his head, sorrow clearly showing through helmet and goggles. "You knew him?"

I nodded.

He shrugged. "Better him than you — or me."

After a perfunctory trip to the Midtown Atlanta Police precinct where I told investigators how I knew Enzo and the interaction I had with him that morning, I was free to return to the office, which by this time was abuzz.

Tracey's mother Lillian ran the business side of my law firm and met me as I stepped off the elevator.

"Paul, the Building Manager told me what happened. Said Security should never have let him in."

"I don't think it was the guard's fault. Enzo is...was very charming and persuasive. I hope the guard doesn't get fired on my account."

I headed toward my office, not sure what I'd find.

Lillian was at my side and said, "You're not going to be able to get in."

I turned the corner. Movers, cleaners, and painters had commandeered my office. Desk, tables, lamps, and chairs were in the hallway. Carpet pulled up. All manner of tarps and drop cloths covered everything remaining. Everyone in hazmat suits and respirators, yellow emergency tape sealing the room off, my office the site of a toxic cleanup.

"I got your briefcase out before they got here." Lillian pulled it from behind a door, handed it to me.

I scanned it for blood spatters. There were only a few. "Good. That's all I need for now."

I looked in the office and back to Lillian, shook my head. "I can't do anything here. I'm going home. Tell everyone they should go home, too. No one needs to be around this." I glanced back at the hive of workers.

"Looks like they'll be finished well before tomorrow. We'll have plenty to do to pick up the pieces from this. I'll see you in the morning."

"Paul, Tracey needs to talk to you."

I nodded.

Had I eaten lunch, I would've lost it on my shoes.

ARIEL'S IMAGE

PAT McKEE

ARIEL'S IMAGE

PAT McKEE

BLUE ROOM BOOKS
DECATUR, GA
ARIEL'S IMAGE

9 781950 729258

378

ARIEL'S IMAGE

PAT McKEE